LITTLE LIAR

Edited by Laura at Ten Thousand Editing and Book Design

Proofread by Havoc Archives

Cover and interior formatting by Justine Bergman at JAB Design Studio

First Edition 2024

LITTLE LIAR

THE WEB OF SILENCE DUET
2

LEIGH RIVERS

CONTENT WARNING

This story deals with topics that some readers may find unsettling.

Malachi and Olivia have a dark story that contains dark themes like non-con, CNC, drugging, dubious consent, heavy somnophilia, possessive and obsessive behavior, stalking, mental health struggles, medication, hallucinations, kidnapping, death of pet due to abuse (spider), suicide, mentions of grooming, extreme violence and gore, death, and death of parents.

It also has multiple kinks like fear play, primal play, mask play, spider play, cockwarming, anal, orgasm denial, exhibitionism, voyeurism, and Malachi's favorite, the sibling kink. They are not blood related. But if calling each other brother and sister is not your thing, please do not proceed. I beg of you.

There are heavy subjects on child abuse that results in mutism and this trigger should NOT be taken lightly.

Side characters from The Edge of Darkness appear within Little Liar, and could contain some minor spoilers to the trilogy, but it does not need to be read first as the storylines do not cross.

PLAYLIST

If We Being Real – Yeat

Apathy(slowed) – Lxzt

VIRUS (Fytch Remix) – KLOUD & Fytch

Dreams – SKUM &Meisym

Bury a friend – Billie Eilish

Time – Dravyn & Altare

Misunderstood – Inadaze & Harvey

Detached from Reality – MEJKO & Arkane Skye

I Don't – Lefty Wingate & guesst

RUNNING – NF

Tentative – Kujah

Thinking About ü – ünü & NAGGA

Crash and Burn – MEJKO & Stephen Geisler

Where I Am – Meisym & Flx

Night Drive – Paapi Muzik

BIRDS OF A FEATHER – Billie Eilish

Listen now on **Spotify**
Little Liar — Author Leigh Rivers

To the book that nearly cost me my life.
I won this time.

PART ONE

CHAPTER ONE
MALACHI
Aged 4

Wind blows in my hair as Daddy keeps me on his shoulders on the way to the playground at the bottom of the neighborhood we live in.

Mommy is at work, so we're going to have some fun before we pick her up in Daddy's new car. We're making cookies tonight!

"Did you have fun at school today?" Daddy asks me, and I scream a "yes!"

I hold his head in a tight hug as we cross the street. Little droplets of rain hit my face, but I have on my raincoat and welly boots so we can jump in puddles.

"Daddy?"

"Yes, son?"

"Can we go for more ice cream on the way home?"

He laughs and flips me off his shoulders. I giggle and scream as he tickles me and puts me on my feet. He wipes the chocolate ice cream from my chin and takes my hand. "If we have time, yes. We need to pick your mommy up from work in an hour."

I grin and skip, jumping in the puddles as we go. A big truck passes us suddenly, and I wince, covering my ears and screwing my eyes shut.

"Hey," Daddy says, crouching down in front of me until the truck vanishes, but my ears still ring painfully. I want it to stop—why won't it stop?

My bottom lip quivers, and when I open my eyes, Daddy is watching me. "It's getting worse, huh?"

I nod slowly. I don't like loud noises—they hurt my ears and make my chest all tight.

"Come on," he says, standing and taking my hand again. "A quick play on the swings and we'll get more ice cream."

A smile cracks over my face, and Daddy skips with me through the playground, lifts me onto the swing, and pushes me high while I smile harder and scream louder.

No other kids are here, which is good. We never come here when it's busy. I think Daddy likes it when it's just the two of us.

Daddy always takes me out to the park. Or we go to the swimming pool where he teaches me how to float.

He ushers me to the merry-go-round. "I won't spin you too fast," he says, pulling my hood up as the rain turns heavier. "Hold tight."

Before he can spin, I gasp and lean forward. "Daddy, look!"

A little spider is making a web on the bar. It's small and

black, and the droplets are getting in the way. Daddy reaches his finger out, and the spider crawls onto it. "Look at that," he says, sitting down beside me, making the merry-go-round creak. He lowers his finger to my hand. "You wanna hold it?"

I nod and even feel a little nervous as I rest my hand on my lap, palm-side up, and giggle when Daddy makes the spider crawl onto my hand. It's so small and helpless and lonely. The rain must be making it all wet and cold. "Can we take him home?"

But as Daddy goes to reply, thunder cracks above us, making me jump. My hands fist, and I accidentally crush and drop the spider. It lands right in a small puddle on the metal.

For a few breaths, I stare at it with wide eyes. It doesn't move.

"No!" I scream and try to get it, but he stops me. "Save him, Daddy!"

"He's asleep, son. Thunder makes spiders sleep. He's okay. Will we go get some ice cream now?"

"But… but…"

Daddy lifts me into his arms as tears start to slide down my cheeks.

"It's okay, Malachi. Don't be upset. He's asleep."

I cuddle into him and cry. Because I know I crushed the spider. I know it's dead because of me. My body shakes uncontrollably until I fall asleep in my daddy's arms while he carries us out of the playground.

"You're such a good kid, Malachi."

I like it when it's quiet. My ears don't hurt, and the bad butterflies don't appear, waiting for someone to yell at me.

The house is never quiet.

When Mommy leaves me in the house all alone, I can play with the boxes she's left sitting around. Sometimes they're big enough for me to climb in and close the lid, then I can hide until Mommy comes home again and takes me to my bedroom.

I'm too scared to look for the boxes now. Did Mommy come home? Daddy? I haven't seen my daddy in so long.

I slide off my bed, nearly falling over the bag of dirty clothes as I make my way to my bedroom door. I tug at the handle, and my bottom lip curls.

Why won't it open?

"Mommy?" I call out, hitting my little fist on the door. I cough into my hand and hit the door again. "Daddy?"

Like every night, nothing. It makes me sad that Mommy doesn't give me cuddles anymore. Daddy used to hug me until I cried and laughed.

Music is playing really loud—Mommy won't hear me again. Tears form in my eyes, and I lower my head as I go back to bed. I trip up on the way—I can't see where I'm going because Mommy took my night light out when I asked when Daddy would come home from work and read a bedtime story to me.

Mommy had said I was being a bad boy by not sleeping, but I wasn't tired. My tummy was sore, and my cheek hurt from Mommy slapping me because I was crying for her to read me the book instead.

I wipe the back of my hands against my wet cheeks and hug myself with my blankie to try to heat up. It's always cold now. Rain leaks into my window and soaks my floor—I tried to clean up the puddle soaking my toys with my teddy bear, and now he's ruined too.

When I fall asleep, I wake to my mommy cuddling me. She smells weird, and the bed is wet. Maybe Mommy needs to wear a diaper like I do. It itches sometimes, especially when I keep it on for days.

I smile as I look up at her face. Her eyes are closed, and she's snoring, so I bury my head into her chest and fall back to sleep.

I'm happy again.

The following night is the exact same.

The next week is the same. It rolls into more weeks. Months.

Am I five now?

Mommy said I'm weird. She doesn't like it when I'm weird. How do I stop being weird? I don't want to be weird. She blames me for Daddy running away.

After school, Mommy holds my hand all the way to the bus. She tells me that my daddy sent me a birthday present, and it's waiting for me at home. I grin with excitement, skipping the rest of the way and having to pull Mommy along because she's barely walking straight and smells like beer.

"Slow down, Malachi," she snaps, yanking my arm hard enough to hurt, making my smile drop.

She has bright red lipstick on today. Some of it is smudged at the corner, and it's smeared across her teeth. I won't tell her—she yelled at me the last time I told her.

"Sorry," I reply quietly and walk slowly all the way home with an ache in my arm—I think she scratched me, but I don't say anything.

There's a box on the table with little holes, and a glass tank beside it. A birthday card with a big number five is on the front, and Mommy goes to lie on the couch while I open the card, trying to read the writing. Although Mommy thinks I'm dumb, my teacher always tells me how great I am with words, so even though the handwriting is messy, I can read the note.

Malachi,

I'm sorry I can't be there for you anymore, son. I hope you can one day forgive me for leaving. You see, Daddy's head isn't a nice place, and he's not good for you and your mother. I tried so hard, but you both deserve better.

6

I wish I could choose you and fight the poison in my brain, but I can't.
I'll see you again one day, but hopefully not anytime soon.
Your new eight-legged friend will protect you, just like I know you'll
protect him. I suggest the name Rex or Spikey. Don't be afraid of him.
After all, you're an arachnophile, just like me.
Love, Daddy.

I frown and look up, seeing Mommy is already asleep on the sofa. What does Daddy mean? Why can't he choose me? Where is he going?

My gaze turns to the box, and I drop the card on the table and inch closer. My long, dirty nails peel away the tape from the top, and I gasp when I open it to see a huge fluffy spider crawling around the box.

My eyes widen. "Um, Mommy?"

She's still snoring, and when I shake her, she knocks me away so I fall on my butt. "Go away."

I get to my feet and look at the box again, hesitating and a little scared before I go back to it, looking down to see the pet my daddy left me. Then I reach in and hold my hand at the bottom to see if it will come to me, shaking a little when it scurries right into my palm. It tickles, but my heart is going too fast to care.

Will it bite me?

I lift the hand with the spider until it's at eye level. "Hi," I say in my squeaky voice. "You're my new best friend."

For the next few weeks, life is a little fun again. Mommy told me my new pet was called a tarantula and I needed to keep it in my room. His name is Rex.

He sleeps in his tank while I lie in bed. I sing to him sometimes. He even watches me while I read him a book, so my mommy doesn't have to.

I don't see Mommy that much now—she's always busy with her friends. I miss my daddy, but he said he'll see me again, so I'll wait for him to come home.

Big bad men are always in the house. One of them came into my room once and tried to take Rex, but my mommy started locking my door again, this time with two keys.

There are loads of people in the house right now, but I need to sleep. I want to go outside. I'm not allowed to go to school because I'm sick. But I feel fine. Why won't my mommy let me go outside and play?

Daddy used to always play a game with me. I would hide, and he'd try to find me. He'd chase me until I laughed, screaming loud enough to hurt my throat, and tears would slide down my cheeks while I smiled up at my hero.

Rex is my only friend now. He's silent. So am I. Mommy hates that I don't talk to her anymore, but I like keeping things to myself. Everything I say always results in a slap across my face or her yelling at me.

He's the only one who talks to me now without using words. My best friend. My protector. My hero until Daddy comes home.

My eyes ping open when I hear a door slam downstairs. Am I supposed to be asleep? I don't know if the stars are out anymore—Mommy painted my window black, and I'm not allowed to leave my room. Not that I want to. The house is very messy, and the dogs poop everywhere, and there's never any food.

I think Rex might be hungry too.

The last time I spoke, I told Mommy I didn't want to wear diapers anymore. I know how to use the bathroom, but I'm not allowed to.

It itches. It hurts when I sit down. She told me to shut up, and I cried to Rex until we agreed not to let anyone hear our voices anymore. He could do it, and since it's been weeks of silence, so can I.

I stand on shaky legs and open Rex's tank, finding my friend burrowed in his little den. I place my palm down, and it takes him a few minutes before he catches my scent and crawls onto my hand.

The yelling is getting louder, and my breathing turns shaky.

Don't worry, I say in my head. *I'll protect you.*

I jump as a loud, bellowing laugh travels through the door.

It's my final warning to quickly hide under my bed. I crawl under and place Rex on the floor in front of my face, then lean my chin in my palms and wait for the voices to vanish.

Then I pause and freeze all over, because someone unlocks and opens my bedroom door. Two someones. I can see their dirty socks exploring my room, then a pair of boots appears in front of my face.

"Fuck. It smells like shit in here. Where is he?"

"Elise did say he was in here. How much did you pay her?"

"Fifty," he replies. "Is the bitch still breathing?"

"Barely. I made sure she took more than enough to kill her though."

Heart thumping heavy in my chest, I hold my breath—it always helps not to cry when I hold my breath, even if it hurts me and makes my eyes water.

The boots come closer to my bed. I gulp and try scooting away.

My heart goes faster as I gather Rex in my hands protectively. I won't let them hurt Rex. I—

A hand grabs at my ankle, and the noise I want to let out makes my lungs burn as I'm dragged from under the bed to see a bearded man grinning down at me.

I close my eyes and scream so loud in my head, my brain aches and I get dizzy.

I hold Rex to my chest, my eyes stinging with tears as the man grabs my jaw. I open my eyes to see the other one grinning with a toothless mouth. His gaze drops to my hands. "What do we have here?"

He grabs Rex, and I panic, unable to pull the words together to tell them to stop as they start throwing Rex back and forth like it's a game. The bad man wraps his fingers around Rex, and I stare at him with wide eyes, desperate for him not to hurt my best friend. I want to scream for them to leave him alone, but I can't.

I can't. I can't, I can't, I can't.

Rex is the only part I have left of my daddy until he comes for me.

"Your mom is dying," he says. "Do you want us to help her?"

I nod, my bottom lip trembling.

Please save her. Please, please, please.

"Use your words, boy."

My lips part, but no sound comes out. I can't. What's wrong with me?

He laughs loudly and looks at his friend. "I think we traumatized the kid."

"Take him downstairs. Show him his whore of a mother taking her last breaths."

I'm grabbed by the shoulder and dragged to my feet, and then he laughs again. "He's wearing a goddamn shitty diaper."

"I want my fifty bucks back," his friend replies, grimacing.

They take me downstairs, and I can hear the dogs barking, trapped in the kitchen. The man drops me onto the floor, and I open my eyes to see Mommy on the ground, vomit dripping from her mouth, unblinking, staring right at me as her chest struggles to rise and fall—she's making a horrible choking noise.

Oh no. Mommy? Are you okay?

I can't form the words.

"Beg us to save her, and we'll get the paramedics here."

I look up at the bearded man, my teeth rattling with fear.

I can't.

I can't save her.

"Hmm," he hums, grabbing something from the table. "The kid has a voice. Elise showed us those videos of him, remember? We just need to drag it out of him. What's in this?" He lifts the pointy thing I've seen my mommy play with, and his friend shrugs.

Pain explodes in my arm—I hold my breath and close my eyes as the men chuckle. "He's stubborn like his mother."

My eyes go funny—I can't control them or my body, and I grow weak and tired real fast.

Hours later, I sit up from the floor. Mommy is still in the same position, but her lips are blue and her eyes are still open. The bad men are sitting on the sofa. "Look, the little fucker is awake again."

My feet hurt. My arms hurt.

They have Rex.

"We need to head off soon, but we have a bet on who can force you to make a sound. You're like a little mouse, aren't you, kid? It's sad." He looks over at the picture of me, Mommy, and Daddy, all three of us happy as I smile wide for the camera in my daddy's arms. Our dogs were sitting nice for the picture too. "Good life turned bad and all."

He sighs deeply and takes Rex in his palm. "Can you count?" he asks me.

I nod once, shakily. My teeth crush together as I keep my eyes on my friend.

Then everything within me screams as he slowly, one-by-one, pulls Rex's legs off. He tells me to count, to speak up, to scream, and then when he realizes I'm not going to make a sound, he crushes my best friend in his hand, drops him on the floor, and slams his boot down.

I should scream. I should cry. I should do something.

But I couldn't protect him, just like I couldn't protect Mommy. I failed.

"He's severely emaciated," a lady says as the doctor shines

a light in my eyes. "He had a soiled diaper on when they found him. Sores and rashes all over him."

Someone tuts, and I'm scared. I feel sleepy, and I want my mommy and daddy. I want to go home.

"The father?"

"Dead. Suicide," someone adds quietly, but my hearing is better than ever since I stopped talking, like I can focus more on my surroundings. "Child services are conducting a meeting as we speak for an emergency home."

"This kid isn't leaving this hospital anytime soon. Can we get more fluids? And we need bloods checked. There are pin pricks on his arms and at the bottoms of his feet."

"He has a dead spider in his pocket." The lady's voice trails off. "Christ," she whispers.

I blink. They keep asking me things, but I don't answer them. They might hurt me too.

A tear slips down my cheek when I think of how long I lay on the floor with Rex and my mommy. They wouldn't wake up. More tears spill, and I feel a hand on my shoulder, making me flinch and pull away.

"You're safe now," the lady says. "Can you tell me your name?"

They already know my name.

I'm Malachi.

I keep my lips still and screw my eyes closed. Maybe if I

count to ten, they'll all disappear.

I count in my head.

I don't know how high I count before I fall asleep again.

CHAPTER TWO
MALACHI
Aged 8

W eeks later, when I go to my first new home, they keep me in my room because I make their kids sad since I don't talk.

I'm sent back to the big building filled with kids until another family comes for me. I'm not sure how many times this happens. How many new mommies and daddies pick up their new children and look happy and mine look terrified, but it keeps going and going. No one wants me as their son. No one ever picks me out of the group. I'm handed to families who are desperate, but it never works out for either of us.

When I turn eight, I don't get any birthday cards or a cake like the other kids in the orphanage—I sit under the bed with a drawing of my spider and imagine a crowd of people singing happy birthday to me, and we blow out candles that I draw.

I close my eyes and make a wish.

I wish someone would choose me.

The footsteps come, and my door opens, and I wait for my leg to get pulled. It won't. It's what they call a trauma response to my past. It's the nightmare I can't pull away from. I glance up from under the bed.

The lady who's the boss of the building glares down at me. "What are you doing?"

I try to sign like I've been taught, but she shakes her head and walks away from me. "It doesn't matter. Get dressed and put all your things into a bag."

I stand robotically, and it takes me a few moments to remember the sign for *why?*

"You're going on a plane," she says, handing me a used plastic bag. "A new family. They'll have the same trial period as the others. Will you behave this time? This family actually chose you this time. I have faith."

I always behave. They just don't like that I'm not normal. They wanted to play and be friends and all that other stuff. I never knew how to—I struggled with communicating since none of them could sign. No one wanted to go through the hassle of learning either. They all just tried to make me talk, and I'm happy with the way I am. It's peaceful and quiet, and I like it.

I was the odd one out at the other houses, and I still am.

Yes, I sign. *I'll behave.*

I was excited the first time they found me a new family.

Not anymore.

It takes a full day to reach where I'll be calling home for the next few weeks. I hate flying, and the lady traveling with me doesn't talk to me once—she doesn't even understand sign language.

"Be on your best behavior, Malachi," she says in an angry tone as I walk beside her with my plastic bag through the busy airport. She's holding my hand tightly. "I don't want to fly all the way back here to take you to another home."

What she means is that I've not to be weird and scare the foster daughter. Everyone thinks I'm weird. They're scared of me. They don't like the way I make them all feel uncomfortable. I've been to five homes, and all of them, within weeks, gave me back like I was a broken toy.

We reach people who talk about me, but I keep my gaze unfocused and on the floor. I wonder how long I'll last here? They'll close me in the bedroom and treat me like I'm fragile— I'll be the kid they'll pretend to feel sorry for until I'm returned.

If they send me back, which they probably will, I'll run away again and make sure they'll never find me.

Because I'll be in heaven with my parents.

I stop in my mental tracks as a little girl with long brown hair appears in front of me with the biggest smile on her face.

"Hi!" She's grinning at me and says, "My name is Olivia. I'm seven!" She holds up seven fingers, and I mentally hold up eight.

Hi, Olivia. I'm Malachi, I want to say or sign, but I just stare at her.

"Do you think I look like a princess?"

Mentally, I nod. But physically, I step forward. I like her— she doesn't make me uncomfortable. She's so happy compared to everyone else. And she's happy to meet me.

I tilt my head.

Her smile drops. "You don't like my dress?"

Without thinking, because I want her to like me too, I lift my hands and sign, *Please don't be afraid of me.*

But the confusion on her face and the look she gives her mom tells me she has no idea what I'm saying.

That's okay. I'll teach her.

I sign the same thing to her again because I need her to know I don't want to scare her—I'm desperate to make sure she knows that.

"Was it scary on the plane? I always cry when it goes really fast and shoots off into the sky! Daddy always makes us go on one. He's your daddy now too!"

I rub the back of my neck, tugging at the long strands of my hair. She seems happy—does that mean she likes her family? I want to talk to her so badly, but I don't think I can.

She goes to look at her parents again, but I touch her wrist to get her attention and sign, *Come with me.*

She's still lost, so I point at the revolving doors, and we hold hands as we run towards it—she's giggling, her hair flowing wild, and I spot the sign for the bathroom. I'll try to talk to her there, away from everyone.

"Where are we going?" she asks, tripping over her feet. I catch her before she falls and pull her towards the bathroom, dodging everyone as we run.

When we get inside, she tries to leave, but I stop her. *I want to talk to you,* I sign, pointing to myself.

Am I already scaring her? Have I already ruined this?

She's still confused, so I point to my mouth and shake my head, because even though it's just us, I can't seem to talk. I point to her mouth and nod.

Her lips part. "You can't talk?"

I shake my head. But I want to talk to her so badly, to tell her I might be strange, but I can be her friend—I'm harmless. I just… can't.

"That's okay! I couldn't talk for so, so long! I can teach you."

I pause then roll my eyes. Why can't everyone accept me for the way I am? I don't need to be taught how to talk.

Her eyes are so alive and colorful. She's nice, and she's being nice to me.

I point to her then rest my palm on my chest, coming closer to her. I want to take her hand and make her do the same sign, to tell me that I'm also hers—hers, her best friend, her new brother—but before I can, the door is knocked open, and my new foster dad is rushing in, the mom picking up Olivia.

"I told you not to be trouble!" he yells at her, and I want to stamp my foot and tell him to back off, but then he turns to me. "And you. You're on a strike, little man. Two more, and your ass is going to *another* new home. You're Malachi Vize now, and the Vizes don't step out of line, so get used to it."

He's not sending me back? He's giving me another chance? I can stay?

I look at the girl then lower my head, signing, *I'm sorry.*

"He's saying he's sorry, sweetie," the mom says. "He communicates with sign language."

"What's that? I want to do it too!"

My head lifts at her words, and a little ball of excitement grows in my chest, especially when the mom tells her they'll teach everyone in the house.

"Malachi will be comfortable in our home. He's one of us now."

I hold back tears, blinking a few times as they lead us out of the bathroom, the dad's hand on my shoulder, directing me out of the airport and into a car. I think they're rich. Their car is huge and fancy, and the house we pull up to is a mansion. My eyes widen a little at the sight, then my attention is back on the girl beside me. I can't stop looking at her. I haven't felt this content since I had Rex, before he was taken from me.

She won't be taken from me. I'll make sure of it. I'll be good. I'll do as I'm told. I'll be the kid they obviously needed to complete their family.

Olivia.

My new little sister. I couldn't protect my mom or Rex, but I think I could protect her.

I will protect her.

Because she's mine.

CHAPTER THREE

MALACHI
Aged 12

When I get off the school bus, I pull my bag up my shoulder and head straight to where I know my sister will be standing. Olivia will be with her crowd of friends. She always is. Always getting attention—the popular girl. She leaves the house earlier than me on Tuesday—her friends have this thing they've been doing for years where they get to school an hour early and sit around gossiping.

As soon as I spot her, I stop walking and hide to the side, leaning my back against the wall. My usual standing position while the world still moves around me. My eyes follow her as she goes to the swings, her friend, Abigail, sitting on the one beside her as they talk. With their heads turned, I can't read their lips—what if she's talking about me?

I won't go to stand with her, but as long as I can see her, I'm happy. The bottom of my foot rests against the wall, and I stop breathing as a group of three boys go to the swings too. They're the year below me, maybe two years, and I tower over them. Being the tallest in my year and the one above, plus not having any friends or talking, I'm not very liked here at school.

They call me a freak.

They say I'm strange and weird.

Olivia doesn't think that, so their opinions are invalid and mean nothing to me. I like staying in my own corner and observing my little sister from afar in public, then as close as possible while we're home. Not in a creepy way—Mom just says I'm far too protective of her, and Dad tells me regularly to chill out.

My blood boils as one of them pushes Olivia on her swing, but she pushes off it and turns away from him. I can't be sure, but I think she tells him to go away and leave her alone.

He pulls the ribbon in Olivia's hair just as the bell rings, and I feel rage rushing when she shoves the boy in the chest and walks away from the trio, Abigail trailing behind. He tries to grab her again, but Olivia runs.

The boy is laughing with his friends.

I push off the wall and head straight for them, gritting my teeth hard enough to hurt.

No one bullies my little sister and gets away with it.

I follow with one thing on my mind—pain. I want to hurt them. All three of them are the last to leave the playground. I move behind them, silent, sliding my bag down from my shoulders.

I grip the arm strap and swing it, the packed lunch Mom made and textbook making it heavy as it smacks into the side of one of their heads, knocking him down.

I smash it off the second's head too when he tries to get away then go after the third, the one who pulled Olivia's ribbon and laughed at her, right into the hallway.

"What the hell?" he calls out as I chase him.

I want to see him bleed.

He pulls a door open, and I run right into it, pain lashing my eye, but I keep going, kicking his ankles to make him trip up and land on his front.

A teacher grabs me just after I punch him in the face.

I'm dragged, kicking and throwing my fists, out of bed in the middle of the night by my dad and pulled from the bedroom I share with my sister—I've been in bed since after school, refusing to see anyone, not even Olivia. She'll ask me what happened to my eye, and she'll find out what I did. I can't tell her I beat up kids for her.

She'll be afraid. I can't have her afraid of me.

Dad drops me and wraps his hand around my wrist tightly,

leading me down the hallway, down the grand staircase, and into his office. He slams the door and paces, his hands running through his silvering hair.

"What the hell were you thinking? I had your principal and parents screaming down the line about you attacking their kids!"

They were bullying Olivia, I sign.

He stops pacing, his hands dropping to his sides.

Then he comes forward and grabs my jaw. "And what happened to your eye?"

Embarrassment has my cheeks turning red. *I ran into a door while chasing one of them.*

"You can't go around beating people up. You're twelve years old. You're not even a teenager yet and you're out there breaking noses!"

This is all I've been hearing all day—how someone my age can be so aggressive. Since when does age count? I stuck up for my sister—he should be grateful.

"What am I going to do with you?"

The question has my spine straightening, and my eyes widen a touch. *Don't send me back,* I sign. *I promise I'll be good.*

Dad walks to his desk, leans against it, and folds his arms. "I'm not sending you anywhere, Malachi. I just want you to behave. I'm a lawyer, and I can't end up on the news because my son is out of control. Why couldn't you have just threatened them? Told them to stay away? Or even better, tell a teacher or me."

All I heard there was that he isn't sending me away.

I silently sigh in relief, my shoulder untensing.

"I think your monthly therapy sessions need to be more frequent. I'll speak to your doctor about weekly appointments. Olivia isn't aware of this incident, and she won't be told. She sees you as an anchor, and we need to keep it that way. I'd rather this stays between us. The boys have all been removed from the school because their parents don't feel like it's safe for them anymore. Please, for crying out loud, Malachi, no more fights."

I nod and lower my head.

"You scared your sister with the way you were kicking around there. Go back and apologize and go to sleep. Your mother will take you to get that eye looked at tomorrow."

I scared her?

I get to my feet and leave, heading to the bedroom. As soon as I open the door, Olivia sits up on her bed, rubbing her eyes. "Malachi?"

I'm sorry, I sign as I lower myself to the edge of her bed. *I'm sorry,* I sign again, this time more firmly as my fist rubs against my chest.

"Did Dad hurt you?"

I shake my head, but I don't think she believes me. Dad hates me—I know he does. Sometimes he drags me to his office roughly for the most minuscule things, and he yells at me way more than he does Olivia, so I know he sees us differently.

I'm the son neither of them wanted but are stuck with. They already think the therapist needs to do more tests—I'm not ready for them yet apparently, whatever that means.

She tips her head, her hair falling in her face. It always smells like strawberries—soft, comforting.

"Do you want a hug?"

Nodding, I slip in beside Olivia. We wrap our arms around each other, keeping each other safe like we have done since we became brother and sister, and fall asleep.

CHAPTER FOUR
MALACHI
Aged 17

Olivia's music is shit, and she's giving me a fucking headache.

We're out running next to the manor, along from the lake we're heading to, and she keeps going in front of me and nearly tripping me up. I might kick her ankles and leave her in the dirt, but then I'll feel bad and apologize, so I decide against it.

Her ridiculous pop music is playing in my ear, Olivia with the other earpiece, while she keeps up with my jogging pace. She's fit. Being a cheerleader and exercising nearly as much as me means we can hang out more. I like to run—so does she.

The perfect sibling fit. And I get to spend more time with her.

Is that weird? I don't care if it is. I'm always in a better mood when I'm around my little sister, like I can be the best version of myself. She doesn't even try to force me to talk or act as though there's something wrong with me, like my asshole friends.

I mean, they aren't assholes, but they aren't *not* assholes.

Shaking my head to focus, my eyes flick to the side, and I try not to look at her chest as I sign, *Dad's teaching me how to drive later.*

She laughs. "That'll be a horrible experience. You should stick to just riding your bike. All he's going to do is yell the entire time."

Probably. He doesn't have much patience, especially since I've been in more fights than I can count the last year—plus the fact he caught me smoking a joint out on my balcony.

He tolerates me now. They've raised me for the last nine years, so they can't exactly toss me back into the system, and honestly, as much as I believe my dad hates me sometimes, I think he still cares about me enough to let me stick around.

We argue and fight a lot though, so maybe I'm delusional.

"Keep up or the Bluetooth will cut out," Olivia calls out.

I blink and realize I've fallen behind, but I linger for a bit and watch her ass, mentally slapping myself because she would never speak to me again if she knew I was even looking at her that way. Plus if her connection cuts, then I can rid myself of fucking pop music by some girl group singing about breaking up with their ex and be saved from the earache.

I catch up anyway, and her music switches to something slow as we reach the lake—she's bending over and catching her breath while I pull my cigarettes from my shorts and light one. She looks over her shoulder at me, still bending over and giving me a full view that I definitely shouldn't be zoned into.

She frowns and straightens. "Why?"

I raise a questioning brow and hope to fucking God she didn't catch her own brother checking her out.

"Smoking is bad for you, especially when you're out running, Malachi."

Hmm. I love when she says my name.

No. Shut the fuck up.

"Mom and Dad will smell it on you when we get home. I'm not sticking up for you again when they corner you in the kitchen."

I shrug and blow a cloud of smoke above my head, leaning against a tree stump while watching her stretch. She's bending over again, touching her toes, and I lift my eyes to the sky before I get caught looking down her top.

This is new.

A little fucked up too.

But over the last few months, I can't stop looking at Olivia and noticing that not only is she as beautiful as she always has been, but she's also really, really attractive. Not in a way a brother should be noticing or thinking about.

I get this feeling inside me when she giggles or when she smiles at me—like a flock of butterflies are going wild. It's addictive. To be happy and excited. I try to be with her at all times to maintain the feeling and try to argue with the voices in my head that it's all kinds of fucked up to have a crush on someone you call a sibling and were raised with.

Dad would hang me—then shoot me to make sure I'm dead.

I reckon I'd still find a way to be around Olivia. The ghost in her closet or the monster under her bed she befriends and cuddles to sleep.

I frown at my own ridiculous and immature thoughts while she types on her phone.

The sun is starting to rise. There's a soft glow around us, peeking through the tree canopy from above. Through the woods, we can see the sun growing brighter in the distance. It's the same view, but we always end up trapped by it.

But this time it seems I'm the only one paying attention because Olivia comes up beside me, takes my cigarette, then tosses it into the lake.

Her narrowing eyes make me smirk.

Do you want to go into the lake next? I sign. *Because I'm seconds from tossing you in too.*

Crossing her arms, she pops out her hip. "You wouldn't."

She squeals as I grab her, lifting her off her feet and throwing her over my shoulder while walking towards the edge of the lake. She's kicking her bare legs, screaming my name, and slapping my shoulders. Standing an inch from the water, I silently laugh, sliding her down my front and pretending to swing her in, causing her to tighten her arm around my neck.

I pause when she wraps her legs around my waist and

brackets her thighs.

"Please don't," she pleads. "I'm begging you."

Fuck.

Too close.

I drop her like she's burned me, and she catches herself before she topples in. She slaps my chest. "You asshole!"

I have the sudden urge to grab her face and kiss her.

It's abrupt and absurd and new. I've kissed Olivia a million times, but not the way I want to right now. It's wrong in so many ways.

I'm attracted to my sister. I must be, right? There's no way in hell I can't be attracted to her—to me, she's a masterpiece.

Realization hits me like a fucking plane crash and makes me blink a few times and look away. My heart beats wildly in my chest at my bad luck. I always knew I was fucked up, but this? This takes the fucking cake. Dad wants me to go back to therapy and get myself medicated. Maybe I should—not for my twisted thoughts, but for the feelings I shouldn't have for Olivia.

Is there medication that stops you from wanting to kiss your sister?

Before, it was all about protecting her—I always felt an attachment, but not like this. I want to kiss her the way boyfriends and girlfriends do.

My breathing changes, and I'm so damn confused by the way I feel—she's still too close to me, and I flex my fingers, needing to wrap them in her top and tug her to me, to smash my mouth down on hers, but I step back instead and swallow hard.

She goes back to typing on her phone while I light another cigarette, refusing to look at her. She's unaffected and none the wiser that her brother is fighting an inner war not to ruin everything by acting on impulse. We're sixteen and seventeen now, but we're still too young for me to be thinking the way I do.

Now I'm angry. Because I have a crush on someone I can never have. I want to explode at the world, or maybe pick a fight with my father and see if he's all talk about beating my ass when he threatens me.

Coming to stand by my side, she nudges me with her shoulder and tips her chin to the sunrise. "I know you have a heart of stone, but you gotta admit that it's pretty."

It is, I sign lazily, my eyes on her as she looks back at the view.

My heart isn't made of stone. It's filled with poison.

What would she do if I did kiss her? Would she kiss me back and become my little secret, or would she run to our parents and get me kicked out of the family?

Maybe she'd pull away from me but wouldn't tell a soul.

The risk is fucking big, but I want to feel my lips on hers so damn badly.

Ultimately, as she wraps her arms around my waist and rests her head on my chest, we watch as the sun reaches the horizon, me inhaling the strawberry scent of her hair and running my fingers through the soft strands like I always do.

Even this isn't normal. I know it isn't, but I don't care.

We can't be close like this in front of our parents or our friends. I was already thrown to the other side of the manor because I kissed her on the lips during a board-game celebration. It was innocent, but Mom and Dad lost their fucking heads.

So we're only close like this in secret. When we go for runs together or sneak into one another's rooms to cuddle, or when I hold her hand while she tries to calm down from a nightmare.

There's a boundary that society created, stopping me from falling in love with my sister, and I want to tear that boundary to fucking shreds and keep her. I'll set fire to it and everyone who stands in my way.

I love Olivia, but I'm not sure it's the same way I grew up loving her anymore. It's stronger, violent, and I have a feeling if she ordered me to get on my knees and kiss her fucking feet, I'd do it. Anything she asked, I'd do.

Fuck. I'm so screwed. Dad is definitely going to kill me because I can't feel this way about my own damn sister.

"I need to tell you something," she says quietly.

What?

"Do you remember a while ago Mom was talking about the tradition of arranged marriages that run in our family?"

My teeth crush together as I think about the first time I was told Olivia would be paired up with someone and taken away from me. Yes, I fucking remember. How could I forget one of the worst things I've ever heard in my life?

"Well, it's already started."

I frown and look down at her, waiting for her to elaborate on what the fuck she means by that. She's too young, too fucking innocent to get thrown into that life.

"Um…" She hesitates then buries her head into my chest, muffling her voice. "Mom is arranging dates already."

My entire body seizes, and I pause stroking her hair.

"The first date is this weekend. Me and Mom are going over to his house to talk with his parents. He's a little older than me and really wants to meet me."

This is ridiculous. She's only sixteen.

Gracing her with any response would result in an argument. I'd tell her no, she'd tell me to fuck off, and then we'd give each other the silent treatment for an entire day before one of us snuck into the other's room.

"I hope he's nice though. Imagine he's mean? I'd need to send my big brother to kick his ass." She's giggling, but I'm still, silent as always, and I think I might pass out from rage.

I'm imagining him in a body bag.

Bloodied.

Ripped to shreds.

Diced and minced and pulverized.

No longer in existence.

No one will ever be good enough for Olivia.

"I've to stay a virgin until the wedding night. Not that I'm sleeping around at this age." Olivia lifts her head to look at me. "Are you a virgin?"

My brows knit together at her question. I am—the idea of sex has never been something I sought out. Yeah, I've jacked off while trying to watch porn, but I never thought of actually going out and fucking someone the way my friends all do. They do try to get me to screw someone, but I always end up leaving the party early and sober, or I get so drunk and unable to even see properly that I stagger home to my sister. She looks after me—a glass of water, a sick bucket, a cold cloth on my head, and she hugs me until I lose consciousness.

She clamps her mouth shut with a disappointed look on her face when she realizes she's getting no response from me. "Sorry. That was inappropriate."

I slide my hand from her hair. *Do you want to get married?*

She shrugs. "Mom has been preparing me for this since I was a kid. She was even excited when I got my period because it gives the arrangement a better value."

I gulp and start to form a plan of kidnapping Olivia away from this life.

"Uhh." She face-palms. "I'm sorry. I'm going to make you vomit everywhere. Sorry."

Don't apologize, I sign. *You can talk to me about anything and I'll never be weirded out.*

I'm furious right now. I might kill our parents and make it look like an accident. I could set the house on fire, trap them both in my dad's office, and be Olivia's shoulder to cry on before I inevitably somehow make her fall in love with me.

Fuck. I just said that.

I can't take my thoughts back now—I want my sister, and I want her badly. I don't know how I'll manage it, but Olivia and I are going to be each other's firsts in everything. Not yet, but in a few years when we're old enough and fully understand how it all works.

When Olivia's ready, then I will be too.

My mind needs to slow down. She might actually see me as her brother, and the thought of even kissing me in a passionate way might repulse her.

Unless I pretend to be someone else? Hide my face?

No, that defeats the purpose.

Fuck.

She isn't getting married to anyone but me. I'll speak to our parents. I'm sure they'd prefer she was with someone they trusted and not some older prick.

I heavily breathe out my nose and pull back, taking her hand and gesturing to the running trail that takes us home. She squeezes my hand before she lets go, reconnects her ear-bleeding music, and we run back to get ready for school.

Mom and Dad are in my father's office when we get home from school. Olivia goes to her room to get changed because she's going to her friend's house to do some routine practice.

I'm trying to go over everything I need to communicate with our parents without her knowing my plan. Or that I'm having a mental breakdown and that my knuckles are still sore from beating the shit out of someone in the locker room.

He told me that if I vocally begged, he wouldn't try to fuck my sister and record it, so I fucked his head off the bench and gave him a black eye.

Dad will know about it by now, but he's long given up trying to discipline me. He'll warn me, try to force me back into therapy, then give a spiel of how I'm making the house unsafe for future fosters. Blah, blah, fucking blah.

I'm sticking up for myself and my sister—I'm not just going out and choosing someone as my next target, but no one understands that. I was labeled an issue, a problem child, the son with a suitcase full of trauma, so it would've been a miracle if I was normal.

When I reach the office, I can hear them. Dad is giving Mom a hard time about Olivia's age and how she's borderline grooming his daughter.

Fuck. Deep breaths.

I knock on the office door, and their whispering comes to a halt.

"Come in," my dad calls out.

I open the door and step into his office, both their eyes on me and filled with confusion. I never do this. Never seek them out. I don't go to them for a single thing or communicate unless it's absolutely necessary.

Not for any particular reason—I just like reserving all my conversation for a certain someone. I know they'd rather step on Legos than talk anyway. Not even my friends get much out of me. One of them knows sign language, and that's enough for him to translate to the group.

Honestly, I'm still unsure why they're friends with me. They only welcomed me into their little group after I started beating up people who messed with Olivia.

"Malachi?"

I blink, realizing I've frozen on the spot and my parents are staring at me like I have two heads.

I mean, I do.

"Is there something wrong?" Mom asks.

Olivia isn't marrying anyone, I sign, closing the door behind me and getting straight to the point. *She's too young.*

Mom scoffs. "Get out, Malachi. Don't you have to study for your test next week?"

I step forward. *Why does she need to get married?*

"Tradition, son," Dad says. "You know this."

Fuck the tradition.

Dad rolls his eyes and pinches the bridge of his nose. "This is of no concern to you. We'll find a suitor who we can trust, and when she's old enough, she'll marry him. This has been in the family for generations."

Even as the words fall from my father's lips, I know he hates them. Regret is all over his face as Mom tries to conceal her smile. They've been arguing nonstop about this. He refuses, yet she wins every time they have a debate.

You can trust me, I sign, not a single nerve going haywire as I keep my confidence. *I'll marry her.* Stepping further into the room, desperate for them to listen, I keep going. *She'll be safe with me. I promise. You can remove me from adoption, and I'll wait until we're both old enough.*

I'm about to turn eighteen—she's just turned sixteen. They can't say no because I'm the only person in the world who can protect Olivia.

Why are they just staring at me? They look… disgusted. Disappointed. Because I straight up offered that they could remove me from the family maybe?

You don't need to look for someone. I'll do it.

Dad laughs. "Very funny."

I stare at him for a long second then look at Mom. *Why can't*

I do it?

"You're serious?" she asks with a revolted look. "That's vile. That's—"

"Not happening," Dad finishes sternly. "But I agree that she's too young." He looks at Mom. "Give her a few years to find her own partner."

"I already have suitors lined up. One I'm especially interested in is your business partner's son. Parker Melrose."

"Absolutely not. He's twenty-one, Jennifer."

Oh, hells fucking no. Olivia left that piece of information out. Why the fuck is Mom trying to partner her up with someone five years older?

Despite the dire need to trash the place to get across how angry I am, desperation seeps into my vein. *Let me marry her.*

Mom glares at me. "No. Don't be ridiculous. You're her brother. She needs someone who comes from money. She needs someone stable who can give her children."

I will, I sign slowly. *I can do that, Mom.*

Her face contorts, but it's Dad who grabs my shirt and yanks me forward, dragging me to the chair. I want to break his fucking hand, but I need them to agree. There's not a chance in hell I'm letting them push Olivia into the arms of a grown-ass man when I'm the perfect suitor for her.

He shoves me down on the chair and steps away, trying to control his rage. "This fascination you have with Olivia needs to stop, Malachi. It's wrong and sick, and I won't stand for it any longer. You're her brother. Start acting like it."

Mom crosses her arms, shaking her head. "We talked about this before when we moved you to another room. Your father has been warning you off her since you were a child. We thought it was a friendship thing and you just needed her to help you… ground yourself. We were worried you'd drag her down with you. But now you're suggesting incest? How sick are you?"

Grinding my teeth, I don't bother responding. It isn't incest. We aren't related by blood. We have different backgrounds. We were just two kids adopted by the same family. I'd happily give up a mother and a father to have even a day of calling Olivia mine.

Remove me from the adoption, I sign. *I'll marry her when we're old enough.* Then I pause, needing to swallow given how fucking much I need them to agree to this. *She'll feel safe with me. I'll protect her. Please.*

I'm repeating myself out of desperation, but I don't care. If they don't let me do this, I'll end up in jail or something for murdering any asshole who comes anywhere near Olivia.

This is probably the most I've ever conversed with my parents since I was a kid—I'm not even sure they realize.

Huffing, Mom crosses her arms and paces to the window. "When you got your diagnosis, we agreed that we'd keep things the way they've always been since adopting you. But if you're looking at your own sister and thinking about—" She stops and spins to glare at me, grimacing. "You can't be attracted to her, Malachi. It's not right."

I'm not attracted to her, I lie. *I want to keep her safe from you.*

She barks a laugh. "Unbelievable."

"This conversation is done. Olivia is sixteen. She's too young to even discuss this." Dad turns to his desk while shaking his head. "Give up on this idea of marrying our daughter off to the Melroses. The family may be rich, but the son won't remain faithful, and he's a spoiled little prick. We'll revisit this when she's finished school and mature enough. And you." He looks at me. "Stay away from your sister. You've already been warned. I do believe that this is you needing to protect her, but it's gone too far. You will go out with your friends, live your life, go on dates, party, until you're ready to work with me. That is all you'll be doing for this family."

He'd look better dead. So would Mom. I'll carve their bodies and stack their limbs into a suitcase before setting it on fire.

"Get out, the both of you."

Mom huffs dramatically and storms out, but I stay put. He sighs when he sees I haven't moved a muscle. I'll fight for this. I'll give up a family, a future he'd hand to me, every single thing the Vize family offers me as their son.

"You have my word that I won't marry her off at this age, and I respect that you want to protect her, but you need to stay in your lane." He rubs his face. "Tell me the truth. Between us. How do you see Olivia?"

I want to tell him so badly about how I really feel. Maybe I am sick and he can help me, or maybe he'll throw me out and I'll never see her again. I gulp, averting my eyes before signing the biggest lie I'll ever tell.

She's my little sister. That's all.

"Protect her," he says. "Be her big brother and keep her safe, but that's all. You can't and won't marry her. You're nearly eighteen—surely you know that's off the table?"

I look at the rug at my feet. My hands are fisting so tightly, my blunt nails are cutting into my palms.

"Look at me, son," he demands.

My gaze lifts, and my chest tightens at the way he's looking at me.

"We're both going to lose Olivia, so we need to just enjoy her presence while we can. Now, get the hell out of my office and never suggest that again."

I know, I just fucking know, whatever relationship we had as father and son is gone. He doesn't trust me. He doesn't think I'm safe enough for his daughter. I'm not good enough either. Unstable. Unreliable. And one word I've heard them using when they didn't know I could hear—broken.

I'm just the broken and deluded big brother trying to marry the fucking sister he has an unhealthy crush on.

I slam the door on my way out, ripping my cap off and running my hand through my hair as I head to my bedroom. I get to the top of the grand staircase when I hear something crash in Olivia's room.

When I reach her door, I open it slightly to see her rummaging through all of her things. She's in her cheerleading outfit, and I know from her naked lips, she's looking for the lip gloss that's in my pocket. I didn't technically steal it, but I like how it smells on her when she accidentally falls asleep beside me during movies, so sometimes, I take the little bottle and sniff it when Olivia isn't near.

Nothing like the addiction the scent of her hair sparks, but close.

I don't make myself known as she slams her vanity drawer and looks under her bed—she's on all fours, ass in the air, and I battle with myself to focus on the mess she's made of her room and not how exposed she is under her cheer skirt.

Pulling the lip gloss from my pocket, I knock on the door, and she straightens and turns to me. Her hair whips, and my heart races instantly.

Beautiful.

The more I look at her, the more I realize how doomed I am. I've never had any luck—but she's the rainbow I'll fucking chase to win something more important than my own life.

I want to kiss her. I want to know what the lip gloss feels like on her lips, to taste it, to make sure no one else in the world gets to know the feeling.

Shit. Why is it getting worse? The need for her.

Mom's right. It's wrong, but nothing has ever felt more right than when I'm around her.

Her eyes light up even though she's frowning. "Why do you have that? Did I leave it in the kitchen again?"

I nod, stepping in and closing the door.

The buzzing of my phone pulls my attention away from the movie I'm watching. I'm half-asleep, my hair still wet from the shower, the towel around my waist.

Olivia

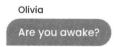

I don't even need to reply—I know what she wants. Olivia has nightmares sometimes, and when they happen, she needs me. She'll always need me to push her demons away.

I get dressed and pull on my hoodie, then pause and pull it back off, keeping it in my hand as I climb over my balcony, crossing the ledge until I reach her unlocked window. I slide it open and jump in, stopping when I see Olivia sitting up in bed, visibly shaken.

Must've been a really bad nightmare this time.

She pulls her duvet aside and takes the hoodie after I drop it in her lap. But when I notice how red her eyes are, I frown.

What's wrong? I sign. *Have you been crying?*

She shakes her head and lies back down, and when I lower myself beside her, she pushes her back to my front and wraps my arm around her, lacing her fingers and holding our hands to the side of her cheek. It's wet from tears, and I feel another slide down against my skin.

Instead of pushing her to tell me what happened in the dream, I hold her tightly to me and inhale the sweet scent of strawberries.

"My tummy hurts," she says quietly. She's holding her stomach with her other hand, curling in on herself, her body shaking with soft sobs. "It hurts so much."

I unravel myself from her after a few minutes, heading into the bathroom to pour her a glass of water from the sink. I stop when I see the underwear and pants discarded on the floor next to the toilet.

Blood. Not too much of it, but it's there.

I stuff them into her laundry basket, not wanting her to feel embarrassed about her period. The gel packs she uses for her cramps aren't under the sink, so I sign to her that I'll be back in a minute and head to the kitchen.

I'll do anything to make her feel better—when she was

younger, her stomach would get sore and she'd cry from eating too much candy, and I'd cuddle her to sleep—I hate it when she's like this.

When she first got her period, she came to me, crying again, and said the pains were everywhere. After a quick internet search on home remedies, I ran her a warm bath, heated up soup Mom had made for us earlier that day, and we lay in bed for two days until she felt better.

We both have school tomorrow or we'd do it all over again.

I stop as soon as I walk in, seeing Mom at the breakfast bar, her head down, drinking straight from the bottle of wine. A box of tissues sits to the side, some scrunched up and stained with mascara-tinted tears.

I should ask her if she's okay, but I don't. I walk in, heat up two of the gel packs, then grab some Tylenol and a bag of chips.

Mom lifts her head to look at me, her eyes dropping to the stuff in my hands. Her lips flatten, then her head lowers again as her shoulders shake.

Dad storms in, ignoring me, and stops in front of the breakfast bar. "What the fuck do you think you're doing? We agreed to wait until Olivia was eighteen to meet Parker!"

Mom scoffs. "Calm down, Jamieson. He wanted to see her in person before agreeing to anything. They got on fine."

My eyes narrow. There's a stab of pain in my chest knowing she met the potential love of her life tonight.

"You had no right. Olivia is just as much my daughter as she is yours. You had no right to flaunt her to the Melrose family."

Mom glares. "Are you done?"

His gaze snaps to me then drops to the stuff in my arms. Just when I think he's going to give me a speech about staying away from Olivia, he fists his hands and storms out of the kitchen, his office door slamming in the distance.

Olivia is still awake and crying when I reach the room.

Her little whimpers are broken, but she sits up and takes the pills, drinks the water, and smiles weakly as I press a gel pack to her stomach for her to hold there. I climb in behind her again and put the other gel pack at the bottom of her back, holding it there with my own body pressing to hers.

After a minute, she whispers, "Thank you."

I nod against her hair, my eyes closing, hoping the pain meds start to work soon. Her low sobs start to settle, then she turns in my arms and kisses my cheek. "You're the best brother I could've ever asked for. I'm glad they adopted us both. You're my best friend too."

I stare at her for a beat, then the corner of my mouth curves even though I want to kiss her tears away and tell her I no longer want to be her brother, that I'd take every suitor's place if she'd accept me. Mom and Dad will allow it if she says yes. They can't deny both of us what we want.

She turns back around, adjusts the packs, then sighs.

Before I fall asleep, I hear her say, "Parker isn't nice at all."

CHAPTER FIVE

MALACHI
Aged 19

After my night-time jog around the manor, through the woods and back, I shower with my music blasting from my speaker—even with the paranoia I've been feeling all night that my sister is at her friends, I manage to stay calm while I wash my hair, rub soap over me, then rinse it all off.

As I step out and into my room, the music stops, and I spot my phone on the bedside unit, flashing with Olivia's name. She never calls me, for obvious reasons, so I frown and answer, pressing it to my ear.

"Hey. Hello. Hi. I think I'm drunk," she says, slurring her words. She lets out a little squeak, and I'm already throwing my clothes on while she's on speaker. "I tripped. Are you there? Can you tap something and let me know you can hear me?"

I go to my dresser, knock on the wood three times, then pull my motorbike boots on.

"O-Okay," she says. "We were at Abbi's, but I left." She

hiccups then laughs. "Why is it even raining? I need, like, a hug or something. Not flowers or chocolates or jewelry—I hate those. A hug... will work just fine."

Once I'm dressed, I type a message to her while she's still connected.

Me

Where are you?

"I'll-I'll show you."

She's silent for a beat then hiccups again, a notification popping up with her location.

"Did you know you're the best big brother ever? I love you," she says. "Like, I s-super love you. It's probably... weird, but I do love you lots."

I narrow my eyes, frowning. She tells me she loves me all the time, but now I want her to mean it in a different way.

"You're never allowed near my friends. Anna's brother had s-sex with Abbi, and now they're all f-fighting," she slurs, hiccoughing. "Do you even have sex? God, don't tell me. It'll be all I see w-when I look at you."

I have no idea how to reply to that.

Me

I can hear you walking. Sit down and I'll come for you.

She giggles and a reply comes through.

53

Olivia

You love me.

"Admit it," she says, laughing like she's told a funny joke. "I'm the best little sister ever!"

Fuck, she's never been this drunk.

The line goes dead. I call back, but it rings out.

Fuck.

Ever since she turned eighteen a few months ago, every time she gets wasted, I nearly die from discomfort. She goes to parties with Abigail, gets drunk, and I nearly always end up picking her ass up and bringing her home. Once, she came to a party I was at—she showed up outside my friend's house and I had to put one of them in their place when they attempted to flirt with her.

Mason. He's the one who can sign, but he likes to push my buttons sometimes when it comes to Olivia. I don't think she even knows any of my friends' names, yet I know everyone who comes within a five-mile radius of her.

Not really. I'm not that extreme.

I don't bother speaking to my dad as I walk by him on the staircase. He won't speak to me anyway—doesn't acknowledge me as I head straight for the garage door. I pick up my helmet, push the button to open the garage doors, and slide onto my bike. It's night-time, and it's raining. The location Olivia sent me was outside a neighborhood not far from here.

By the time I reach there, she's gone, and I try not to think of all the ways someone might have taken her. They'd see a pretty girl, falling around and drunk, and want to take advantage.

What if that fuckwad Parker got to her first?

I get off my bike and hunt around the area, silently praying she isn't in a bush; that she hasn't fallen victim to a hit and run.

She's not here.

I open up my group chat with my friends and type out a message.

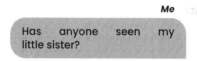

Me

Has anyone seen my little sister?

It's a ridiculous question. Their paths never cross—my group is a bunch of punks, and she's the popular girl far too beautiful for her own good.

Taking a deep breath, I drive around more, ending up outside Abigail's house. It's in darkness too, but the room light is on.

I've climbed up to that window more times than I can count. It takes me no more than two minutes to get up onto the tree directly across from the window, but I grimace and look away when I see Olivia's friend kissing some guy while his friend watches on the bed.

Okay, so she isn't there, but I might need to bleach my fucking eyeballs out after seeing Abigail's tits. My sister won't act like that—she's still innocent, nervous around guys, and

O

she's technically not allowed to fuck around.

I shiver at the thought of her with someone else.

I'll kill them.

Where the fuck are you, Olivia?

I try to call her again, but still no luck. After searching the streets for another hour, seeing the sun is already starting to rise, panic turns to full-on anxiety, and I decide I need help.

I head home, fully intent on getting Dad to call the cops and start a hunt for my sister—she's not even with Abbi anymore, and I have far too many scenarios running through my mind to even worry about the speed I'm going on my bike.

What if she's hurt?

I should turn back and go to her friend, pin her down and force her to tell me where Olivia is, but the fact she's probably being rammed by two cocks has me deciding against that idea.

Reaching the house, I silently swear when I see it's in darkness again. Mom is at some event, and I was certain my father would be home still, but his car is gone. I rush in, check his office just in case, then head to my room while typing out a text to him.

Our last messages to each other were four months ago, when he asked me to pick Olivia up from practice in her car and then to show him pictures of what was wrong with my bike. I'd crashed it, and he was going to fix it, but I ignored the texts, giving him the cold shoulder until I sorted the bike myself.

Before I click send, I stop a few steps from my door, seeing it's open.

I closed it on my way out.

I push the door fully open, and my shoulders untense, my heart rate slowing when I see Olivia asleep in my bed. I breathe, lean my back against the door frame, and drop my helmet on the ground.

She's going to fucking kill me one day.

I delete my message to Dad, toss my phone onto the weight bench, pull off my jacket, and kick my boots off. Then I pinch the bridge of my nose and count to ten, trying to talk myself down from strangling her for making me panic like that.

Her dress is dirty as if she'd fallen, and her mascara is smeared down her cheeks like she's been crying. I think she's been crying every day for the last week, but she won't tell me why. She's doing that a lot lately, and I don't think it's from the nightmares. She's usually honest with me when it comes to them.

I pull open the bottom drawer of my dresser and grab sleep shorts and a top from her pile. They have snowflakes on them, a Christmas present from one of the house workers who never gets me anything. Not that I care. No one in this house sees me the way they see my sister or my parents.

After making sure my door is locked, even though I know no one is home, I shut the main light off and turn on the lamp beside the bed, giving her pretty face a glow.

Her lips are parted a little, and she doesn't stir as I slowly run the pad of my thumb along them, smearing the red lipstick I hate. Soft, yet sticky, I watch the color move onto her skin, then rub the stain between my thumb and fingertips.

She looks better with her lip gloss on.

Once I pull her shoes off, I try to figure out where the zip is on her dress to remove it. Her hair gets caught in the material as I slide it off and toss it into my laundry basket.

She isn't wearing a bra.

Pausing, I stare at her chest.

I see her in her underwear a lot. Fuck, I see her naked a lot—she just doesn't know it. I have five cameras set up in her room, one in her bathroom, and one in my own room so I can watch her sleep in my bed when I'm not there. I never thought to check the feed to see if she was here while I was out hunting for her. Fucking idiot, Malachi.

The number of times I've stroked my cock while watching her through my laptop screen is embarrassing and wrong. Initially, when I set the cameras up, it was just so I could look at her. Obsessively. I always checked to see what she was doing.

But then it all changed because one night, she was in bed, and I was in my own room. We were going to go to sleep. Like always. But she pulled her top off, then her shorts, so she was lying on the duvet in just her panties.

Then her hand slid under the waistband, and my hand copied absently.

It was the first time I ever jacked off while watching her touch herself. I didn't have any sound, but I could tell from her mouth shape and the way her back arched that she was moaning. Her hand sped up, so did mine, and she grasped at her own breast until we both came.

I've lost count of how many times that's happened now.

She's perfection.

She's mine.

Or will be. My claim is there, but no one knows. Our parents have accepted that it was just me being possessive of my sister. I haven't asked to marry her since, and I usually keep my distance from her when they're around and aware. They think I want to protect her, to keep her safe.

I mean, I do, but I also want her under me, writhing, screaming while I fuck her into oblivion until her brother's cum fills her up.

I'd need to wear protection, right? I have no idea if she's on birth control—but she has no reason to be, unless there's another use for that stuff I'm not aware of.

If I don't wear a condom, I might knock her up, and imagine that fucking diabolical mess?

But that could be my way of trapping her—a tether to me forever. Mom and Dad would never split up a mother and father with a newborn kid.

Hmm. Something I definitely need to look into. Technically, it wouldn't be fair on the child, since I don't have a fatherly bone in my body and Olivia is far too controlled by our mom.

Olivia shifts on the bed, her legs falling open, and I need to hold my breath and bite my knuckles to halt my lungs as I stare at where her pussy is concealed by her panties. Barely. The material is a strap going up her ass and only just covering where I want to bury my face.

My tongue tingles at the thought of tasting her sweetness. I can already imagine her fingers grabbing a fistful of my hair and forcing me to devour her pretty little cunt until she unravels against my mouth.

I come closer, sitting on the edge of the bed, and push her legs more apart, checking she has no bruising on her inner thighs. If I find out someone took advantage of her tonight, I'll hang them from the tallest building by their fucking nostrils.

Her skin is soft, and as I drag my thumb across her inner thigh, my cock twitches, making me pull back and close my eyes. I'm seconds from cracking.

I can't do this. Not when she's unconscious. Imagine she woke up to her brother's fingers near her pussy?

I've zoomed in on camera, screen-grabbed her with her fingers buried deep, and walked in on her in showers and bathtubs, but this... this is the closest I've gotten where she'd never know if I touched her.

I shouldn't.

She'll never know. Touch your little sister, Malachi.

She wants it, Malachi.

She'll scream your name, Malachi.

Do it, you fucking pussy.

The voice in my head and temptation win over when I look at her tits, the way they rise and fall as she breathes, in a deep sleep with no idea as I lower my head and let the tip of my tongue glide over her nipple. My dick thickens in my pants, my balls aching as I suck on it lightly. With no experience, I still manage to make her back arch a little, and she moans quietly as I trap it between my teeth and release it.

What the fuck am I doing?

I pull away and stand.

Shit.

I can't. It's a total violation. Not that the cameras aren't, but I'm not physically doing stuff without her consent; I'm only watching her.

A part of me, the sick and twisted part, licks his lips and gloats inwardly from feeling her nipple in my mouth. I could do it again. The damage is already done, right?

One more lick and suck.

No.

Fucking no.

Staring between her legs again, my mouth waters, but I take a few steps back until I'm far away enough to catch my breath, running my hands through my hair and turning away.

I could fuck her.

Is she unconscious enough that she'd never know that I was inside her?

But she'd bleed on my bed from losing her virginity.

She would know. I might get her pregnant. She'd never forgive me.

I want her awake when it happens. I want her to know that we're each other's firsts and that she's mine forever. We'll leave the Vize family—we're old enough anyway.

Patience has never been one of my strengths, but I applaud myself as I walk to the shower. I let the cold water calm me, my dick soft again, needing the thoughts to stop. I might hurt her if I do it, and I don't want to. I'm not like that. I'm not a bad person. I can be good.

I can be good.

I can.

But you're not good, the voice in my head says. *You're weird and dead inside, so use that as an excuse to steal her from the family robbing you of your happiness.*

I leave the bathroom and keep my eyes unfocused as I put Olivia's sleep clothes on, using a damp cloth to rid her cheeks of smeared makeup, then turn off the lamp and climb into bed beside her. I keep my distance. Usually, I'd be wrapped and tangled in her, but I need to stay as far away as possible. I can't let those thoughts win.

It doesn't matter what I decide to do, because in our sleep, we gravitate to one another naturally, and I wake in the morning to her lying on my chest, her legs twisted around mine.

Despite drinking and rolling about in the damn dirt last night, her hair still smells the same as it always does. Some of it is in my face.

Her leg is hiked, her thigh dangerously close to my cock.

Olivia doesn't talk, but I know she's awake. She sighs a few times, adjusts herself against me, and lets her fingers explore.

I pretend to stay asleep as her fingers slowly graze across my chest. So gentle, so fucking soft and innocent, yet my mind is picturing her touching my cock the same way, my lips around her nipple again, hearing her whimpering. Of her moaning above me as she bounces. Her tits in my face, her tongue in my mouth, her pussy grinding up and down every inch.

I can't stop my cock from reacting. It's hardening, and she definitely fucking knows. Her head moves on my chest, looking down, and she lowers her leg, resting it across my thighs instead.

Is she… staring at my dick?

Is she mortified? Intrigued? Hungry? Will she touch me without me being awake like I did to her?

I can't see her face to know, and it's killing me.

It's all yours, Olivia, I want to tell her, but it might result in her telling our dad and him putting a bullet in my head for being an incestuous dickhead.

But thankfully, just as my control starts to slip and my cock pulses, Olivia pulls away from me, doing her best not to wake me as she sneaks out of my bed like she's just had a one-night stand. She doesn't go out the door—one of our parents will see her and get suspicious, so she goes out the balcony doors and vanishes.

CHAPTER SIX
MALACHI

I nearly got arrested for assault.

The guy was staring at Olivia like he wanted to taste every inch of her body while they talked, and no one fucking looks at her like that but me.

It bit me on the ass though, because in order for the family not to press charges, Adam and Olivia now have to go on dates, him being another potential suitor for my sister.

I was already planning the death of Parker Melrose, so this is just annoying.

Olivia did come to my room two months ago, and that seemed to have changed things between us. She was curled up in bed with me after nearly having a fucking heart attack when I tried to place Spikey, my new tarantula, in her hand, and she somehow stayed, even when I was rock solid and pressed into her.

She even pushed her ass into my dick while we slept.

It was a sign. The first cemented sign that there's a chance for us. Even though she's still in a mood about the whole Adam and Parker thing.

I don't understand why she was so upset. It's not as if she needs to fuck them or actually marry them. The kiss part pissed me off, but I can work past that if she doesn't do it again, but no dicks will go near her.

She can say no.

Mom isn't going to twist her arm and force her to spread her legs or push her into marriage—not at this age anyway. I'm still working on a plan to make her mine.

It's been years of standing on the sidelines and watching her, touching her skin while she sleeps, kissing her cheek and smelling her hair, overhearing her and Mom discussing me going back to therapy, but I need more. The cameras, hiding under her bed and watching the phone screen while we both masturbate. I could actually hear her, and it only made the cum decorating underneath her mattress that much messier.

The drive to the mountains takes forever. I'm bored out of my skull, and I'm pretty sure I'm still fucked up from last night—Mason managed to talk me into taking a few pills, and honestly, the last thing I remember was me sneaking away so I could go see my sister and tell her I was into her.

She didn't understand my signing. Neither could I. My hands wouldn't coordinate properly, and I grew frustrated as I staggered around the room, pulling at my hair. I wanted to use my voice, but I couldn't. And then she stripped me, gave me a glass of water, and put me to bed.

I was so fucked up, I nearly ruined it all by telling her how I felt.

Idiot.

Waking up with her body pressing to mine, on the verge of fucking her, I had to leave. It's a good thing I did, since Dad went around hammering all the doors and demanding we all pack for this camping trip.

Now I feel like I'm on the edge of death—my head is falling off, my body hurts, and my vision is blurring.

Whatever Mason gave me was fucking strong.

Olivia is beside me in the car, checking her phone and huffing—I know it's one of them. Adam or Parker. They're both fighting for her attention and her approval. I don't like them. I hate Parker more, though. He's a sleazy bastard who I've already encountered a handful of times. Apparently, me standing outside his house while smoking a joint made him uncomfortable—Mom told me to back off and let my sister live her life.

But Olivia isn't living her life—she's in my mom's shadow and doing as she says, obeying her every step of the way like the good little daughter she was raised to be.

It pisses me off.

The group chat is far too active—everyone's sending memes and GIFs.

They're still awake and partying. I left when the sun was starting to rise, and those assholes were still popping pills and taking lines from tits and dry-humping on the stairs.

I'm ignoring them. They're trying to grab my attention, but I exit the chat and open my messages with Olivia. Call me needy, but I'm feeling rough, and I want to hug her in bed.

Me

Hold my hand.

She looks at me after staring at her screen for far too long.

Me

Don't make it obvious.

Olivia

Why do you want to hold my hand?

Me

Do I need a reason? Give me your hand, or I'll tell Mom you touched my dick while I was asleep.

She chokes, and I try to hold in my smirk and look to the side. Was that too far? It's not a lie. Her hand slid under my waistband and touched me while she thought I was asleep. I'd basically kidnapped her from her friend's house and made her come home because I was feeling off and needed her. That was the next sign that things had changed between us.

She never knew I was awake, but I was wide awake and desperate for more.

Dad glances over his shoulder. "Are you okay, angel?"

"Yes," she replies, far too eagerly. "Perfectly fine."

My phone vibrates again.

Olivia

You were awake?

Why does the fact she thought I was unaware make me hard?

Me

I'm always awake. Give me your fucking hand.

Always awake. When you drag your nails across my chest, lower your lips to my cheek for a fraction too long, pushing your leg between mine while pretending to still be asleep, even though my cock was stuck between your thighs.

I know how much you stare at me without me being aware.

So many moments I've been awake, ever since that night she touched herself while I showered then grinded her ass over my dick when, again, she thought I was asleep.

I think my sweet, twisted little sister has a kink. Or multiple kinks, considering her slim fingers were wrapped around her brother's dick, and she's not even trying to defend herself.

Olivia

Not when they can see.

We only really hold hands now if we're calming the other down, or if we're asleep and it unconsciously happens. Not like we used to. I like it though. I can protect her and feel at ease if I have her in my hold. It's like being able to breathe that little bit easier.

I pull off my flannel and put it between us, and I fight a smirk as she lets me pull her hand underneath the garment. When I squeeze it, she squeezes back.

Rubbing my thumb over her skin, I draw my attention back to my phone, to the group chat that's still just full of memes and ridiculousness from a bunch of high assholes. I can tell she's trying to look, can sense it, and a part of me gets excited that she's curious, maybe even jealous that I could be texting someone who isn't her?

Technically, she has no right. She's gone on dates for a while now, been out fucking kissing them too, and I've been doing fuck all and watching her from afar. The only orgasms I have are when I cause them, and the only time I think about sex is when my sister is lying beside me in bed, half naked most of the time, and rubbing against me like a horny sleepwalker.

For the next few hours, Dad and Mom talk over the music, argue over fuck knows what, and then Olivia nearly pulls her hand away when Dad mentions a girl he's tried to set me up with, but she was too scared of me.

Good. The glaring worked, I see. Maybe she didn't like all

the tattoos and piercings I've been getting, or the joint hanging from my lips? Cutting lines in my eyebrows definitely sealed the deal of making her run in the opposite direction, and my dad never arranging that shit for me again. Olivia gets jealous, I fucking know it, even if she denies it.

When we reach the destination, we set up the tents, which are far too small for two teenagers or two adults to share. I'm not complaining. I get to be closer to her.

Plus, something is different. Everything is different, and I feel unsettled—unsatisfied with how we're progressing so slowly, she might not even realize that we're gravitating towards one another with a mighty pull that'll clash and keep us together forever.

She's laughing at something Dad says while I help her shove a marshmallow on the stick for her to toast over the fire we're sitting around.

Olivia's thigh hits mine.

My fingers curl in, making fists at my sides as my knees bounce.

I'm agitated.

I need something.

You need more, Malachi. Take more.

Take.

I blink a few times and glance around the darkness, then at the parents who raised me. They don't want me here, not really, and Olivia… I'll lose her soon.

She'll forget about me.

I'll be alone again.

Breaths growing heavy, I grind my teeth and stare at the flames.

Dad says something, and Mom laughs, but Olivia just hugs herself with one arm and continues to toast her marshmallow.

Mason told me last night that sometimes, I scare him, because when I focus on something in the room, my eyes don't leave it, even when he's trying to talk to me. Apparently my eyes go void, and I look like I want to be anywhere but there. Is that what my parents see whenever I'm around them? Void—and scary?

Olivia hasn't ever mentioned being afraid of me. She seeks me out more than anything, but Mom hates being alone with me, and Dad avoids me at all costs.

They raised me, but they don't love me.

I only care a little, so I internally shake my head and look at Olivia, and not the two older adults bickering over Olivia potentially burning her fingers on the stick. Her bottom lip is trapped between her teeth, a smile peeking through while she unravels herself and pulls the sugary goodness from the stick and sniffs it.

Her eyes flicker to me, and I dodge back when she tries to put the marshmallow to my mouth. I capture her wrist, and she giggles as I knock it out of her hand, dropping it on the dirt surrounding us.

"Asshole," she mouths, giggling again as I find the biggest

marshmallow and stab it with the stick before handing it back
to her.

Smiling while she quietly laughs, she looks like she's blushing.
Hmm.

I could listen to her laugh forever, but there's something else
I want to hear. For me. Caused by me. All for me.

Olivia moaning my name while she's over me, dropping her
sweet little ass down on my cock, telling me it's too much even
though she keeps going regardless until she comes—

"Who wants to take a walk?" Dad calls out, interrupting
my thoughts.

Mom raises her hand. Olivia doesn't.

So I don't either.

"Come on," Dad says. "I think we can get a better view of
the stars near the cliff. Are you coming, kids?"

I shake my head, very aware that my sister is doing the same.
My blood is rushing so fast in my veins, fucking burning, and
if I don't light a smoke within the next minute, I might throw
myself in the fire.

Thankfully, my parents fuck off, and as soon as they're gone,
I pull my cigarettes out and light one, enjoying the way the
toxicity burns inside my lungs.

My eyes close as I take another draw, and I open them again
to see Olivia staring at me.

You aren't allowed one, so don't ask.

She scoffs. "I don't want one. Smoking is bad for you."

No idea what she says next because I feel like my soul is slowly connecting with hers—a connection that, I fear, may kill me one day. Her lips are moving, and I want to taste them. I silently laugh because the world certainly hates me. Why, out of the entire universe, do I end up adopted into the same family as the girl I'm madly in love with?

I can't ever have her. Not really.

Now I'm mad. Who the fuck is anyone to say what I can and can't have?

Tossing the smoke, I stand, grabbing Olivia's hand and pulling her with me towards the tent. The same one we're sharing, all night, just the two of us.

Once I throw her in, there's no counting to three in my head or stopping to think about what I plan to do. I zip the tent back up, slip the padlock on, and then turn to her while she tries to figure out what the fuck is going on. "Jesus, Malachi," she hisses. "Do you need to be so damn rough?"

Yes. You never listen, stubborn ass.

Despite being thrown around, she doesn't look afraid of me. Good. It'll make it easier for me to do what I want her to do. She's given me more than enough signs that she wants me.

She says something, but I'm trying to figure out how exactly I start this off. Do I just kiss her? Pin her down, rip her clothes off, and do what I want with her? Do I ask her how she feels about me and if she wants to be a secret behind our parents' backs until we're comfortable to come forward about our relationship?

Do I ask her if she wants to see my dick, since she's so engrossed in touching it while I'm asleep?

Maybe I should just kiss her.

I drop to my knees, chewing the inside of my cheek. A sudden weight is on my chest. How do I do this?

How do I kiss her?

I want to kiss her.

So. Fucking. Badly.

Unless we start slow. First base, I think it's called.

Can I see you? I want to add that I want to see her naked, but nerves win, so I leave it at that.

Her brows knit together. "You can see me?"

Cute.

I tug her collar as I get closer. *Without this,* I sign, then touch her pants and raise my hands again. *And these.*

There's a possibility I might die tonight. My heart shouldn't be going as fast as it is. "Death by nerves" sounds horrendous next to my name on my headstone.

"Why?" she asks.

I want to see you. I promise not to touch you, I sign, now officially the biggest liar in her life. I'll touch her. I'll do a lot more than touch her.

She'll love it too.

"I'm sure you've seen plenty of girls without clothes on. You don't need to see me."

How delusional is this girl? The only naked person I've ever seen is Olivia, but she isn't fully aware of how much I stalk the living daylights out of her.

I have pictures, videos, and soon, I'll have footage of me fucking her into one of our mattresses. Or both. Or maybe in multiple places. Maybe I'll chain her up and record me fucking her ass while she screams for me.

Then I click on to what she just said and shake my head.

"You haven't?"

No. Plus, it's your body I want to see. Why won't you show me?

Her nervousness makes my impending anxiety attack lessen, and I watch her fidget. "What if our parents catch us? You know it's wrong."

They won't. We'll hear them coming.

"But... I'm... Really?"

Why can't she see what we are already? Without even being together, we are stronger than our own parents' marriage—fuck, we're more powerful than the entire world.

"I'm your sister."

And that's your war cry. Take your clothes off, Olivia.

My patience is vanishing with each word.

I expect her to slap me, but she only chews her lip nervously. "I'll do it, but under one condition."

Did she just say… She'll do it? She'll actually do it?

Now what the fuck do I do?

"We make a game of it." She's grinning, tipping her head, leaning back. "I ask you questions, and if you answer them honestly, I'll take something off. If you don't answer, or I know you're lying, then you take something off."

Shit.

Fine, ask me something.

Her few seconds of confidence slips as she hugs her knees. "Did you take drugs last night?"

I expected questions a little more… explicit. What the fuck is this?

And how the hell does she know?

Wait. What if she's stalking me the same way I stalk her? What if she has cameras, hides in the shadows, and sneaks around to watch me dress and work out and even jerk off?

Yeah. Some of my friends were trying it, so I did too. I pinch the sleeve of her hideous sweater that would look better set on fire. *Take this off first.*

"I think I get to decide what item of clothing comes off first, thank you very much." She's smug as she kicks off her shoe. "And don't take drugs. They're bad for you—way worse than smoking cigarettes."

The silent laugh shocks me. It's unintentional, and I almost forget I'm terrified of what the fuck I'm doing right now.

Ultimately, I want her naked.

Then what?

"Do you remember how to talk?" she asks, her tone full of curiosity. "Like, do you know how to pronounce words and stuff?"

I haven't heard myself speak in years. I tried once, and it felt unfamiliar, and I hated it. Trying to talk to myself in the mirror at the age of ten and needing to seek out my sister for comfort after isn't something a guy my age should be proud of.

A little. I haven't spoken out loud for a long time.

Her other shoe comes off.

"Is your voice deep?"

Mason asked me the same thing. His voice is deep, and so are the guys' voices, so I assume mine would be too.

I think so.

Her sweater comes off, and I want to rip her shirt off too. It's tight against her body, the curves I want to drag my tongue against, to hold on to while I shove deep.

"Can I hear it? Even just say my name. Or, like, laugh."

No.

I draw closer, nudging her with my shoulder. *You need to take something off.*

"You said no, so you take something off."

Would she hate me if I strangled her?

I answered your question honestly.

When she takes off her sock, I imagine all of her clothes in the fire outside, melting into nothing, while she lies exposed to me.

But then her next words catch me off guard.

"Do you see me as a sister? Because a lot of my friends have brothers and they're... different than what we're like together. I can't imagine them cuddling in bed or playing this game, for example. So, yeah, am I a real sister to you?"

Without thinking, because am I fuck going to answer that, I remove my flannel and drop it with her clothes.

"You won't answer my question?"

No.

I play with my rings for a second, watching her gawk at me. I need more. I need her to ask me something that triggers me to kiss her. Not ask me if I see her as a sister and then have her run away from me.

Your questions are boring.

Her eyes roll, and I want to spank her. "Do you have any piercings?"

Not visible to the everyday person, no.

Yes.

Her brows narrow. "What? Where?"

I pull off my shirt, anxiety starting to disappear at her cheeks going a bright red. She's affected by me. That's a good thing, right?

Or is she embarrassed?

Fuck.

Just when I start to abandon ship, her eyes drop to my chest, my abs, studying my ink. Her breathing is growing heavier.

Why are you staring?

"I wasn't."

Liar.

"Mom and Dad are going to be so weirded out if they walk in and see us."

I shrug. I'll blind them if they see her like this. *Ask me something else.*

"Why do you want to see me?"

I already told you. I want to look at your body.

Her face is even redder now. I'm not sure how it makes me feel.

"Why? You've seen me in swimwear, and there was that time you walked in on me in the shower."

And when you're not aware. I have close-ups and everything, but none of that is enough.

I want to see all of you.

I need to. I think if I need to wait another day, I'll do something I'll regret and she'll never forgive me. My urges are bad, extreme, and powerful. The strength I have not to just make her mine already is hanging on by a thread.

My brain short-circuits as she hesitates only for a second before taking her shirt off, sitting in her sports bra.

More. I need more. Now. I can barely breathe properly without her realizing my restraint is wavering.

Another. I answered two.

My dirty little sister takes off her bra, holding it to her flushed chest. Her nervousness makes my balls tingle, and I can feel my cock thickening in my briefs. Her nipples are hard, from what I can see, and fuck, I want one in my mouth again so badly, it waters.

Give me it.

She hesitates again then quietly says, "Promise you won't laugh?"

Is she fucking joking? In what world would I laugh about anything about Olivia or her looks? She's beautiful—every atom of her being was made for me and only me.

Why the hell would I laugh?

"They're… small."

They're perfect. I might need to check this girl's head if she thinks anything about her is bad.

Show me. Or I'll make you show me.

"Stop being a caveman."

Her head turns, averting her gaze as she drops her sports bra, and everything around me stops. The world grows quiet now I'm allowed to look at her exposed beauty with her

O

permission. Her nipples are hard, pebbled, flushed pink, her breasts big enough for a handful. Her little tremors of nerves have me coming closer, my dick fucking solid as she looks back at me.

Ask me something else.

Her silence, the way she's just looking at me… I'm about to break. I'm going to grab the back of her head and kiss her if she doesn't do as I say.

Fucking ask me something.

"Why did you attack Adam in the gas station? We were just talking, and you stormed in and went crazy."

He was trying to take what was mine.

"I'm not yours," she replies, and the world goes dark.

She keeps talking, making the hole in my chest grow more hollow.

"I'm your sister—that's all. We're the Vize kids."

No. You were mine when we were kids, and you're mine now. You'll always be mine.

Even when we're dead, our souls will belong to one another. The sooner she realizes that, the fucking better.

"Do you see me as a sister?"

Don't cheat your own rules. I already answered a question.

She lets out a low "okay" and slowly takes off her pants.

Her pussy is right there, hidden behind a scrap of pale pink material, and I'm in front of her. My sister is basically naked, and my dick hurts with how hard it is. I wonder if she'll tell our parents she's finished with the dates and that she'll just marry me, or will we run away?

How many kids will she want?

Does she want the life we've had growing up, or do we get an apartment somewhere, a small kitchen and bathroom, with a spare room for any guests?

Precum is leaking from the tip of my cock, my sweats not even slightly hiding the evidence of how much I need her.

"I think you need to start asking questions. I'm one answer away from being naked and that's not fair."

Technically she is naked.

Enough for me anyway.

She likes to masturbate. Olivia does it a lot when she's lying in her bed, all alone, either watching porn or reading a book, with her big brother watching her fingers slide in and out of her perfect little cunt.

My jaw tenses, and I push myself to sign the words that might ruin this entire night.

If I asked you to touch yourself, would you?

Her silence is deafening, her mouth parted as she stares at me. Maybe she's waiting for me to say I'm joking or to move on to the next question.

I've watched you before. You fuck yourself with your fingers a lot with your curtains open.

"You've watched me through my window?"

And with cameras in your room.

I just gave away one of my biggest secrets. Such a fucking idiot.

The shock is evident all over her face. "You have cameras in my room?"

Yeah. Stop changing the subject. You didn't answer my question. If I asked you to touch yourself, right now, would you?

"First, you'll remove the cameras!"

Not a chance in hell am I removing them. They're my safe haven when she isn't around, or when she's in a mood with me and I can't go to her.

She slaps my arm after I shake my head, and I grit my teeth, wanting her to hit me harder. Slap my face. Spit on me. Fucking pull my hair and call me the best big brother ever.

Answer.

Her next words light something inside me. "I think I'd do anything you asked of me." She pauses. "Under the condition that it stayed a secret."

Am I dreaming?

Did the drugs I took last night put me into a trance? Am I hallucinating this all? Is Olivia… agreeing to this?

If she's answered honestly, I need to strip off another piece of clothing. I stare at her, unblinking. Did she actually say those words, or did I imagine them? Can I ask her to repeat it? To clarify she did, in fact, say she'd do anything I asked her?

Olivia goes to grab her clothes, but I stop her, getting to my knees to pull down my sweats, not caring how hard I am—my cock is pitching my briefs and I'm struggling to conceal what she's doing to me. My precious sister, naked before her deranged big brother, telling me she'll fucking finger herself for me as long as I don't tell anyone.

The fact she's staring at my dick and licking her lips has the tip throbbing.

There's a long, dragged-out silence between us, yet everything is so damn loud in my head—she's looking at me in a way she's never done before, and I feel… nervous.

She terrifies me.

What do I do now? Tell her to do as I say and lie back, stick her fingers in her hole and show me how she gets herself off?

"Should we get dressed?"

Not yet, I sign, anxiety building in my gut because I haven't the faintest clue what to do here. *And that was another question, which I answered.*

I don't give her a chance to argue—I tug the string of her panties and snap them right off her body as she gasps out my name, but I cover her mouth with my hand and push her down onto her back.

I part her legs, so fucking close. Would she let me fuck her? What if I hurt her? We're virgins, inexperienced, but we can learn. I'll teach her what I like, and she can do the same.

I sign to her to stay still, kneeling between her legs, my heart accelerating as my eyes land on her pussy. My mouth waters; every hair on my body rises. She's wet. I can see how much her pussy needs attention. Even as she tries to shut her legs, I keep them open.

"You said you wouldn't touch me."

I'm not a good guy—I don't keep my promises, and I lie. I lie every single day. Because I don't want to be the son of a Vize; I want to be married into the family. I want her. All day. Every day.

She shakes as I nervously place a kiss to the side of her knee. *Can I taste you?*

"You said you wouldn't touch me," she says again, trembling even more as I kiss her other knee, trying to hold it together— my heart might blow out of my chest, and I need a smoke to calm me.

Or something else—her.

Then touch yourself.

"Really?"

Yes.

"You're not trying to mess with me? If you're fucking with me right now, Malachi, I will hit you."

I want her to hit me. I want it to hurt too. *If I'm not allowed to touch you, then you need to do it yourself.*

"What if I say no?"

I love this girl, but she sure knows how to push my buttons. She won't say no. She wants it as much as I do.

"Okay, okay, okay. But you need to promise not to touch me."

I raise my pinkie, hooking it with hers like we used to do as kids. Is that fucked up? I used to do this when we'd keep petty secrets from Mom, or when we'd promise to always be best friends—now I'm doing it to prove I won't touch her while I watch her fuck herself with her fingers.

I never usually break a pinkie promise, but there's always room for more firsts between us.

"And don't tell anyone. This isn't what siblings do. We'll be in a lot of trouble."

I won't. Our secret, little sister.

She slaps my hands from her in disgust despite blushing more as her pupils expand. "Please don't call me your little sister right now."

But you are my sister, I sign, smirking, my own words driving me fucking insane. *My dirty little sister who's going to touch herself in front of me. Show your big brother what you sound like when you come.*

My heavy gaze follows her movements—movements I never thought I'd get to witness in the flesh. Her fingers slide down, parting herself, and I struggle to breathe as she gives her clit the attention it deserves.

Mason's pills have fucked me up because there isn't a chance in hell this is happening right now. My sister isn't pleasuring herself while I'm between her legs. She can't be. If I blink, she might vanish, so I keep my eyes focused between her legs as she speeds up. Her back arches a little, her eyes closing, and my skin grows far too fucking hot despite having no clothes on.

Olivia has no idea of the danger she's in. I could pounce, shove deep, make her come all over my cock, and she'd have no choice.

I eventually blink because I'd never do that to her. I want her permission. I want her to want me back.

Am I forcing her right now?

Does she want to do this?

My body absently draws closer, magnetizing to hers like it belongs. I need her to tell me what she wants me to do to her. I need… something.

Can I touch you?

"No," she pants, still circling her clit. "Please don't."

Why?

I don't get a response—Olivia is far too deep into a trance. Her other hand slides down, one working her clit while she sinks two fingers into her pussy. My dick pulses, and I can't take it any longer. I wrap my hands around it, over the material of my boxers, and squeeze. My balls ache, my brain is short-circuiting again and again, and I feel like if Olivia even as much as put her lips anywhere near my body, I'd come.

She's whimpering, and I imagine she's saying my name, fucking moaning it while I stroke, listening to how wet she is as her fingers plunge in and out of her depths until she hits her climax.

Fuck me. I want to be the cause of that heavenly sound.

Her mouth is open, her back arching, her little gasps and cries making me squeeze my dick hard enough to hurt. I refuse to come yet. I want her lips around my dick or her fingers replacing my own.

She's staring at me through her orgasm, sinking her teeth into her lip, her inner voice tormenting her, probably giving her shit for her position and the way I'm so fucking close to being on top of her.

Each breath is forced out of me—I could die right now, and I'd be borderline happy about it.

"Do you still want to taste me?" she pants.

Is she delusional? Why would I say no?

I nod because I'm not a fucking idiot who would ever turn down that offer. My heart ricochets all over my ribcage as she lifts her fingers to my mouth, and I pause as she rubs them across my lips.

Whatever drug is still in my system could never come close to the hit I'm getting right now. I grab her wrist and take her fingers into my mouth—licking, sucking, biting—her taste exploding on my tongue as my dick fucking begs for her warmth.

Anything I can get from her is more than enough.

I inwardly groan, my eyes closing, my free hand hardly able to move around my dick from the sensations running through my veins. Too sensitive. Too fucking much.

As soon as her fingers vanish, I'm on her. She stops me with a hand over my mouth before I can kiss her. "No," she gasps, her eyes wide. "We didn't agree to that!"

I frown, because she's saying these words, yet I can see all over her face how much she wants me to keep going. I can feel the way her body is beneath mine, how hard my dick is stabbing into her thigh. I snatch her wrist, removing her hand from my mouth and taking her jaw. My mouth lowers to hers a second time, and something deep inside my hollow chest, my fucking black heart, snaps in two when she dodges my kiss by moving her head sideways.

"No, Malachi."

She's fucking with my head.

She's... killing me.

I get up, figuring out what I want to say but not knowing how to explain it—she's hurt me. She's making me feel shit I can't control, and I don't like it.

I hate myself for not being able to just tell her how I feel and why we should be together. Rather than running away, like I want to, I lift my hands to sign, but she obliterates every ounce of my confidence by turning around.

"Let's just go to sleep," she says, bathing us in black by turning off the flashlight above us. "We're obviously not thinking straight."

In an instant, because rage and pain and sadness win over every emotion, I turn it back on and snatch her throat, feeling her pulse fucking racing until I squeeze. Her lungs will start to struggle. Her eyes will go wide and red and bloodshot. Her lips will turn blue. Then she'll grow cold. Unseeing. Unblinking. No air passing her lips. No more love to throw out to everyone except the brother who would literally die for her.

Realization washes over me that Olivia is struggling. My Olivia. My girl. My sister. I let go of her, and she's shaking, trying to clear her throat quietly after a few seconds of strangulation.

Don't silence me like that. Don't ever fucking silence me, Olivia.

How dare she look confused? How fucking dare she, not even a minute after breaking me?

"I... I didn't."

I gesture to the flashlight. *I can't fucking talk to you if you can't see me.*

How ridiculous is this? Why can't I be normal? Why?

"Oh. I'm sorry. I didn't realize I did that. Just... We can't kiss—it's not what siblings do. Regardless of what just happened. Please don't make this awkward."

I'm giving myself internal whiplash. Running is all I can think about. Vanishing from this shit. But I grab her hair and pull her to me, closer, but not close enough. Never close enough.

Never.

You used to always kiss me.

"When we were kids, and the kisses were innocent. You… We… No, Malachi."

No? You just— I stop, defeated. My chest hurts.

"Mom has me going on dates with guys for me to marry them, Malachi. I can't chance being caught kissing you."

If she doesn't understand that she can't be with anyone else but me, I might need to kill everyone in the world so it's only us two remaining. Then she'll have no choice but to be with me. It's not exactly a good or healthy way of starting a relationship, but she sure as hell ain't marrying someone else.

Imagine her having a different surname from me? Not a damn chance.

You aren't fucking marrying anyone.

Her eyes are watering like she's trying to make herself cry. They're fake tears. Or pity tears. Or she's upset because her dreams of marrying her prince have been crushed by her lunatic brother. She feels sorry for me. The lost kid with no life ahead of him—the defective, black sheep with more baggage and psychotic tendencies than most teenagers. She doesn't want me—she's been put in this position. By me. I made her do this entire thing. This isn't consensual.

My teeth grind together, and my muscles burn with the need

to explode—why is she doing this to me? Why doesn't she want me the same way I want her? Her next words only cement it all as her lip trembles.

"We can't," she whispers, making my thoughts worse—shoving the dagger deeper into my chest. "You're Malachi Vize and I'm Olivia Vize. We're sister and brother."

Why did Jamieson and Jennifer need to adopt me?

Fucking why?

Stop saying that. We aren't blood related. You aren't my real sister, so what's the goddamn problem?

She covers herself with the sleeping bag as if I haven't just been all over her, my eyes taking in every inch and curve and random freckle on her naked skin. "This was a mistake."

I need to recalculate how to win her because this isn't working.

"Are they already sleeping?"

Mom is coming. I can hear Dad's footsteps far behind her.

She'll see how dirty her daughter is if she manages to get in. She won't. I have it padlocked, but I secretly wish I'd forgotten, so I can see the embarrassment on her face when our parents catch us naked together.

I want them to see that their perfect little fucking angel is messing with their son's head—that she's making their son worse; that his sickness is manageable, without Olivia as a factor.

I shake my head. Ridiculous. Olivia is the reason I breathe.

She hides under the sleeping bag, pretending to be passed out.

"Are you guys asleep?"

She looks up at me. I want her to tell me she's sorry, that she feels the same, that we can be together. To kiss me and fucking choose me.

"They must be asleep," I hear Mom say in the distance. "Since when are we the ones staying up late? Grab the beers!"

Raising my hands, I contemplate apologizing for putting her in this position. Then I drop them because fuck her for making me feel this way. Fuck Olivia Vize for making me fall in love with her when she has no intention of doing the same with me.

I lie down, but I don't want to be here. She's too close. I can hear her adjusting her clothes, her breaths, until she falls into a deep sleep and her breathing turns heavy.

It takes me an hour of calming myself to the sound of her light snores before I unzip the sleeping bag and get the hell out of the tent. The fresh air hits me, and I run my hands through my hair, grasping the strands hard and not letting go as I head straight for the woodland.

My lungs burn from how much I need a good breath. My brain hurts—pressure all over—and my mouth is dry.

As soon as I'm a few yards into the forest, I give in to the attack and drop to my knees, head still in my hands. I can't breathe. Everything is tight as fuck, and my head is lowering, burying into the dirty forest floor.

"Breathe, son."

A hand rests on my back, but it doesn't make anything better—I still feel like I'm spiraling, like I'm losing my fucking mind while Dad kneels beside me.

"Slow your breathing. You're hyperventilating."

I try to push him away and fail—he's gripping the back of my neck, trying to make me calm my overworked lungs, to listen, to do something other than lose my shit.

The world ripples as I fall in and out of consciousness, a fucking battle to stay awake as he rubs my back, saying something else in my ear as he tightens his grip on my nape and shakes me.

I think he's saying my name. I can't understand him. I try to focus, to slow down my breaths, but then I give in, slipping into the darkness of the void where I belong.

CHAPTER SEVEN
MALACHI

S taying away from Olivia has been hard since the camping trip.

While she's awake and aware anyway.

I usually slip into her room when she's asleep to lie with her, walk with her to practice from afar, or watch her on my one remaining camera that points right at her bed. Sometimes I think she's left it there intentionally. She wants me to watch her, to see the way she touches herself night after night. It's like an addiction now, watching the way her fingers slip between her thighs, her red-painted nails circling her clit while she stares right at the lens.

I want to fuck her. So damn badly.

The decision to step back wasn't my own. I mean, it was, but it also wasn't. If it was fully up to me, I'd grab her in front of our parents and show them just how unlike siblings we can be.

I don't want distance from Olivia, not in the slightest. But it's for the best. I'm losing myself—even my friends have been concerned. Mason texts me more often to meet up on our bikes, and asks me constantly how I'm feeling and if I'm going to off myself.

Obviously not—imagine leaving this world without Olivia? She'd need to be dead already for me to willingly leave this earth.

The thing is, the moment I realized I had to put myself first was when Dad found me losing my shit that night of the camping weekend. I passed out from lack of oxygen, woke up a few minutes later, and we sat in silence in the woodland for hours. He didn't tell Mom because he knows she'd want me to do the therapy and medication crap again. Dad knows I hate it, that I'd never stick it out. It would be a waste of their money and everyone's time.

Dad asked me what happened to trigger the attack, but as has been the case for months, I couldn't answer. Even signing to him would've made me look weaker than I already am. He has an idea of how messed up I am from when I was younger. My diagnosis solidified that I wasn't mentally wired the same way as the rest of the Vize family. Still, they kept me under their wing despite being afraid of me, of the dark thoughts I'd get.

Honestly, I have no idea why they didn't throw me back into the system.

I certainly deserved it.

I'm the son they never wanted, and they're all stuck with me. I think Dad is starting to catch on to the way I am with Olivia. That he was right when we were younger. The obsession I have with everything about her is unhealthy and wrong.

I've noticed him watching us a lot since the camping trip, and he definitely knows something is up. Me and Olivia don't communicate—I only look at her when she isn't looking, and I don't follow her around like a lost puppy anymore.

Even if he does find out my true feelings, there's nothing he can do.

They can dope me up with meds, force me into an institution, try to cleanse me of my fucking sins. I'll still be living and breathing for my sister, waiting for her to choose me. It's been too long since I was so damn close to touching her, kissing her, claiming her, and I'm dying to communicate with her, but this is more fun.

She's in the bathtub right now while I lie on my back on her bed. Usually, when her music stops, I'll leave before she comes out or slip under her bed and vanish when she's fallen asleep.

Keeping my balcony doors locked, knowing when she's having a nightmare and seeking me out yet ignoring her, has been hard. But when she does pass out, I'm always sliding into her room and watching her sleep.

It's kind of creepy.

My friends would have my balls if they knew what was going

on in my mind.

My eyes fall on the glass of water filled with ice sitting beside her bed. The little frozen cubes are nearly gone. I decide to make myself useful and change it while my sister takes forever in the tub.

When I'm in the kitchen emptying the glass, Mom walks in and huffs, "You left the garage door open again, and there are marks on the driveway from the wheels of your bike. Do you ever listen?"

I ignore her. Her voice grates on my nerves—like nails on a chalkboard.

She opens the medicine cabinet and grabs a bottle of pills, taking two out. "I usually only have one, but I need to be in a deep sleep for the next twelve hours. Don't ask me for anything until I resurface."

Is she drunk or something? When do I go to her for anything?

She swallows the pills with water, her eyes focusing on me, narrowing as if she wants to talk to me more, to ask me something, but then she rolls her eyes and puts the glass into the sink and walks out.

An idea comes to the forefront of my brain at my mom's words. Her pills. The idea is depraved and wrong, but I don't know how much control I have left. If I don't do this, I might have to kiss Olivia while she's awake, and it might ruin everything if she pushes me away or even fucking slaps me for attempting to kiss her.

But if she's asleep…

I could kiss her, and she couldn't tell me no.

It might stop my obsession. Stop the craving for my little sister. Scratch the itch to stick my dick in someone I grew up with as a sibling.

I pop four tablets in then a fifth, leaving them to sit until they're fully dissolved. Stirring with a spoon, I add in a few ice cubes, the smallest amount of orange juice to hide the medical taste, then head upstairs to Olivia's bedroom.

Thankfully, she's still not out of the bathroom, so I place the glass where it was, hurrying into her closet when I hear her music stop.

Her footsteps might as well be on my chest.

A towel around her, she rubs a second one into her hair. There are little droplets leftover from the shower making wet trails down her skin, and my mouth waters, my breaths heavy through my nose.

She takes forever to dry her hair, my throat closing as the towel wrapped around her body drops to her feet. Her breasts, her pussy, her fucking body.

Fuck.

Sadly, she pulls on a nightdress, my entertainment keeping me awake as she practices one of her routines in the mirror before she calls Abbi, tells her to meet her tomorrow at the mall, then downs the glass in one go, making the remaining ice cubes hit her teeth.

Her nose crinkles with a grimace, and she glances down at the empty glass. She licks her lips, then goes into her bathroom to rinse the glass and set it aside.

It's done. Pretty soon—in minutes even—Olivia will lose consciousness.

My cock shouldn't be hard. Nothing has happened, yet it's standing at attention, nearly nudging the closet door open. Maybe I should be honest and tell her she's mine instead of drugging her into a sleep for my own enjoyment?

I shrug to myself. Too late.

I stare at the clock opposite where I'm hiding. The arms seem to be taking forever to make their way across the face, and tick by tick, Olivia's breathing grows heavy as she bundles herself under the duvet.

I should feel bad. I should feel disgraced with myself for drugging my sister, but there's only so much control I can have until it snaps. I'm not a good guy—never have been. I'm an asshole, controlling, and I don't deserve the life I have. I'm certain I should be locked up in a psych ward or something.

I think, by the way my excitement is growing the less lucid she becomes, I've definitely snapped and dropped off the cliff with no return to reality.

The door creaks open, and I leave my hiding spot, moving

to the side of her bed before slowly lowering to my knees. I'm nervous. I've never been so nervous in my life. Because I can do what I want, but I have no idea where to start.

Olivia's face is sweet and relaxed. Beautiful. Stunning. Breathtaking.

Anyone would be lucky to call her their wife, mother of their children, the person they get to grow old with.

Her chest rises and falls with each breath she pulls into her lungs. Her lips are so full, and I want to kiss them. I want to hear her gasp against my mouth as I devour her, to feast on her tongue and trap her bottom lip between my teeth. I'd rather she was aware that it was me, that she could watch me as I slid down her body to taste her, but this will do.

Dad's voice is in my head, telling me to stay away from Olivia. He's never really trusted me around her. Ever. And he isn't wrong—but now she's just turned eighteen, me about to turn twenty, the innocence is gone, and I know exactly what I want.

I adored my sister. She was, or is, my anchor. She's the only person in the world I want to communicate with or care about. But I don't want to cuddle her and talk and act like I don't want her. I want every inch of her more than I need air.

It's not right, but I don't give a fuck. I'm well aware that it's not allowed, that my dick shouldn't twitch and harden at the thought of sticking my cock between her tits until I paint them with my cum.

I slowly pull down the blanket, my breaths catching in my throat when her soft, delicate skin comes into new.

Olivia's nightdress has ridden up to her hips. She's intentionally been wearing less and less clothing to bed, and I can't say I have any complaints. She could be completely naked and I'd still need more. Watching her naked, showering and even pleasuring herself isn't enough. I need to be the cause of those fucking beautiful moans.

I've never touched a girl before—never felt the need or wanted to. But I want to touch my sister so badly that I can't stop myself as I pull the blanket completely off her and stare at her bare legs; at those perfect damn thighs that I want wrapped around me as I drive into her hard enough to smack the headboard off the wall.

The desire is too much. I let my fingertip drag over her collarbone, hooking under the strap of her nightdress and pulling it down off her shoulder. The curve of her breast appears, then her pink nipple, and a thud hits my balls. A pulse. My dick is struggling in my boxers, especially when the pad of my thumb circles her nipple, making it pebble.

It's still not enough. I pull down the other side, both breasts free, and shift myself onto the mattress, between her legs, and pull the nightdress completely off her. Her panties are plain, white and innocent, and I remove them too, my tongue swiping at my lips as soon as my eyes land on her pussy.

I glance up at her face, still asleep, and keep my gaze on her as I press my thumb to her clit. If she wakes, she can slap me, and I'll apologize. Her brows knit together a little, furrowing deeper as I apply pressure, slowly circling around the sensitive area.

The fact she isn't waking up and yelling at me has me smirking and circling again, learning the feel, the physiology of her most private part.

I use both thumbs to spread her pussy lips, seeing how pink and pretty she is, then lower my face so I'm an inch from her and inhale.

Better than fucking drugs, or the adrenaline I get on my bike, or when I drive my fist into some asshole's face. Her cunt is my new favorite toy.

I run my thumbs up the sides of her pussy, parting the flesh around her clit, opening her more for me.

Circling her with my thumb again, I slide my finger down to her entrance, keeping my eyes on her as I feel how wet she is despite being asleep. A little whimper escapes as I ease a finger in, my lips parting as I study how warm she is inside, just as perfect as her exterior.

I huff out a deep breath, needing to free my cock, then stroke it as I push my finger in deeper.

My hands are much larger than her own. Will this hurt her? I know when a girl loses her virginity, it can hurt, make them bleed, but will a finger cause her pain?

I pull my finger out to make sure there's no blood, but it's just wet.

Gulping, squeezing my dick as I stroke from base to tip, I suck my finger into my mouth, my eyes rolling on a silent hum. She tastes like heaven.

I bend her knees then push her thighs apart and tug down my boxers, kicking them to the floor, my shirt joining them. If she's naked, it's only fair that I am too.

I ease two fingers inside her, pausing as her body tenses, unable to blink or move or anything. She tightens around my fingers for a second, getting even wetter.

Wake up, little sister, I say in my head. *Wake up and see what your big brother is doing to you. Feel how much you want him with his fingers buried in your cunt.*

I should fuck her. Be her first. If I fill her with my cum and keep it in there, she might fall pregnant. Then she'd be stuck with me.

It's three in the morning. Mom is out cold from her sleeping pills, Dad is working on an appeal case that's all over the news, and the staff are all off. No one can catch me violating my sister as I lower myself over her body, burying my nose into her hair and inhaling.

Addictive. I inhale deeper, making sure I don't crush her small frame as my cock presses to where my fingers are easing in and out. Slow. Shallow, not even to my first knuckle. Wet. Growing tighter with each thrust.

My other hand rests in her hair, and I close my eyes, my cock thickening with how delicate and soft she is. I push two fingers deeper and pause when her hips rock upwards, taking my fingers to the knuckle. Whatever she thinks her dream is, she's trapped, keeping her asleep.

Part of me wants her to wake up and beg for more, to moan my name and admit her feelings. Though I'm not sure how she'd react if she woke up to me on top of her, my dick thrusting against her thigh, my fingers deep inside her, making her whimper even more.

She did grind her perfect little ass against me, then chickened out when I tried to put her hand down my boxers. She confuses me. I know my little sister has a crush on me; that all these dates that Mom sets her up on are pointless.

Pointless because she won't marry any of them. I'll make sure of it.

My Olivia groans in her sleep again as I remove my fingers, sucking them clean.

I hike her knee to my hip and slide the underside of my dick against her pussy. And fuck, she's soaking, and from Mason's over-the-top detail about all the people he's fucked, and from basic common sense, I know it's a good sign that her body is moving absently, that her breathing is stilted.

I think I'm doing it right, and the way her hips lift, chasing the smoothness of my dick, I know my unconscious girl enjoys it. Such a twisted little sister chasing her brother's cock while he practices on her.

She won't even remember in the morning as I bury my nose in her hair and thrust harder between her legs. I won't push my dick inside, even as my precum-covered head slips against her entrance. I want Olivia to be aware of who's inside her when we lose our virginities together.

My spine twists with the sensation. At each light thrust and inhalation of her scent, my heart speeds up, and I feel my balls tingling, my dick throbbing and thickening. I'm covered in her arousal, my precum all over her pussy.

The sounds she makes against my ear makes my dick pulse and harden even more as I dry-fuck her sleeping body.

I kiss her throat, half wishing she'd wake up and accept what we are. The other half of me wants her to stay asleep and not ruin this. She'd say that we were siblings and that it's wrong.

I capture her earlobe and suck on it lightly as I keep dragging my cock between her legs, needing more, needing to know what it's like to actually fuck her, to have the warm flesh of her pussy wrapped around my cock, but I hold back.

I hear her phone buzzing on the bedside table. I'm so damn close to release. When another buzz comes, I stop, panting, and curiosity wins on the third message. I lean over and put in the passcode—my date of birth. It unlocks, and I frown at the messages from the asshole I attacked a while ago.

Adam

What time are you coming to my parents' house tomorrow?

I don't want to cancel and annoy our parents. How do we get out of this?

Or we could pretend again? I'll make sure my maid doesn't overhear us this time.

I grit my teeth and glare at my sister. Then I delete the messages and toss her phone back onto the table. She's going on a date tomorrow? Does she like this guy? He's a potential suitor for my sister now because of me. But if she likes him…

I lean over her again, fisting my dick as I perch my elbow against the pillow beside her head. Her lips are parted. I've thought about kissing those lips for far too long—but now I'm pissed, and the idea of someone else kissing her makes me want to hurt her.

Positioning my dick so my swollen head is right against her soaked entrance, I snatch her bottom lip between my teeth, sinking them in until she flinches then soothing the flesh with my tongue.

I regret it as soon as I do it, so I close my eyes and press my lips fully to hers. Her still, statue-like mouth is unmoving as I inhale deeply and take her chin, angling her head to kiss her harder.

I silently hum as I slip my tongue between her lips. She's not kissing me back, but that's okay. I hike her knee further up my hip as I keep feasting on her mouth, careful not to push into her and cause her any damage.

Firstly because she's never had sex, and also because I don't exactly have an average-sized dick.

Does she even know I'm pierced? Mason got it done, so I went with him, and it was the worst pain imaginable, especially at that age. But now it's all healed, I'm a virgin with a pierced dick and an obsession with my sister, and I'm still going to argue that I'm not going to go to therapy or take any medication.

It'll be fine. As soon as she realizes and chooses me, I'll be normal.

Her cheeks are flushed, and I nearly die as she rocks against me, the tip nearly inside her. I pull back a few inches, my forehead to hers, and bring the head of my dick to her entrance again.

Fuck, I want her to be mine so badly. How do I stop this dating bullshit? Olivia is mine. The sooner Mom realizes that, the better.

I kiss her again, forcing my tongue in until I feel hers, my balls pulling tighter. My lungs burn, and I need to thrust so fucking much, but I hold back, even as my dick gets harder and starts to throb.

I've come to the thought of Olivia millions of times. From watching footage, pictures, or being physically near her while she touches herself. I've coated my hand, my duvet, my shower wall. But now, as I keep kissing Olivia, and her tongue reacts, moving against mine, I falter as she starts to tense beneath me. Her back arches, and she releases a moan loud enough to wake the dead as her cunt throbs against the head of my dick.

I release so hard, I need to sink my teeth into her lip again as I pulse, my cum painting her pretty little pussy.

Just to add to the pressure behind my eyes, I slip my hand between us, pushing two fingers in, needing some of my cum to be inside her. I gather more and push it in, until I'm satisfied.

She's going on a date tomorrow with my cum inside her virgin cunt.

I pull away from her, my breaths heavy as I get to my feet and tuck my dick away, my heart racing. I run my hand through my hair then grab my phone, snap a picture of Olivia, and send it to my laptop. I'll store it with the other images I have of her asleep, naked, eating, dancing, and when she's smiling. If anyone found the shit I have on there, they'd think I was a creep and stalking my own sibling. And I guess, in a way, I am.

After taking one last look at her body, I don't bother cleaning my mess as I put her panties and nightdress back on, already planning what I'll do to her tomorrow night.

CHAPTER EIGHT
MALACHI

Olivia is hovering above me, our pinkies hooked together, after I've told the biggest lie of my life about having no experience so she'd show me how to kiss.

Technically, it is a lie. I've kissed someone before. Her. While she was drugged and absently kissed me back, completely unaware that her brother's fingers were in her pussy.

It was messy, definitely not something to brag about, but still a lie.

When her text came through, asking how my date was, I smiled at the screen, ditched my friends, and headed straight for home—her room window was open, and I climbed up and waited for her to get out of the bathroom.

The date was shit. It was planned to make Olivia jealous, and it worked. Anna asked me to go to her friend's party when we met up. I had agreed, nodding because she hadn't a clue how to sign, and I made sure Oliva's friends saw me go upstairs with her.

It was perfect. Until I got into the room, the door closed, and Anna tried to kiss me. It wasn't part of my plan, but for some reason, when I stepped away, she kept fucking coming at me until I put my hand on her forehead and shoved her back a few steps. She wasn't happy about my refusal, but I gave no fucks and got the hell out of there.

My heart might explode through my chest because as much as I've been all over Olivia for years—as much as we've cuddled in bed since we were kids, and everything else, I'm so damn nervous, I struggle to swallow.

She tries to cover herself, tightening her towel around her body, but it barely matters. I've seen her naked too many times.

The fact she's done this before, while awake, with someone who isn't me, doesn't sit right with me. I'll blame Mom. That way I don't need to blame Olivia.

All I can think about is her kissing someone else. I always knew, since I overheard on numerous occasions, but it still feels like a dagger to my cold, barely functioning heart. Especially hearing her say it—or even the fact she thinks she can "teach" me how to kiss because she has so much fucking experience.

Fuck. Now I'm mad again.

She leans up on one arm. "Are you sure? It doesn't bother you that we're brother and sister?"

I quirk a brow. This is the best day of my life—why is she

even having to ask this? Was it an issue when we were in the tent, or when she was grinding her pretty little cheerleader ass against my dick while she thought I was asleep, or when she actually did touch me?

I think my little sister has a somnophilia kink. Not that I'm complaining.

Stop saying that.

A blush creeps up her chest and neck, her hair like a dark curtain around us. I wrap a lock around my finger, wondering if she can see how much my hands are shaking. I pull it enough to draw her closer to me. The redness spreads to her cheeks, and damn, does her nervousness make me feel less anxious about this entire thing.

"Remember Mom told us not to kiss on the lips when we were younger? You said we were allowed to because we were siblings, but it got us into trouble. This will, undoubtedly, get us into even more trouble."

All I can think about is how kissable her lips are, how soft her facial features are, even when she comes. I keep playing with her hair, bringing it to my nose to inhale the scent that keeps me grounded. Her. All her.

Since I was a kid, it's been a thing to seek out when I was feeling in my head—holding my new foster sister while sniffing her hair and feeling far too confused about why she was my anchor.

I'm tugging her hair harder, and she's lowering onto my body, closing the infinitesimal distance. "Malachi," she whispers nervously. "Are you sure?"

Shut up, I sign, needing her closer, closer, until we can't even breathe without sharing the same air. She looks at the door, then back down at me before her nose nudges mine, sliding down further.

My lungs aren't working, and I think I might go into shock— she's right there, tilting her head, and everything ceases to exist as her lips press to mine.

I hope Olivia is aware that everything is now changing.

Us. Her life. Mine. Our future.

We're going to be together now. I'll make sure Mom and Dad understand, because Olivia's willingly kissing me, and I think if she stops, I might die. Her kisses are soft, gentle, and I follow her lead while trying not to be pathetic and pant uncontrollably into her mouth.

There's a sharp tug in my throat, and I think it might be a silent moan as she sucks on my bottom lip, scraping it with her teeth.

Olivia breaks the connection, looking down at me. "Will I keep going?" she asks, and I'm momentarily stunned, unable to communicate, as I study how beautiful she is.

I swallow. She wouldn't be doing this if she knew the things I've done to her unconscious form, right?

Of course not. Why would she actually want to do this? I'm getting annoyed at myself. The voice in my head is mocking me that she's being forced.

No. Olivia wants this. I know if I dropped my hand between her legs, she'd be soaked. She would. She's always wet for me.

You aren't allowed to stop yet. Keep going, little sister.

"Put your hand here," she says, taking it and resting it on her cheek. "Or you can put your hands on their hips or in their hair. People like touch, especially while being kissed."

What do you like?

For some reason, she's speechless for a long second, and I want to narrow my goddamn eyes and tell her to answer carefully, but she only grabs my hand once more, my cock twitching as she places my hand on her throat.

Her fingers squeeze around mine, and fuck.

Fuck, fuck, fuck.

"I like to be choked," she tells me. "I like rough kisses that hurt."

I want to kill her.

She screams as I flip us over, so I'm hovering above her, grasping tightly around her fucking throat as I smash my lips down on hers.

My tongue pushes past her lips, and I suck on hers, kissing her deeper while she struggles for a full breath. I can hear her choked gasps as she wraps her legs around me, my dick stabbing into her thigh.

I snatch her wrists and pin them above her head, using my hold on her to keep her in place as I grind the underside of my cock between her legs—she whimpers; sinks her teeth into my lip until it hurts.

She rips the skin, making us both taste copper as a trail of blood drips from my small wound.

It's not sore, but it aches, and for some reason, the pain has me growing even harder while I lean up, watching her as I drag my cock against her core. Her moans are driving me insane—I might accidentally make her pass out from how tightly I'm gripping her throat.

She moans louder, and I have to cover her mouth. Our mom is next door painting with music playing, probably too loud to actually hear us, but I can't take any risks. Doing this, and being caught, is a one-way ticket out of this house, and it's the only thing keeping Olivia strapped to me.

Whimpering into my palm, she meets each thrust, her eyes rolling, and she tenses up everywhere when I lower to her throat and sink my teeth into her flesh. I suck on the skin, tasting her, devouring her, her muscles going rigid. She's seconds from release, but I'm not ready for this to be over.

I flip us until she's on top, straddling my thighs—her towel gone, so I can get a full, perfect view of her body.

The body I own.

Before I can take control, Olivia fists my hair and brings her mouth back to mine. I touch everywhere I can. Her hips, her breasts, her thighs, her neck and face. My tongue moves with hers, following her, copying her, and she starts rocking her hips, grinding herself down on my cock. Needing more friction, I grab a fistful of hair at the back of her head and drag her down harder, firmer, until she's lightly groaning when I suck on her throat again.

This is the most explicit kissing lesson I've ever heard of. We went from our lips touching to seconds from fucking within minutes.

We must have that much chemistry. We're going to screw like rabbits soon, if not now.

"I can show you how to do this," she says, taking my hand and guiding it between us. She presses my fingers to her clit, teaching me because she has so much fucking experience.

The more she talks, the more she shows me how to circle my fingers around her clit, the more a dagger buries into my chest and buries deep.

Does that mean she's been touched by someone who isn't me?

I stop kissing her and look down between us, imagining someone else doing it. It's not my hand; it's someone else's, and I have to grit my teeth and blink so I can see my own hand again.

Why is there pressure behind my eyes? Why, while I pleasure

my sister, do I feel like running out of this room and finding who the fuck has touched her before?

"Have you done this before?"

Fuck. I need to lie again. Or should I tell her the truth? I can't look up at her—I watch my fingers circle her clit as I shake my head.

"Girls love this," she continues, making me want to murder someone. "Do it while you kiss them. If you do it right, you can make a girl come on your fingers." Despite my apparent inexperience, she whimpers so loud, I fear for our privacy. "Fuck, yes. Just like that, Malachi."

I guess, in a way, I am inexperienced. I've only fucked around with her body a few times since the first time I drugged her. I've licked her, had my tongue inside her, and even nearly tongue-fucked her ass.

I kiss her again to stop her asking any more questions. Harder. Taking her throat because I love how she sounds when she struggles to breathe—I love having control of her life force, not that I'd ever risk it.

"Faster," she moans. "You're doing so good."

Maybe, just maybe, she'll let me fuck her tonight. And maybe, just maybe, I don't use protection. And maybe, just maybe, she'll fall pregnant and never be able to leave me.

Irrational, but realistic.

Fuck. No. That's ridiculous.

"Malachi," she gasps as I pinch her clit between my fingertips. "You're making me so wet."

Her pussy rocks against my fingers until she sinks down on them a little, and though I've already fucked her with my fingers and thought it was heaven, having her lucid and awake and moaning above me has me nearly coming in my boxers from the feel of her.

I need my clothes off. My dick is rubbing against her ass with each gyration of her hips, deepening my fingers, and I need to go further. Anything. My balls ache, my lip is pulsing from her biting me, and I think I'm falling more in love with my sister every time she drops her hips onto my fingers.

Her eyes are glazing over, her pussy tightening around my fingers, and I know from before that she's about to reach her euphoria. I grab her neck, kiss her, her moans against my tongue making precum leak from my tip.

I'd fuck her ass. I love her ass. Imagine having my cock inside it?

I want to so badly.

Would it be too much to tell her that it wasn't true? That I don't need lessons and that I'm in love with her?

Then I'd ruin the moment.

Fuck. My mouth connects with hers again.

A picture falls from her hand slamming against the wall above us as her body convulses through her orgasm.

"Fuck," she pants, her voice shaking. "Keep going."

My girl is so vocal. I'm so glad my camera is recording all of this, but it's a shame there won't be any sound when I watch it back. I should really update my system and buy cameras that also record noises.

Just as I'm about to remove my boxers and fuck her through the rest of her high, a knock sounds at the door. "Sweetheart? Are you okay in there?"

Olivia freezes and tries to get off me, but I catch her by the hair and arch her back enough to suck a nipple into my mouth. I suck hard enough to mark the skin around it, my fingers curling inside her pussy until she's trembling.

Another knock, and I switch to the other breast, giving it as much attention. She's silently crying, her pussy gripping my fingers like a vise while her ass rubs against my cock.

I'm not sure if another orgasm hits, or the first one is just exploding, but she tenses all over, as if she's been turned to stone. I go to kiss her again, swallowing her moans while our mother knocks on the door. My tongue lightly grazes hers as her muscles start to weaken, her inner walls gripping me, my hand and fingers soaked with her cum.

She shoves me away as much as she can. She's breathless, her eyes wide as they study my mouth.

Does she want to kiss me again? That's fine. I'm all hers.

"No, I think she's snuck out with Parker. I'll be calling his parents to tell them that we're setting them up for an arranged marriage, not to fuck around at all hours. Plus, she was with Adam last weekend, remember? I had to go get her the morning-after pill." There's a long pause while I think my brain fails to work. "Is Malachi in his room?"

I'm certain I heard that wrong. I must have.

There's no chance in fucking hell Olivia would need the morning-after pill, right?

Then Dad replies, "I'll go check."

What the fuck did they just say?

Olivia gets her towel and jumps off the bed. "Go!" she says silently. "Hurry before Dad gets to your room."

I'm tasting her from my fingers at the same time I'm trying not to lose my shit. My heart was already racing from what just happened, but now it's accelerating to an unhealthy pace, black dots obscuring my vision. I rise from the bed and walk towards her with my fingers in my mouth, cleaning them of her taste.

Why did you need the morning-after pill?

I back her into the wall. So many voices are going wild in my head, but I manage to angrily sign, *Fucking answer me!*

She's shaking, covering her breasts, looking innocent and shy and fucking guilty. She's not telling me because that means she needs to admit that she's fucked someone. That she lost her virginity to someone else. That she's been intimate with somebody who isn't me.

I pull on my shirt, getting the fuck away from her before I strangle her. I don't want to hurt her. I love her. Why do I want to hurt her?

Will I go out there right now and ask them why you needed a plan B?

Her eyes are watering. "They wanted me to sleep with him to prove my loyalty."

Glaring, I crush my teeth together, grinding them to dust as the black dots nearly take over my vision from the rage filling my veins.

What?

"Don't look at me like that. You know what they're like when it comes to me being partnered up with someone wealthy. I wasn't going to tell them no, Malachi," she hisses, like I'm the one in the wrong. "I don't have that luxury."

I look at the door, deciding which parent to bury first— maybe Dad, so our mom can have the horror of watching me skin him alive, ripping away the love of her life like she's trying to do to me.

Was Adam your first? The one who made you realize you liked to be choked?

"No," she replies.

My heart sinks, needles stabbing into my eyes. *No to which part, Olivia?*

Who else has she slept with? Why do I feel like I'm about to pass out?

You fuck him again, or anyone else, and I'll kill them.

"I'm supposed to marry one of them," she seethes, like she has any right to be mad at me. She should have told me these fucking dates were more than just going out for dinner together or watching a damn movie—if I knew Mom was arranging for her to fuck people to prove her loyalty, I would've put a stop to it.

Fuck. Even now, I want to go out there and trail our mom all over the house, but then that means I'd hit a woman, and as much as I can be a dickhead, I wouldn't stoop so low.

This is Olivia's life. She's been raised this way by this fucking witch.

For what? To have her marry the wealthiest family to make sure ours stays out of debt? Dad doesn't even know how much she's driving them into being broke.

My sister looks terrified, so instead of getting even angrier, because I know it isn't her fault, I go to her, slide her hair behind her ear, and kiss her lips before I grab my clothes and disappear out the window.

I balance across the ledge until I reach my balcony, drop my clothes, and lean against the brick wall. Lowering my head, I squeeze my eyes shut.

My body is confused. My heart even more.

I'm in fucking heaven because I have the taste of her on my mouth and my fingers, and I've never felt more alive—but I also have a twisting feeling in my gut.

Betrayal, it feels like.

I think.

It must be.

I can't be Olivia's first because someone else got to have her before me, and I don't know if I'm angry, jealous, or if I'm slowly dying inside that she didn't wait for me.

My phone dings with a new message. I hold the smoke in my mouth while I read it.

Dad

> What the fuck happened to your bike?

He's attached a picture of the handlebars hanging off—the wheel beveled. It wasn't my fault. I had to get home to Olivia, and the gate was in the way. I'm unharmed, but I can't say the same for my damn bike. I crash it all the time, so it'll be another bill they cover since they refuse to let me get a job.

The only time he contacts me is to yell at me, or to express his disgust. It's been gradually getting worse. He didn't even ask if I was okay. I could have a broken fucking arm or a missing finger, and he's more concerned about a damn motorbike.

His next message has me grinding my teeth and throwing my half-smoked cigarette away.

Dad

> Get your ass down here right now.

Despite needing to have space, I shower and head downstairs, and for the fifth time, we arrange for a mechanic to come fix my bike while I sit in silence, trying to calculate when and where and who got to have Olivia first.

CHAPTER NINE

MALACHI

Mom and Dad have far too many friends here—the pool is packed with cheerleaders, music is blaring, and the barbeque has a queue of people I've never met before in my life. Some of them haven't even spoken a word to my parents.

It's Mom's birthday. I think she paid people to be here because there's not a chance in fucking hell this many people tolerate that woman enough to celebrate her day of birth.

In a way, I used to worship Mom for saving me. I'm still thankful, which is probably why I put up with her shit. She raised me, put clothes on my back, gave me money whenever I needed it—birthdays and vacations were always extravagant, and she lets me do whatever I want. Unlike Olivia, who has extremely strict rules, even at the age of eighteen.

Going from having nothing to everything, I know I owe Mom a lot, but because of her, I lost someone who belonged to me from the moment we met in that airport.

She let my sister fuck someone else, and for what? To prove she's got what it takes to marry into a wealthy family? Or so Mom could finally solidify how much control and influence she has on the life of a girl she raised since she was a kid?

My jaw tenses at that thought, and I gulp half of my beer, needing something stronger to banish the bitter taste of betrayal.

Mason is standing beside me, but I didn't invite any of my other friends—not that they'd fit in with these assholes anyway. They'd end up taking drugs and wrecking the place. Plus, one of them would flirt with my sister since they think she's pretty, and then I'd be arrested for multiple murders.

I trust Mason now that he's stopped trying to annoy me by commenting on how hot my sister is. But given the way he's staring at Olivia's group of friends in the pool, I'm starting to think inviting him was a mistake. If I find out he's looking at my girl, I'll fry his eyeballs and make him eat them with ketchup.

Not really. Mason can handle himself and puts up a good fight against me. We've had a few scraps over stupid shit where neither of us came out the winner, and I'm in no mood for a bloody nose or broken bones.

Who's the purple-haired girl? he signs, gesturing towards Abigail.

I roll my eyes. *Don't waste your time.*

Sometimes he'll sign with me, and other times, he'll speak. Mostly, though, it's so we can slaughter our company with words without any of them knowing what the fuck we're discussing. He learned sign language as soon as we became friends—he asked his parents to bring a tutor in, so I'd have a friend in school.

But if he fucks Abigail and breaks her heart, I'll need to hear about it from Olivia for the next few months until she gets over him. Mason isn't monogamous and likes to have more than one partner at a time—a recipe for disaster when it comes to him having any interest in one of those cheerleaders.

She's the one who keeps looking at me. He presses the heel of his boot against the wall, dragging smoke into his lungs as he studies Olivia's friend.

She's a headcase, I tell him, finishing the rest of my beer and heading over to the ice barrel filled with bottles to grab another.

When I get back to Mason, he signs, *I think your dad is in a shitty mood.*

My eyes drift towards him. Dad looks like he wants to disappear or set himself on fire as he watches Mom socializing like the butterfly she is. He's the total opposite of her in every way. He hates people and has no patience despite being a high-profile defense attorney.

That makes two of us though. I can't stand being around Mom's friends. We're more alike than we both would like to admit—Dad hates people; I hate people. He won't fake a conversation; neither will I. Our friend groups are small. In fact, I don't think he even has any friends.

We even glare at each other the same way. If I didn't have memories from before the Vize family, I'd truly believe I was his biological son.

Mason shifts beside me, sighing. "I know you told me not to go there, but the little purple-haired cheerleader is looking at me like she wants me in every hole. Give me three good reasons why I shouldn't."

I silently laugh. *She's clingy.*

She can cling to my dick.

Searching for more reasons, I chew my lip. *She flirts with everyone.*

So do I.

I breathe out an annoyed huff and glare at him until he rolls his eyes.

Just in time, Abigail climbs out of the pool and tells Olivia she's running into the house to use the bathroom—it's the first time I've seen Mason put out a cigarette and give himself a few breaths before telling me he'll be right back with a pat on my chest.

I quietly tut and shake my head. He has no idea what he's getting himself into with that girl. She'll eat him alive, from the stories I've heard from Olivia.

Drawing my attention back to the pool, I ignore the irritation in my gut. Has the music gotten louder? I become hyper aware of my surroundings the longer Mason is gone from my side—I hear giggling from Olivia, a scream as someone splashes, and the sizzle of the grill.

So many faces, so many eyes, so many voices, and all I can fully focus on is my little sister. She keeps screaming and splashing her friends, then climbing out the pool in her tight black bikini and cannonballing back in.

I know people are watching her. How could they not?

She's looked at me a few times, caught me looking back at her, but it doesn't put a frown on her face or spoil her fun—if anything, she grows more comfortable and confident, and fuck is she beautiful when she believes in herself.

I've noticed her mood depleting recently. Even her kisses are growing more desperate while she lies to herself that she's only teaching me.

Annoyingly, she's always at Parker's house, or at Adam's. It's like they're just passing her to each other, despite none of them knowing the other exists.

Adam is terrified of me. I've followed him on my bike, slashed his car tires, held him against the wall by the throat until he begged me to believe that he doesn't even want to be with Olivia. Both our parents are forcing them.

I haven't bothered with him much the last few weeks. He's no threat, as much as I want to beat the shit out of him out of pure jealousy.

The emotion is pointless. I have an ugly green monster

on my shoulder, angry about the guy even though I get to kiss Olivia whenever I want—when she comes to my room or I go to hers, her "lessons" getting more handsy by the night. My anger issues about Mom's obsession to marry my sister off have been overshadowed by the joy I feel every time Olivia whimpers against my lips while riding my fingers like my own little whore.

Four times.

Five tonight, once everyone fucks off and leaves me alone with her. It never goes further than a fingering, despite what I signed to her the morning after that first night—that I wanted her to teach me how it felt to have her lips around my cock. She went out with Parker later that day—feels like she has been out with him fucking constantly—so I couldn't make good on my threat, but every moment I've been able to steal since then, I've taken things as far as she'll let me.

She still hasn't touched me properly. She always grabs my dick through my shorts but never skin-on-skin or stroking me. Apparently, the lessons are about *teaching* me and not her *doing* stuff to me, and I'm not going to argue, as much as I can't wait to shove her to her knees and watch her eyes water from choking on my—

My thoughts are interrupted as another family walks down the side of the house, drawing a huff and a muttered "fucking hell" from my dad. My beer nearly cracks in my grip when I see my dad's business partner, Victor Melrose, and his imbecile son, Parker. He's a preppy asshole. Shaggy blond hair, clothes too big for him yet he thinks he's a style icon. Looking like he smells of sweat from five days ago although he's never lifted a weight in his life.

He'll look so good covered in his own blood—still a dickhead but unmoving, unseeing, silent, dead. I'll drag it out. Make sure he's aware of his attacker and feel every bone snap while I engrave me and Olivia's names into his skin before I remove that too.

His eyes are studying the yard and the pool. His father shoulders him and points to Olivia. She's concerned and questioning the purple-haired girl she calls her best friend and spends a lot of time with.

I hate her too. I don't like the immature influence she has on Olivia, but my gaze is pulled to the guy who thinks he can have my sister. The guy who, no matter how many times I threaten him, keeps appearing and getting on my fucking nerves.

His eyes clash with mine, and I see him paling before turning away.

I run my tongue across my teeth as Mason appears once more—he looks pissed, my gaze flicking to Abigail as she rolls her eyes and gives him the middle finger.

"I think she likes me," he says even though he looks like someone shoved a knee against his nuts. *I need to come over more often.*

No he doesn't. And he won't. I'll tell Olivia her friend is no longer welcome because I refuse to have our groups tangled up in drama.

Who's the preppy guy?

I grit my teeth. *Someone my sister might be marrying.*

He snorts, smirking at the evil look in my eye. *You wanna fuck him up?*

I nod. Parker is three years older than me, four if you count the random few months because my birthday is before his, but I tower over him and have nearly two times the muscle mass. I could squash him like a bug within a minute.

Olivia hasn't noticed Parker yet—she's too busy gossiping with her friends and eye-fucking me when no one is looking. Her hair is down her back, halfway to her perky ass, and her bikini clings to her curves. I can't stand the thought of everyone looking at her, including Parker.

Has he fucked my sister?

I look at him again, watching him push his hands into his slacks and laugh at something my mom says. To the left, my dad is drinking a non-alcoholic beer, scowling at the same person I am. His gaze moves over to me, then he glances at Parker again, his eyes darkening with a deadly glint.

Good. We both hate him.

That means he doesn't have Dad's approval. He'll never get to marry her. But will he give me his blessing? Should I ask again, but this time tell them that we're together and in love? That I'll treat her right and make her happy?

Someone else appears at the party—they greet the Melrose family then my mom, and my heart pounds at the anticipation of fights breaking out.

I swear to fucking God, if Adam shows up, I'm blowing up this yard and everyone in it.

The party goes on for the next two hours. For 120 minutes, I scowl at Parker and the way he keeps attempting to get Olivia's attention. She goes to the food table, dodging him when he says something to her, and then when she sits on the ledge of the pool, she jumps into the water when he tries to crouch beside her.

Good girl. At least I know she doesn't like him.

His dad will be forcing him to approach her. Mom is openly flirting with the guy, her hand going to his chest while she laughs at something that isn't even funny, and then whispers stuff in his ear. I go to stand beside my dad near the back door to the kitchen while Mason floats over to the cheerleaders to flirt with Abigail again.

"Your hooligan friend better not cause trouble," he tells me. "I'm in no mood to beat the shit out of a teenager with more tattoos than my insolent son."

Mason is twenty, but I don't correct him.

I take a big gulp of my beer, not gracing him with any response. The fact I'm even standing beside him is good enough after he basically called me arrogant.

The sound of giggling has me glaring in the same direction as him.

Surely he's aware of Mom's obvious flirting? She's seconds from taking Parker's dad into the house. He's staring at my mom's tits like his wife isn't five feet away with their son.

Fed up with the blatant disrespect, I step forward, but Dad grabs my arm. "Don't bother," he says with no emotion. "Let her make her own bed and lie in it."

Glancing back at my mom, I huff and lean against the wall, checking my phone to see if our friends are out riding. Not that we'd be leaving until Parker fucks off and Olivia is in my bed, already coming down from her orgasm, waiting for me to return to cuddle her to sleep.

The music gets even louder, and my skin itches from all the voices.

Dad notices. "You don't need to be here if it's too much."

I swallow.

Blank him out.

Blank it all out.

"Your mother will understand."

No. Mom is too busy fucking up her marriage by batting her eyelashes at a married man, and my dad isn't doing a damn thing about it. She wouldn't give a fuck if I was here or not—but Olivia would be disappointed.

Shocker, Mason and Abigail go back into the house, or more like, he follows her, and she has a smile hidden behind her scowl.

If they fuck in my bed, I'll burn them alive.

"Malachi!" my sister calls out, my eyes already on her. "Can you help me?"

I tilt my head in confusion.

"The filters won't turn on for the pool," she clarifies, pushing her sunglasses to the top of her head. "Please."

I down the rest of my beer and head towards her, feeling Parker's eyes burning into the back of my head—Dad's probably are too as I vanish around the side of the pool house to where all the filters are. She can never fix them herself.

As soon as I'm out of view, Olivia grabs me by the shirt and yanks me towards her, backing herself up against the brick wall and cupping my cheek in her palm. "Hi," she says, smiling. "This is a lesson on spontaneous kissing."

I smile back and wrap my arms around the small of her back, pressing our bodies together.

"Kiss me," she whispers.

My mouth comes down to her, chaste, gentle presses of our lips turning open-mouthed until our tongues are moving together.

I can taste her fruity drink, and she can probably taste mint from my chewing gum and smoke, with a hint of beer. Or she's not focusing on that because she's turning us around and sitting me down on the ledge, straddling my thighs in her tight bikini.

She's either drunk or she's confident no one will come around here and catch us. The place is crawling with people, yet she's got her tongue down my throat and making my eyes roll by just kissing me.

Fuck. This girl owns me.

"You're angry," she says between strokes of her tongue against mine. "Because he's here."

I nod, biting her bottom lip. I can't sign because my hands are all over her, and plus, words couldn't describe how angry I feel right now.

I hold her tightly to my body, devouring her mouth like it could be the last time she wants to teach me something intimate. Her skin is smooth and warm from the sun, yet wet from being in the pool—she molds into me like she belongs in my lap.

The drastic opposite between us is glaringly obvious. It's hot as fuck out and I'm in black combats, boots, and a white shirt, and she's wearing a scrap of fabric and glowing from tanning on a lounger all day.

She pulls back, her gaze on mine. The way she's looking into my eyes momentarily stalls me. I've been feeling like I'm trapped within a dream since the moment I knew I could push my boundaries with her—the tent, since she fell asleep in my arms in a non-sisterly way and made my heart pound, when she touched my dick and made it hard, when she kissed me back for the first time and had my chest tightening at my luck. The first damn smile that gave me butterflies at the age of seventeen— when the attraction escalated into fucking heaven.

I always had a thing for Olivia. Since I was a kid. I had no idea it could get stronger. So much so, I think I'm a health risk to myself and everyone around us, because I would kill for this girl without thinking twice.

Olivia's smile grows. "If you're not mad, then you're jealous."

My eyes narrow, and a fire lights and spreads like wildfire within me as she hums, grinning against my lips like she's genuinely happy.

"I like it when you're jealous."

I squeeze her hips, making her giggle some more.

Then she tilts her head. "Keep Mason away from Abbi."

I give her a glare that silently tells her to keep Abigail away from Mason.

"We should go before someone sees us."

I shake my head. *Not yet.* This is the highlight of my day so far—I'm not done with having her attention yet.

Her eyes light up when my fingers play with the string of her bikini, which is resting on her hip, and I tug to loosen it. She traps her bottom lip between her teeth as I do the same to the other side. The scrap drops to the ground beneath us with a slap of wet material.

"Take yours off too," she orders, pulling at the waistband of my combats.

I let her unfasten the buttons of my pants and slide her hand under my waistband to feel how hard I am. She palms my dick, and the gentle touch sends shocks straight to my balls, drawing a muted groan into my throat.

"Have you ever been touched, Malachi?"

She knows the answer. But the way her pupils expand when I shake my head has me wanting to worship her until the day I die.

Olivia has groped me through my clothes, touched me, but she's never gotten me off using her hand or stroking my cock until I found my high. So when her fingers wrap around the thickness of it, I gulp nervously, wanting to touch her but leaving my hands on her hips. My fingertips dig into her skin as she goes from base to tip, twisting her wrist and back down.

"This can be another lesson," she says. "A lesson on receiving."

She can call it whatever she likes. I blink far too much, watching her hand move up and down on my dick while warm euphoria wraps around my spine, making my legs and stomach tense.

Using her free hand, she snatches my throat, forcing me to look at her. "Touch me while I'm doing this to you."

Fuck.

Fucking fuck.

I gulp against her palm, my pulse hammering, as my fingers

leave her hip, shakily sliding between her legs to feel the heat of her pussy.

She must get off on the way she's making my eyes roll because she's soaked. I push two fingers in at the same time she rocks her hips, taking me to the knuckles.

Humming a soft moan, her eyelids fall shut, and I'm mesmerized with how beautiful she is while she rides my fingers at the same time she jerks me off. I thicken from her touch, and I flinch as the pad of her thumb swipes over the bead of precum at my swollen head.

I mouth a "fuck" and pull the cup of her bikini down under her breast and suck a nipple into my mouth, causing her to tighten around my fingers and let out a whimper.

So warm and tight and fucking mine.

"You don't need any more lessons on touching," she breathes. "I guess I'm just selfish and greedy for my big brother's fingers."

My cock twitches, dying to dip into her pussy. To have her mouth. Her ass. Fucking anything. The way she talks only has me shoving my fingers even deeper, grabbing on to her skin for dear life while she rocks into my touch.

The sounds she makes when I add another finger has me snapping, my balls going firm, and I have to sink my teeth into her nipple from how intense the powerful orgasm hits me.

Lashes of my cum coat her thighs as I suck hard, and her free hand goes to my hair, tugging while I curl my fingers deep inside and stroke a spot that has her tensing all over as her high smacks into her like a tidal wave.

We ride it out together. Her dragging my mouth back to hers and me swallowing the loud cries until we're both panting the same air and holding on to each other.

After a few minutes of catching our breaths, she lifts her head from my shoulder, bites her lip nervously, then smiles.

Olivia climbs off my lap, looking down at the mess I've made of her skin—her cheeks and chest are flushed a deep red, her pupils dilating even more as I slip off my white shirt and clean my cum from her thighs.

In a daze, her fingers trace up and down my arms until I'm sure I've gotten rid of the proof the Vize siblings have been fucking around.

"The filter wasn't broken," she admits before snatching up her bikini bottoms and fastening them back onto her body. "It was only an excuse to get you alone."

I already knew that. She's not very creative, since it takes less than a minute to fix the damn filters and we've been around here for over ten.

Like nerves are sinking in, she fidgets then kisses my cheek and runs back to the party, leaving me feeling like I'm the luckiest guy in the world with a stupid smirk on my mouth.

It's when I stand, checking if I'm able to put my shirt back on, that Mason walks around the corner, calling out my name with a tone filled with concern.

He pauses.

Stares at me.

Looks back at the party, then to me again.

"No. Fuck no. Tell me you weren't doing what I think you were doing."

My nostrils flare as I run my hand through my hair. *Then don't ask.*

Mason's lips part to say something else, then he flattens them and stares at me.

"That's fucked up, Vizey."

Rolling my jaw, I shake my head in annoyance. *Tell a soul and I'll kill you.*

It makes so much sense, he signs. *So much fucking sense.*

I flip him off, and he laughs like he's been told the best joke ever.

Well I pissed off your sister-turned-girlfriend's friend and I think she might throw a drink in my face or hit me with a glass bottle, so can we go?

We both grab one last beer and head out, and Mason promises to keep my secret, as long as I figure out a way to get him and Abigail in the same room again.

The blackmailing dickhead.

CHAPTER TEN

MALACHI

I'd never had a blowjob before.

Well, since Olivia is balancing across the ledge to get to her window with her throat coated with my cum, I can cross that off my list of things I want Olivia to do to me in this life. I can still feel the warmth of her mouth around my cock and hear the way she was gagging while Dad yelled at me to get inside.

She waited until he vanished to go back to her room.

Imagine he found out it was her? I'd be a dead man.

The fact she's even going to see that asshole Parker makes me want to rip his fucking head off.

How many times do I need to threaten him before he backs off? I don't give a shit if his family made a deal with mine—he'll walk away unless he wants his balls to replace his eyes.

Adam took one look at me in his driveaway, my hood up and smoke falling from my lips, and he's not been back at the manor since. I think Olivia still goes out to see him when she's forced to though, but at least he's not under my damn roof, pretending to play happy couples with my girl the way Parker does.

She might think these lessons are real, but they're the furthest thing from the truth. I don't need to be taught a single thing, considering I've done stuff to her while she's been unaware— the excuse worked though, so my inner Malachi is gloating at the other voices that tried to talk him out of it.

Those voices are calling me a little liar while a devil chuckles on my shoulder. I'm a sneaky prick, and I don't care.

My phone buzzes, and I fully expect a message from my sister, but it's the group chat. Everyone's planning a meet-up on their bikes, so I decide I might as well kill time until she gets home by joining them.

Mom and Dad don't ask where I'm going when I pass by them in the hall. They're arguing, as usual, and Mom is pointing in his face, but he doesn't seem to give a shit at how angry she is.

The guy has become so indifferent to her. They were loved up and happy on the camping trip, and somewhere, it fell apart.

I pull on my helmet, hit the button for the garage door to open, and head out to the meeting point only five blocks from here.

Mason is on his way there too. He said he was at some chick's house and needed to clear his head. He hasn't said much about me and Olivia since catching us last weekend. The only time he mentions it is when I don't reply right away, and he asks if I'm too busy fucking my sister.

Most of the time, I'm ignoring him because I'm kissing her, watching a movie, or we're jogging at our usual spot while she blasts pop music through our shared earphones and I stare at the ass that I'll soon enough get. I think so anyway. If she's going through everything else, surely she'll let me near her ass?

So he's partially correct. I'm not fucking her. Not yet. But I know the lesson is coming soon. There's only so many times we can get each other off with our hands before it gets deeper— I've finally had my dick sucked, so we're moving forward. I'm certain Olivia will bring me to my knees to return the favor any day now.

I'm starting to think I have an unhealthy fascination. She's all I think about. Whenever something happens, I think of her. When I'm bored or busy or just lying in bed or hitting some weights, I try to imagine what she's doing and if she's thinking of me too.

I'm definitely in love with her. Soon, I'll make her fall in love with me too.

"Are we heading to the lake?"

Some of us nod, and we speed off towards the water. The adrenaline I get from squeezing the throttle isn't even close to how it felt having her lips around my dick, flicking at my piercings, her eyes on me, but I go even faster and overtake

Mason and Rory.

The latter is new to the group. He's still learning how to ride a bigger bike and crashes more than me. Even though he's the height of a child, he's the biggest party animal with booze and drugs, and the one who always asks me to invite him over so he can look at my mom.

He's never been allowed near my house.

Three hours later, we end up at Mason's place. His parents turned their garage into a hangout spot for us all. We order pizza, play games, and pass joints between us until someone turns white and vomits everywhere.

Mason is scowling at his screen beside me. I glance over to see the middle-finger emoji sent from a contact called "Cheerleader" below a message telling him he was just a quick and easy fuck.

I stifle a silent laugh and shoulder him. *Did you actually get used?*

He shuts off his screen and takes the joint from between my lips. "Fuck you." *Have you screwed your sister yet?*

My eyes lift to the group. None of them can sign or understand it, but I still get a wave of paranoia at what he's asked me in front of them all.

"Relax," he says. "Your secret is safe with me."

"What secret?" one of the guys asks, and Mason shakes his head as a reply.

My phone buzzes, and I pull it out to see a message from

Olivia. I frown at the location pin drop, swiping through to see if there are any other messages.

"What's up?" Mason asks, noticing the way my body stiffens.

I show him the screen. His eyes narrow as he reads.

Then it hits us both at the same time. Olivia is in trouble. We jump to our feet.

"Vizey's sister is in trouble. Grab your bats and masks and let's fucking go!"

Beats of panic smash into me while we speed to the location I've shared with them all. We nearly get wiped out by a truck on the way.

As soon as we reach the pin drop in the middle of an expensive neighborhood, the bikes are ditched, the balaclavas are slid down to hide our identities, and we sneak into the house.

Voices and music come from the basement. Everything happens so fast, I barely register kicking in the door, hearing Olivia tell me what they were going to do to her, and ordering her to get out before my bat connects with far too many faces. Parker's my first victim—I break his fucking nose while he tries to argue his position.

I grab an ashtray filled with joint ends and crack it into the side of someone's face, following with a knee to the chest and a punch to the back of the head.

A fist misses me by an inch, and the guy squeals like a pig as I shove the handle of my bat down his throat, jerking it to break his jaw in several places.

Warm blood splatters over my face and down my clothes. He vomits crimson on the floor by my feet, mixed with cries and snot. If he doesn't get to a hospital right away, he's screwed. I don't care enough right now to bother with the repercussions of my actions. They were going to hurt her, so I'm going to make sure they never even breathe in the same direction as her again.

Mason and the guys are beating the shit out of everyone while I grab Parker by the scruff of the neck and kick him in the midsection, knocking him back towards the basement door.

I smirk under my balaclava as he runs up the stairs, falling to the ground when he reaches the kitchen. He throws open the patio doors and escapes into the backyard, and that's when I decide he'll never walk again.

I like the way he begs me to leave him alone—I have all the power now, and this asshole spent his last day getting too close to my sister.

The earlier rainfall has turned the yard to sludge, so he doesn't get very far before I catch up to him, swinging my bat and knocking him off his feet.

He's face down in the mud now, and I press my boot on the back of his head, suffocating him in the dirt where he belongs. He fights—his arms and legs are thrashing as he chokes, but it only makes me push his face deeper.

This piece of shit. I want to kill him. I want him to suffer.

I only let him up for air so I can get a good swing at his leg, inwardly laughing as I hear the bone's sickening snap. It only brings me joy.

He wails in pain. "Fuck! You fucking psycho! Who the fuck are you?"

I pull off my mask, screwing myself over by ensuring he can identify me, and watch his eyes go wide. With blood staining my face from his hopefully dead friend, I drive my fist into his jaw once, twice, three times, until the motherfucker is crying for me to stop.

His leg is broken, so he can't get up, and the mud beneath him is swallowing his body while I grit my teeth and break his other leg by slamming my heavy boot down as hard as I can. Again, and again, and again.

"Fuck!" he cries, probably pissing himself while he starts begging me to leave him alone. He'll do whatever I want. But it's too late. He already messed with the one person who means more to me than life itself.

I punch him one last time, knocking him out, before I let up and pull my bat to my shoulder, spitting on him.

If I could talk, I'd tell him it was for Olivia. And if I could laugh, I'd do it while telling him she was fucking mine.

CHAPTER ELEVEN
MALACHI

O livia's idea of going for a drive and doing something away from how hectic the house is wasn't what I planned today. We'd spent hours wrapped up together. She was between my legs, and I was between hers, before we were rudely interrupted by our parents arguing right outside my bedroom door.

She huffed and told me to get dressed. Since her bossy side is adorable, I showered, got dressed, and met her in the garage. Now she's staring at me, at my hands tight on the steering wheel, her eyes glazed over.

We never got to finish. She needs something to tide her over until we get back home later. I slip my hand to her thigh, and she fights a smile and averts her eyes to look out the window.

The girl can't even handle me touching her fucking thigh from how needy she is. I dig my fingers into her flesh, and she opens for me while I try to keep my attention on the road. As she takes my wrist and slides my hand up further, I swallow, gripping the steering wheel at the feel of how soaked she is.

Still so wet.

Always wet for her big brother.

"Eyes on the road, Malachi," she orders, trapping her lip between her teeth. "If you crash, I won't suck your dick again."

I do as I'm told as I press my fingers to the wet patch on her panties, right where her entrance is throbbing for me. Whimpering, she moves her hips into the touch, guiding my fingers under her panties to feel the warmth of her pussy.

Maybe we should fuck already? What else is there to learn? There's nothing stopping us from pulling over somewhere discreet and sleeping together. Then I'd tell her the truth. Everything.

I'd tell her that I'm madly in love with her and if she has patience enough to have me as a brother with no voice, she'll accept me as a partner too. Maybe I'll tell her how much I've fucked her over. How, even though she shows me what to do, I still like to touch her when she's unaware. Lick her. Suck her. Everywhere.

All of a sudden, she yanks my hand away. "Pull in here."

I frown and look at where her gaze is directed, and it's a restaurant in the middle of nowhere. Releasing a sigh, I put on my blinkers and turn into the busy parking lot.

This is not even slightly what I had planned. Why aren't we going somewhere to make out until our mouths fall off?

She unfastens her belt and gets out of the car without saying a word. I follow, pulling my phone out to see if I have any messages and notice a missed call from Mason. I'll call him back later.

Olivia goes into the restaurant, asks for a table for two, and we go with the waitress to a booth in the middle of the room— we're surrounded, the place busy, and I think I might kill my sister for even thinking about coming here.

"I'm hungry," she says. "It's basically the evening, and we've been in bed all day."

For good fucking reason, I want to tell her, but I'm frozen in place, watching her look through the menu and order us both a water with ice. I'm uncomfortable—there are too many people here, and I'm certain some of them are looking at us.

We don't look like siblings, but we don't look like a couple either. She's a pretty little cheerleader, and I'm the furthest thing from the jock all the other cheerleaders are supposed to date. But I care more about how she feels with these people staring.

She's talking to me about food. Her lips are moving, but I'm taking none of her words in. They're so soft, shaping around each syllable, each time she licks them and lifts her eyes to me. I stare at her, focusing back on her mouth.

Her shoe hits my boot, and then she's rubbing her foot up my ankle, my knee, gasping when I capture it under the table.

When I let it go, her lips part, and she stares at me for way too long.

Run, I sign.

She frowns. "What?"

Unless you want me to fuck you on this table in front of the entire restaurant, then you better run.

She gulps, glancing around. "We aren't on that lesson yet."

I fist my hands on the table, my gaze burning into her, and sign, *Run, Olivia. I want to chase you. I want to catch you. I want to fuck you until you scream so loud, you lose your voice just like I have.*

She knows I will. A twisted part of her knows that I'm not joking. Everyone can either leave or watch me lose my virginity to my little sister while I bend her over this fucking table. Screw the consequences. She told me she wanted to be chased and fucked. That's exactly what I'm going to do to her.

My eyes darken on her, at the way she's still sitting in her seat.

As soon as I stand, she jumps up, grabs her purse, and runs straight to the exit. I leave a few notes for wasting their time and follow after her.

I spot her hair swishing in the wind as she vanishes into the woods next to the parking lot—she's running like I'm going to kill her.

I set off after her. The onlookers getting out of their cars watch me push into the woods and hunt for my little sister—who's seconds from being owned by every part of me.

Cracking branches beneath my boots, I follow the sounds of

her heavy breaths and footfalls. It's growing darker the further we get into the woodland, damper, the birds chirping overhead as they burrow into the canopy of trees.

I stop and listen. She's not running anymore. My heart is pounding in my ears, adrenaline lacing my veins with determination to find her.

"You're not very good at this, are you?"

Gritting my teeth, I move towards her voice, in the direction I can hear her footfalls again. She's fast. Usually, when we go running, I like to think I could get way ahead of her, sometimes making her sprint, but right now, she's like a damn rocket.

She giggles, stopping again, and I go slowly, branches still snapping under my weight. Olivia is behind a tree trunk, thick enough to conceal her, but close enough that I can hear her gasping for breath. Fitness is never an issue for her, so I'd like to think she's panting from anticipation of what will happen when I catch her.

Just before I can grab her, she spins around from behind the tree and jumps into my arms, hands in my hair as she drags my mouth to hers. I stagger backwards until my back hits another tree, steadying my balance, then snake one arm around the small of her back and grab her thigh with the other to hike her up more.

Her tongue delves into my mouth, and she's humming, smiling, tightening her thighs at my waist. Then she shoves at my chest until I drop her.

"Close your eyes," she tells me, and I do.

I furrow my brow at the sound of her running again, huffing as I open my eyes to see her vanishing into the distance once more.

I inwardly curse and shoot after her. She looks over her shoulder and lets out a shriek when I grab her by the hair and throw her on the ground.

I want to make sure she's okay, but the grin on her face and the way she's trying to scurry back tells me she's fine and enjoying this way more than any normal person would. I walk up to her, fisting her hair to tip her head back.

Smiling, she digs her nails into my wrist, which only makes my dick hard and my body lower onto hers until she's pinned into the dirt by my hips.

Grabbing her throat, I force her down and straighten my arm beside her head. The last time I saw this fear in her eyes was when Spikey dropped on the floor and she launched into my bed to escape him. She's scared, but her pupils are blown.

My cock is as solid as a rock, prodding right between her legs. And she opens them so I slot between her thighs perfectly.

She can barely breathe, her pupils dilating even further, and I grind my teeth to dust as she rocks her hips against me. She does it again, and again, and a third time, watching me as my hand tightens around her throat to cut off her air.

Olivia trying to take control is cute. In all fairness, she's been the one controlling us from the start, but this is my turn.

Not being able to breathe doesn't scare her, even though I can see pressure behind her glazed eyes. She keeps moving against me, keeps dragging herself up and down the underside of my dick.

She whimpers out a choked cough as I release her throat and rip her dress right down the front, exposing her braless chest and baby blue panties.

Soaked, as expected.

She gasps as I snap off her underwear and pocket the material, then drag my fingers up her pussy, spreading her, nipping her clit between them. She's so wet, so needy, and I think I might pass out if I don't feel what it's like to be inside her.

I lean up and tug down the zip of my combats, freeing my hard, thick cock that's already leaking with precum.

"If anyone sees us…"

I'll blind them and hit them hard enough to forget what they saw.

Laughing, she goes to wrap her fingers around my cock, but I snatch her wrist then take the other. A breath falls from her lips and touches my own as I pin both hands above her head.

I line our bodies up, but nerves start to take over as I grind my cock against her pussy, feeling the heat, the warmth, the way she's already ready for me.

My precum and her wetness mix together, making the

underside of my cock slide against her too fucking perfectly. The piercings rub her clit. She moans, tries to free her hands, but I grip them harder and thrust faster.

"This is so wrong," she says, gasping as I keep grinding into her. "Wanting you." She gasps again, rocking up to meet my thrusts, my tip nearly pushing into her. "My big brother."

Groaning inwardly, I close my eyes. Whenever she calls me her brother during some sort of sexual act, I nearly come all over her. It's wrong. It's deranged. Fucked up to want to feel the inside of your baby sister. But Olivia is mine, so I deserve to know what it feels like to have her come around my cock. I deserve to hear her cry my name while I fill her with every drop of me.

I lower my head and kiss her.

It's not soft or gentle, or anything romantic. We devour each other like we're starved, tongue and teeth and lips and moans, breathing each other in as my dick nearly pushes into her.

"Malachi," she whispers against my lips as my swollen head settles at her entrance, desperate to ease in, to thrust. One push and I'll be hers forever. "Not yet."

I let go of one of her wrists, and she automatically lowers it between us and grabs my cock, stroking it while the tip stays pressed against her entrance. I can barely move, inhale, anything as she slips her tongue into my mouth and strokes me from base to tip.

Every few strokes, she reaches the tip and rubs her hand, covered in my precum and her own wetness, over her clit and circles it.

We're both melting into one another as she continues. Stroking. Kissing. Rubbing. She cries into my mouth when she comes, and I feel her cunt quivering against the head of my cock, and it only drives me straight into my own release. Pulses of cum coat her pussy the exact same way it did when I messed with her sleeping form, and I watch as she slides her fingers inside, pushing my cum in and moaning, still in her high.

Fuck.

"I might have messed up," Mason tells me.

I inwardly sigh and lean my forearms on my handles, pulling up my visor so he can see my eyes. I raise a brow, needing him to elaborate, though I'm sure I already know what he's going to say.

"Abigail." He throws his leg over his bike, fixing his helmet on while his mother tells him to drive safely. He waves her off. "She won't talk to me."

And? I reply.

"I'm starting to think she really is only using me for a

good fuck."

I silently tut and shake my head. He's been so damn hung up on the girl since my mother's birthday party. He either shows up at her work, outside her cheer practice, or stalks her social media until he gets her on her own and somehow gets her into bed. It's tiring to watch, even though it's only been a few weeks.

Mason gets bored easily, so I'm waiting it out. The next person to pique his interest will take over, and Abigail will be forgotten.

I'm the total opposite from Mason. I was created for one girl and one girl only. The thought of even thinking about another person makes me uncomfortable as fuck. I would never betray myself or Olivia by entertaining someone else.

I can still see the way she lay beneath me in the woods. How she pushed my cum into her and made me lose my mind. It almost makes me want to drug her again, just so I can continuously fuck her, to watch my cum leak from her cunt until she's carrying my offspring. However, she might not like that—I feel like that's something I definitely need permission for.

I frown at the caller ID that pops up on my phone. Olivia never calls me. Instantly, my heart races, and I pull my helmet off and put the phone to my ear.

She's crying.

Fuck.

If someone hurt her—

"How dare you, Malachi. How fucking *dare* you? You lied to me. You… Y-You lied. You lied and tricked me into teaching you everything, you goddamn *freak*. I thought I was helping you, and I was falling for you in the process, yet all along you knew damn well what to fucking do! What sort of sicko does that? I'm your sister! And I… I was…"

She's silent for a beat, and my brows furrow even further. Mason can hear everything she's saying. He's frowning too. Maybe because he's a little protective of me and she called me a freak. Her cries are loud enough I don't even need to have her on speaker.

"I hope screwing Anna was worth ruining whatever fucked-up relationship we had. You'll never get near me again, Malachi. Never. I hate you. I h-h-hate you so fucking much."

Rapidly, I fire out a text while trying to control each panicked breath that leaves my lungs. She can't end this. I won't let her.

Me

Where are you?

"Fuck you," she snaps before hanging up.

My gaze lifts to Mason, my mouth dry, pulse rattling in my ears.

He lets out a heavy breath. "Fuck. Family drama. You need to go, man."

Patting my back as I shove on my helmet, he signs, *Don't do anything stupid. Let her yell at you and then explain your side. We both know that shit with Anna isn't true.*

I nod, barely able to think straight. He adds, *Good luck.*

It takes me five minutes to speed home. I ditch my bike in the drive, climb up her side of the house to get to her room faster, and jump through her window, which is unlocked. I keep the curtains closed, pacing, waiting for her to come home. She's not answering my calls, but Dad texted to tell me he'd bring food home for us both, so I know she'll be here soon.

What the fuck do I say?

I didn't fuck Anna.

I didn't even kiss her, so why is she accusing me of this shit?

I go over and over everything I can say. I'll let her shout, scream, even fucking slap me if she needs to, and then I'll sit her down, just like Mason said, and explain that I didn't do anything, and that whatever she's heard is a bunch of lies. I bet Anna got her ego hurt because I wouldn't go near her, and this is her way of retaliating. I swear, I'm going to strangle the bitch when I see her.

"Okay," I hear her say on the opposite side of the door. "I love you, Dad. Thank you."

My nerves spark into flames as I wait, matching the lighter I keep flicking. She doesn't open the door right away, although I know she's there. I move to sit on the bed, my gaze shifting back and forth from the window to the door, and I flick my lighter faster, feeling the burn on the pad of my thumb but unable to stop. If I feel pain, then maybe it'll coat the panic in my gut.

The door opens.

I hold my breath; I'm looking at the window.

"Get out," she snaps. "I don't want to even look at you."

Shakily, I turn around, but she refuses to look at me. She's standing aside, holding the door open.

"Leave, Malachi," she continues, falling against the door, drained, her eyes red from tears. "Whatever we were doing is over. I want you to leave my room, and don't ever come near me again."

Fuck no.

I haven't lied about anything, I sign, but she isn't looking. It's partially true. She came on my fingers in her sleep, and I've touched her more than the times she's been conscious, but that's not why she's mad.

I go to her and snatch her chin to make her look at me, but she won't look me in the eye.

"Can you please leave?" Her voice cracks. "You hurt me, and I can't look at you."

No. No, no, no. This isn't happening. It can't happen. I press my forehead into hers, silently begging her to stay with me, to keep me close while my palms hold her face in place. I try to kiss her, to show her how much she means to me and how I can't fucking breathe without her, but her hand swipes at the air, slapping me across the face.

"Get the fuck out!"

I try to sign and tell her to let me explain that Anna is lying, but she grabs my hands to halt me. The backs of my eyes burn, a mixture of rage and heartbreak. I'm seconds from shackling her to the bed and forcing her to understand.

She pushes me, and from the force of her hands on my chest, I actually take a step back, unable to dodge the perfume bottle launched at me.

"Leave!"

I'm getting annoyed—Olivia is being erratic and fucking selfish. She can be mad at me, yell, hit me, but if she silences me one more time, I'm going to blow the fuck up.

Shaking my head, I go to her again. *Let me fucking explain.*

"Fuck you." She slaps me again. "I hate you; do you understand that, you fucking freak? I hate you for tricking me. For manipulating me into doing things for you."

Olivia called me a freak again. And manipulating? Is she being serious?

She's been manipulating me since the day I fucking met her.

I didn't do anything, I sign, but she grabs my fingers and twists them. I grit my teeth from the pain, but she keeps going, her eyes filled with a fire I plan on snuffing out when she eventually begs on her knees for hurting me, for not fucking listening to me.

She'll calm down soon. Mason said to let her ride it out. For once, since I haven't the slightest clue how to fix this, I'm going to take my friend's advice.

Olivia shoves at my chest over and over again until I grab her and push her into the wall. I try to say her name. Actually say it—I can't get the pronunciation or get the words out. I'm useless in this fight. I can't sign because she either won't look at me or grabs my hands; I can't talk because I'm unable to actually do so. How do I win here?

She dodges under my arm and pulls the door handle.

"Go. Just… just go, Malachi. There's nothing to resolve here."

We were going to be each other's firsts, I sign, finally getting her to look at me properly. If she's done with her mood swing, I can get it out. *We were—*

She shakes her head, laughing as she leaves the bedroom. "I'm not a fucking virgin, Malachi. I haven't been since I was sixteen!"

My hands fall to my side. Sixteen?

I already knew she wasn't a virgin, that I didn't get to be her first and only, but hearing it from her mouth is like being hit by a truck.

"And apparently neither are you!"

I'm not a liar, I sign desperately. *Believe me.*

"I'll never believe you again."

The only thing I have left to do is force her to believe me. My least favorite way, from all the scenarios in my head, but I fist her hair and turn her to face me, then crush my mouth to hers in a last-ditch attempt to win her over.

She slaps my chest, fighting me while I kiss her harder, keeping her against the wall as I snake my arm at the small of her back. Slowly, I can feel her giving in.

Her body relaxes even as her nails sink into my cheek and rip downwards. The searing pain has me hissing into her mouth, catching her thigh when she attempts to knee me in the balls.

I bracket it to my hip, my chest tightening when Olivia gives in and starts kissing me back nearly as desperately as I'm kissing her.

We both need this.

She needs to move her hips to rock against my hardening cock. She needs me to nip and bite and suck on her tongue while she hums in pleasure into my mouth. As my hands slide down to grab at her ass, she grinds against me.

"I hate you," she pants as she bites my lip, hard enough to make me flinch. She pulls back to look at me, a tear sliding down her cheek that I lick away, then I drop my head to suck her pulse hard enough to leave a mark.

I silently groan against her throat as she wraps her fingers around my cock. Her grip is tight, the strokes forceful, but I seem to enjoy the pain as I thrust into her hand while I palm her ass.

Olivia releases me, eases me back, then drops to her knees. She tugs down my combats, looking up at me as she wraps her fingers around my dick again.

This isn't exactly what I intended when I kissed her—I wanted her to calm down, to sit with me until I explained everything. I need her to know what she means to me. How much I'm in love with her and how my entire world revolves around her. But the way she's looking up at me with the head of my cock inches from her mouth, I suppose I can wait till we've finished our fuck around.

But then she talks.

"I hope when you see others on their knees for you, you see me, your innocent baby sister, with your cock in her mouth. I hope when I'm out of your life, you miss this sight, because as soon as you finish down my throat and I swallow all your big brotherly cum, you're going to pack all your shit and leave."

Gulping, my hand goes to the wall above her head.

"Do you understand?"

Not even slightly. If she tries to run, I'll find a way to keep her. She'll be locked in a box next to Spikey.

Her nails sink into the flesh of my dick, and fuck, does it make me twitch and need her to keep going. I love her more than life, but the way she tries to overpower me is adorable, and a total turn-on.

I need to remind her who's the dominant one in our relationship. I might be weak for this girl, but I can have all the control too. I grab her hair with both hands and prove just that as I thrust my cock into her mouth, gagging her.

I hammer into her throat, not giving her a second to breathe until my forehead presses to the wall, my chest heaving to fill my lungs. Her eyes are watering from choking on her big brother's cock, and I wish I had my phone on me so I could take a picture of the sight.

But I refuse to come in her mouth. I need to be inside her—if she truly thinks this is us done, I need to fuck her and prove it's not. When she realizes that I can make her feel better than anyone else who's been inside her, she might give in.

She might choose me.

The way she's glaring up at me from her knees, a wet string of drool from my dick to her lips… My mouth waters; I need more drool all over her pretty lips. The act happens before I can think, and I spit on her face.

"What the f—"

Cutting her off, I shove her to her back and come down on her and kiss her again. It's deep, definitely controlling, and she gasps to push me off yet whimpers as I thrust my cock against her jeans.

I remove her jeans and throw them behind me, not paying attention to where they land. I'm going to make her feel good. I need her to come, to cuddle me in bed to scare away the unwanted feelings creeping all over me like spiders, and tell me that I'm hers and she's mine. I need it all. And I need it now.

Tell me you're in love with me, little sister.

"No," she grits out, and rage washes over me so hard, my fist drives into the marble next to her head.

Say you love me. Say you feel the fucking same way I do about you!

"I don't love you, Malachi. I could never love someone like you."

She might as well have shot me in the heart, or fucked someone in front of me, because it hurts more than any bike crash I've ever had.

I've never been enough. Not for my bio-parents, my adoptive parents, not even the sister I fell in love with.

Because I can't talk? Because I can't tell you how fucking breathtaking you are every second of every day? Because I can't breathe without being near you? Someone like me… I'm different—I can't be normal for you. I can't defend you without using my fists or my bat, and I can't touch you at the same time as telling you that you're everything to me. I can't whisper sweet nothings into your mouth, and I can't fucking marry you because not only am I your brother, but I'm defective.

My eyes burn as I sit up on top of her. Everything spills out. Everything.

Believe me or don't, but you're the only person in my life, and you always have been. And when you take your last breath, or I take mine, that won't fucking change. You. Are. Mine. My goddamn property, do you understand?

She's silent for far too long. Then she lets out a soft cry, as if the information is breaking her heart more than I'm dying deep down.

"You can't even feel love, so everything you're saying is another lie."

She covers her face and sobs into her hands.

As if she knows it's true, and I've yet to figure out that we'd never have a chance at a happy ending. I'm too fucked up. Too weird. Too much of a *freak*. I'll never make her happy. Not because I'm a Vize or because I can't talk. I'm just... not enough to be chosen.

I love you too much to walk away, Olivia, I sign then tap her arm because she's not looking.

All she's doing is crying, and I have no idea what to do.

My breaths shake as I do the only thing I know she'll like. The only thing to put her mind at ease. I shift on top of her, lower myself to between her legs, and drag my tongue over her pussy.

Without moving her hands, she moans while I slide my tongue over her entrance, circling her clit, pulling back to spit on it and suck on her lips. I part her with my thumbs, my eyes on her covered face as I drive my tongue into her entrance and devour her. I push her legs apart, and her whimpers grow louder.

"Oh God. You're going to make me come, Malachi. Fuck. Fuck, fuck, fuck," she cries, her words pushing me to keep tonguing her pussy, licking her clit, trapping it between my teeth as I slide my fingers back to her ass. I don't let her adjust. I don't even give her a warning—I push a finger inside the tightness of her hole as I thrust two fingers inside her pussy, and fuck her in both ways with her clit throbbing against my tongue.

"Angel?"

Ignoring my dad's voice—because I'm far too deep into this and need her to finish—I pull my fingers free and grip her thighs while she soaks my face.

She's grinding against my mouth despite whispering, "Daddy?"

I can hear footsteps, and then my father's voice is bellowing. "Malachi!"

He tries to pull me off, but I'd rather die than break this connection we have. I don't care that our father caught us, or that he's gripping my shoulders and tugging me, dragging both me and Olivia across the floor. My mouth sucks on her clit harder, and I hear Olivia moan.

Her taste is on my tongue as her orgasm starts to flush through her. But before I can finish her off, Dad manages to pull me away from her, a fist smashing into my face so hard, I see dark spots.

This asshole.

Warm liquid leaks from my nose as I grab Dad by the jaw and spit Olivia's juices in his face.

Your daughter tastes fucking delicious, I sign, regretting he can now taste her as well. *Too bad she's all mine.*

Dad wipes his face with a look of revulsion. "You disgusting piece of shit!"

He launches himself at me, and everything I've been holding in erupts from my mind—like a dark storm soaking me in nothing but evil. Like I know this is it. It's all over. I'm about to lose everything.

The second my fist drives into my dad's face, I feel it happen. The mental slip. The void drawing me in. I try to stop hitting him, but I can't. I want to tell him that he needs to get the fuck away from me, that I can't control the darkness taking over me, to shoot me if he can.

Despite the internal war with my demons, all I can do is hit him harder while my sister cries for me to stop.

But then…

Everything within me snaps completely.

The void in my mind grows.

Dragging me down until I'm trapped.

CHAPTER TWELVE
OLIVIA

My hands are covered in my father's blood as Malachi leans against the wall.

He's unbothered by the mess around us and obviously doesn't regret his actions—he just pulls out a cigarette, lights it, and watches me while the sirens grow louder.

I try to ignore the blood around me, my brother's cum leaking out of me and soaking my panties as the flashing lights glow through the windows.

In a few seconds, I'm going to lose Malachi and my father.

I'm losing them both.

For what? The sake of a forbidden fuck?

He's staring at me, not running or trying to flee his impending arrest. He's crossing his ankles and watching me cry over our father's body as life drains from him with a cigarette in his mouth. Uncaring, unflinching as the door's kicked open, or when the officers storm in and grab him.

Malachi lowers to his knees, his hands behind his head, and I can still feel his burning gaze searing into the back of my skull—he wants me to look at him, but I can't.

All I can do is slide back, smearing the blood on the marble ground, while my dad is surrounded by medics.

Malachi is read his rights while being handcuffed—there's no resistance or fight, but as soon as I hear the clicking of the cuffs, I know his only form of communication is gone, so I look at him.

Our gazes clash, and I feel everything within me shrivel to nothing—he's not even blinking as his eyes stay on me, even when he's dragged to his feet and pulled away from me.

It's Malachi, yet it's not. I have no idea who's looking back at me. Emotionless, with no humanity, he turns his head to look over his shoulder at me when the officers lead him out, and for some reason, I wish I could scream at them to let him go.

I want to cry for him—the brother who was always misunderstood and left behind, silenced, in need of so much help, yet I'm the one who breaks eye contact by closing my eyes and letting the tears fall.

The car door shuts in the distance, an engine roars, and I know my brother is gone forever.

Why, as I sit here with my father's blood all over me, with paramedics working hard to keep him alive, am I filled with so much regret, I wish I could vanish?

This morning, we were happy—we were going to take the next step in our lessons, and I was going to teach him how to say my name. I was even going to tell him that it was never about teaching him but because I loved him. It was perfect, the dynamic we had. It was fun, exciting, and I was happy.

Now I feel empty.

An officer takes my arm and pulls me to my feet—they're saying something to me, but I can't hear them. Another one appears, shining a light in my face, and then I'm taken out of the house just as my mother speeds into the driveaway and throws her door open.

"Olivia! What's happened? Are you okay?" She reaches me and pushes my hair from my face and looks down at my body. "Is that blood on you?"

But when my dad is wheeled out on a stretcher, the scream she lets out nearly blows my eardrums, and she runs to him. She's crying, demanding answers from the medics and officers as they load him into the ambulance.

More sirens blare, and my body starts to shut down, drowning out the sounds surrounding me. I don't think I even blink as I trap my mind away, trying to wake up.

I need to wake up.

This is a bad dream—Malachi will be lying beside me when I open my eyes. He'll hold me close, promise me that we'll be together forever, and this will all be a dream.

But I never wake up.

CHAPTER THIRTEEN
OLIVIA

Mom calls my name, but I don't respond. I keep my eyes on the mirror while I apply my lip gloss as slowly as possible, as if taking my time will make the day pass, and I won't need to walk out of the door and ruin my brother's life.

It's inevitable that my mom will come into my room in a matter of minutes and yell at me for what I'm going to say.

She's looking for me—I can hear her opening the main bathroom door, then the walk-in closet.

"Olivia!"

By the tone of her voice, she isn't happy. Ever since Dad woke days after his surgery, Mom's been on a mission to control everyone and everything. I've become the target of her anger, so I've been keeping my distance.

After all, Malachi did nearly kill our father, and she did overhear me begging my comatose dad to forgive him. I was crying, pleading for him to help me get his son the help he so desperately needs.

I wanted my dad to live but secretly hoped that the brain damage the doctor spoke of after his MRI meant he wouldn't remember the truth.

The thought of losing him was worse than him waking and remembering what happened that night a month ago, then cutting ties with me forever.

Luckily enough, Dad had some brain damage and only remembers being on the phone to me that night. And flashes of Malachi hitting him, but that's all. My statement probably solidified Malachi's confinement. I couldn't lie about who attacked Dad. Malachi was covered in blood, his knuckles cracked, scratches down his face from my nails, and didn't even try to deny anything.

He could have run out of the backyard and got away, had time to himself before this all struck, but he just stood there, silent, staring at me like he was committing me to memory.

Emotionless—gone from reality, even when the cops and paramedics barged into the house. My heart slowly breaks, remembering the betrayal I can never take back—I should have protected Malachi.

I still can.

Mom walks into my room and huffs when she sees me; how swollen my eyes are. "We need to leave. Are you ready?" She looks at my outfit—a simple black dress and tights. "Why are you crying?"

I take a deep breath and sit on the edge of my bed. "I can't do this."

A beat of painful silence, and she crosses her arms. "Can't do what?"

"I can't testify." I hold my breath, awaiting the storm brewing in her eyes to hit. "I won't."

Her gaze drops, and she lets out a disbelieving laugh. "He has you so badly wrapped around his finger, you don't even realize how much he's manipulating you."

I frown. Mom has never spoken to me like this before—of course she's yelled, but never in this tone, like she's sickened by me. Not when it comes to my brother. Sure, she's heavy when it comes to the dates and my lifestyle, but she's never looked at me with so much… disgust.

"He's not manipulating me," I say, standing and taking two steps towards her. "I'm not testifying against him. He needs help, not to be locked up with criminals."

"He *is* a criminal, Olivia."

Malachi isn't a bad person. Everyone has this image of him now because of how he reacted—but he lost himself, that's all. Everyone's afraid of my brother. Even his own friends bailed on him when the news broke online that he snapped and nearly killed his adoptive father.

Everyone but Mason.

If my brother knew that his best friend died the same night he was arrested, while speeding to the manor to make sure Malachi was okay, it would be the final straw. Abigail is devastated and hasn't left her house to see me. Not that I blame her. We've had news reporters and onlookers standing outside our house since the case went global. Thanks to my father's high-profile name, it's been all over social media.

I miss Malachi. And I feel selfish for missing him, considering what happened between us. A part of me wishes I hadn't overheard the girls in the locker room. I'd be none the wiser that Malachi was pretending to be inexperienced so he could mess around with me.

Another part of me also thinks that, maybe, it wasn't true. I didn't let him explain. I silenced him and watched him get arrested.

Dad was dying—his blood was all over us both. He was my main focus when I broke our eye contact for the last time. I can never look at him again.

I could be the person who sends him to jail. The reason he'd be charged with attempted murder and put behind bars for a really long time. I might never see him again. I have no doubts that he'd be done with me if I do this.

So…

I won't.

Mom stares at me—I'm too determined to back down. I'm not going to. Testifying against the one person I love, the one person who's always protected me, would be like stabbing myself in the heart and leaving the blade there to twist every time I think about him.

She can see the determination and love in my eyes as I think about potentially saving my brother, or at least refusing to testify. I'll take back my statement. I'll make him walk free with me. I need to.

"You don't remember much about your childhood, but I do. I have your reports. Do you know how badly your real mother and father treated you? They were more interested in their next hit than feeding you and your baby brother. They were investigated for years. The only reason child services had a fireman break into your house was because they didn't attend a drug test, then failed to answer calls, and then a neighbor contacted them to tell them that a baby had been crying for days on end before it fell silent. You were so thin and barely had any energy, yet you held your dead brother in your arms until you were found."

My eyes burn as she keeps going.

"I saved you from that life. If it weren't for me and your father, you would've stayed in the system. I gave you this life, so be a good daughter and defend your father against the monster who tried to *kill* him."

Tears slide down my cheeks, and my body shakes with anger. "How dare you use my past against me like that! I didn't ask to be adopted by you. I didn't ask for this life you're forcing me into."

She laughs. "Forcing you into? Open your eyes, Olivia. Has Malachi warped your mind so much that you don't see the bigger picture? You're refusing to stand up for the man who raised you against a disgusting beast who we never should've adopted."

I have to stop myself from slapping her. "That's enough, Mom."

"Is this how you thank us?" she grits. "You're just as bad as your brother."

Malachi isn't disgusting or a beast. But Mom is right about one thing. She did save me.

I bite my lip to stop it from wobbling, and my chest burns. Everything she's saying, every damn word, hurts me. I try to push away the memory of how cold my little brother was before he was taken from my frail arms, how sore my body was when a fireman lifted me from the soiled crib and carried me out into the sun that burned my eyes.

It's the only memory I have.

The only one that sticks with me.

Mom sees my inner breakdown, and her shoulders sag as she takes mine. "I'm sorry, sweetheart. Malachi will get the best help away from the public. He's a danger to you, himself, and society."

Tears soak my cheeks, every atom within me colliding.

"Promise me you'll make sure he's safe. Promise me he'll get help." I sniffle and drop my head to her shoulder. "I'll do it, but only if he gets help."

"I promise," she says, moving back and wiping my eyes. "Get cleaned up, fix your hair, and let's go."

On the drive to the courthouse, I don't speak a word, even when my mom asks me if I'm okay—she tells me to lift my chin when we stop the car as cameras flash outside, reporters waiting to get their five seconds of shoving themselves in our paths as we push through to the front entrance. Dad being a well-known attorney only makes this all worse. Entitled people think they can yell disgusting words at us, even though we're the innocent ones. It makes no sense—Malachi was the one who attacked our dad.

A part of me feels nervous, as if someone might be able to read my mind and see the full image of what happened that night. Someone will find out the truth, and I'll lose the family who saved me forever.

Malachi was charged with attempted murder and sentenced

to prison. He refused to plead insanity, no matter how much we tried to push his lawyer.

He's sent me letters. Some I can't read fully; some are so heartbreaking that I keep them under my pillow. He's losing himself in there. He can't understand why I'm not there, visiting, being there with him. Some letters are concerning, so I've given pictures of them to his in-house psychiatrist. In some, he begs me. Those are the ones that are covered in tears. Both of our tears. I can tell which ones are angry, which ones are sad, and which ones he struggled to write.

After his tenth letter, I've been sitting at my father's desk, staring at a blank piece of paper. If any of them knew what I was going to do, they'd call me a traitor to my family.

My fingers shake too much to start, so I drop the pen and flex them, closing my eyes and imagining his face; the room he'll be trapped in—four walls he's going to be staring at for years. He's already described his cell, the dinners he hates, and how he can hear my voice, see my face when he closes his eyes.

I can see him too. I force images. I force myself to feel his hand on me even though it's my own. My heart beats heavily at night, and sometimes when I hug my pillow, I pretend I can feel his beating against me.

He'll know what I'm trying to write. My handwriting is terrible, but he'll know. He knows me more than anyone, and he'll decipher this if he has to.

The pencil moves over the page, and the words spill out nearly as fast as the tears fall from my cheeks and onto the page.

Malachi,

What happened to us? We had everything. A family, friends, food in our stomachs and a roof over our heads. We had love. Real love. Did it ever exist? Was it all fake? Am I an idiot for wanting your love, in whatever form anyway? I was mad at you for lying to me about your date with Anna, but I never wanted this to happen. We were supposed to argue, yell, kiss, and make up. You would've explained your side if I only let you. I shouldn't have silenced you the way I did. That was terrible of me and I'm sorry. I'm so, so sorry, Malachi.

I know what happened with Dad was a mistake. It was the sign we all needed from you to show how much you're struggling, and I'm going to help you, I promise. Give me some time to talk to our parents. I'll tell them the truth about us. Once Dad is doing better and Mom isn't on the warpath with everyone, I'll tell them that I'm in love with you and everything you said was true. I'll spare them the details of that night though. Let's agree to never talk about that. We'll do everything as new. Everything.

Mom is hellbent on me marrying still, so I need to try to get her to stop. I'll refuse. I won't marry anyone who isn't you, Malachi, because you're the one I want to spend the rest of my life with, even if I have to wait a while. Please keep yourself out of trouble. I'll visit as soon as Mom lets me. I'm so sorry I did this to you. You don't have to forgive me. But I hope you do.

I love you more than everything: It shouldn't have taken me losing you to realize that.

I should've chosen you.

Olivia

I stare at the words. Some of them are distorted by my tears.

I turn the page over and pick up a picture of the two of us. I'm kissing his cheek while he carries me on his back. His expression is blank. No smile, no emotion whatsoever, but I know he was happy. One of many good moments together, proof we have a chance.

But what happens if I can't talk Mom out of marrying me off? I was so delusional when my big brother gave me butterflies, and I knew he felt them too. We were just too young to realize our feelings. Too confused by the ridiculousness of falling for someone we grew up with and called a sibling.

This letter… It represents false hope for us.

I don't have a shred of hope, but Malachi has every opportunity to move on from me. When he's released, he can find someone he can truly be with, and not someone already manacled to someone else.

The realization breaks my heart so painfully, I let out a sob.

Through my bated breaths, I grab the lighter, flick it, and hesitate as I read over the words one last time. I wish we lived in a world where I could give him this letter, that I could stand in front of him and watch him read word for word what it says before having the rest of our lives together.

I watch the flames engulf the corner of the letter, spreading to the edges and eating all the words I'll never speak of. Malachi will never know about my feelings. He'll never receive the apology he deserves, and he'll never feel any sort of hope for us. He can't. If I send this letter, I'll be leading him on while marrying whoever our mom forces me to be with.

It's emotional suicide for our hearts—they're fragile, important organs that need protected, and this is me protecting Malachi's by burning the letter into a pile of ash.

Thanks to Mom, I've never had a choice in my future. It's inevitable that I'll become who she raised me to be. Wife to a rich man. Silent. Compliant. The perfect daughter. The worst sister.

At least with me burning my final bridge to my brother, I can protect him from ever being poisoned by me again.

CHAPTER FOURTEEN
MALACHI
Present Day

My back presses to the tree as I drag in heavy breaths to my starved lungs.

Sweat clings to my body like a second skin, dirt splattered all over my legs and ruining my shoes from how fast I've been running in the rain. Clearing my head and drowning out the voices only works when I'm exercising or when I'm wrapped up with Olivia, but something wasn't right when I woke up. I had to detangle myself and slide out from under the covers.

That was hours ago. I think I've been running all morning.

My mind is in overdrive. I'm not sure why.

Anxiety has been eating away at me—the kind that wakes you through the night as if you've been strangled. The kind where you can't find your appetite. The kind that makes you think you're losing your mind.

To be honest, the third point is most likely true.

I roll my neck, savoring the cracking sensation, and pull out my earphone, listening to the woodland's noises, then hold in a smile when I hear the rushed footfalls of my girlfriend hunting for me.

I told her to wait twenty minutes before she came looking for me when she called and asked where I was. She managed a whole five minutes.

I didn't want to wake her when I snuck out, but I also wanted to drag her from our bed and demand she deal with the rock-solid cock I'd woken up with after she'd rubbed herself all over it for hours, keeping me awake.

I almost slid inside her while she was lightly snoring.

Almost.

It would've helped with how I'm feeling. Maybe it would've eased everything, even for an hour.

Fucking her again while she's not aware is apparently off the table—she's given me strict rules not to touch her while she's passed out unless she gives me prior consent.

As boring as I find the restriction she made since coming back to me last week, I'm listening—I even covered her naked body before I went to work out though the voice on my shoulder yelled at me to ravage her.

See? I can be nice.

Olivia doesn't know it yet, but I'm starting to—

Whack.

"Fuck!"

Something hard hits the side of my head, then there's a burst of pain and warmth trickling down my face as I pull away from the tree and turn to see Olivia hauling off my gas mask and dropping the baseball bat to the forest floor.

"I'm sorry!" she yells, her eyes wide. "I was supposed to hit the tree, not you!"

I wipe blood from my wound then stare at my red fingers before letting my eyes slowly lift to her. She gulps, taking a step back, but I shake my head and she stops.

"It was an accident."

Put the mask back on, I sign, because I'm still more comfortable using sign language than speaking. She picks it up and slides it on while I ignore the trail of blood reaching my shoulder and most likely staining my skin. *Now pick up the bat.*

She lowers to grab it, her movements slow, calculated, as if she's ready to run any moment.

"What now?"

She stiffens a little as I walk towards her. Branches snap under my shoes—MEJKO is still playing in one of my AirPods, the other safely in my shorts pocket.

Olivia lets out a whimper as I tug the front of her shirt, popping the buttons at her breasts. She's shaking, but I don't know if it's with fear or with the anticipation that I might touch her.

I won't. Not really.

She's not wearing a bra, and her nipples go hard from the cold air. I lightly trace my blood-covered fingers over the perfect skin there, the pad of my thumb circling one of her nipples.

Her tits look perfect any other day, but with my blood on them, painting them red? Wearing my mask and holding my bat? I think I might give up on my plan and fuck her right here.

I release her and step back. *Take your clothes off. Keep the mask on.*

Slowly, she traps the bat between her thighs, unfastens the last two buttons, and lets her shirt fall to the floor, then unbuttons her pants, the bat dropping as she slides them down her legs so she's only standing in her panties.

White lace.

Now I'm fucking harder.

You'd think having been inside my sister more times than I can count, seeing her like this, basically naked with my blood on her, I'd be used to it. Nope—I'm still very much obsessed with her, even when she's in her PJs, with knotted hair, and smelling like garlic or some other disgusting thing.

What twenty-eight-year-old gets butterflies like this?

Damn, I love this fucking girl.

"Are you going to just stand there and stare at me all day?" she asks, her voice muffled beneath my gas mask.

The same mask I wore on Halloween night. She likes it— apparently it reminds her of how she let go and allowed herself to fully have me and not worry about the repercussions.

I think I might stand and stare—she's a fucking masterpiece.

I gulp, knowing my shorts are tented as I drag my teeth over my bottom lip.

Olivia's terror shines out of her.

Beautiful. Scared. Fuckable.

I want to devour her fucking soul. If she asked me to, I'd do it. Whatever it means. I'd pin her down in the dirt and fuck her so hard, her head would end up buried in the forest floor. Even if she screams for me to stop, I won't until she's passed out from lack of oxygen. Leaking. Fucking filled with every drop of my cum, and if any escapes, I'll finger it all back in and drag another orgasm from her corpse.

"Malachi?"

But then if she's a corpse, she'll be dead. Then so would I.

We could haunt our house together.

My sister is very much stuck with me forever. If she tried to run again, I'd chain her back up in the basement and she'd never see the light of day again.

Mine, always mine. And I'll mean it. Not just a claim of property or a claim on life. Everything about her will be mine.

Already is.

"Malachi?"

If anyone gets in my way, I'll kill them. I'll finish off Dad, snap Mom's neck, and if that little sister of hers gets involved—

"Hey," Olivia says softly, and she's right in front of me now on the rug, the mask and bat gone. "Look at me."

Her clothes are on. Different clothes. Sleepwear.

I blink, disorientated all of a sudden, confusion ripping through me when I look around to see we're standing in our bedroom.

CHAPTER FIFTEEN

MALACHI

The smell of strawberries fills my senses as I rouse from my sleep.

There's tangled hair all over my face, limbs spread over me, a leg hooked around my own, and a gentle hand resting on my chest. For a split second, I think I'm still dreaming and in a memory from when Olivia used to sneak into my room when we were teenagers. I'm still in that place I used to go to when I was in my cell, alone, pretending Olivia was asleep beside me, talking to me about our future.

We were going to get married. Have kids, if she really wanted them. We were going to go on vacations and find careers we loved. As long as we had each other, no one else mattered. We were a unit. A strong fucking unit that would disintegrate when someone interrupted my thoughts.

I wasn't losing my mind like the guards had said. I was latching on to memories of her to keep myself sane. All the times we snuck into each other's rooms played like a broken record in my head. The prison guard overheard me talking to Olivia—the imaginary version of her who smiled and kissed me while we lay in bed together for hours. They heard me arguing with myself, begging no one while I dropped to my knees, crying, and asked Olivia to forgive me.

Tears that no one in the world would ever see but her.

They thought I was insane, and I was sent in for further evaluation on my ASPD diagnosis. All that came back was that I had depression, and I was given more call times and an extra visitation slot, but everyone who tried to call or visit, I didn't agree to see. My parents hated me, and I only wanted Olivia there. I didn't need to see any of the fake assholes.

My friends vanished. Even Mason didn't attempt to see me. My relationship with my sister died. And I lost my parents again. It was a miracle I didn't lose my mind, commit myself to a noose, and end it all.

When she kept refusing my calls and not writing back to my hundred-odd letters, and when I sat at that table, waiting to see if she'd visit, another piece of me would shatter. I'm not sure how I'm able to lie with her in my arms now and even think I can be normal again. If I ever was.

During therapy—the four meetings I've attended so far since being released—they try to talk about my childhood. They ask questions based on what they've read in my report.

Do you still think about your biological family? Do you remember what happened to you? Do you get nightmares? Can you remember the day you nearly killed your adoptive father?

Regardless of what went down with us, I still saw him as my dad. Biology or not. Jamieson Vize raised me, not the guy who gave up and left me with the woman who birthed me.

I sometimes remember her face. I know it's probably a made-up image, since she died when I was young. She had long blonde hair that was almost yellow, bright red lipstick, and smoked far too many cigarettes.

The therapist always pushes for me to talk about her.

It's like he can hear her telling me that I'm weak and useless and weird and fucked up. He can see the abuse I suffered. Hear me crying for my mom and dad when I was a kid.

Am I supposed to say I had an awesome childhood and that I miss my real mother? That my father should have taken me with him when he threw himself off a bridge?

If I still had them, I wouldn't have met Olivia. No one could save me but her. She's the only person in the world who understands me, even when my voice is locked away and I struggle in every aspect of communication—no matter how many times she's called me it, she doesn't think I'm a freak.

I'm not normal. I know that. My mind isn't the same as hers, or any of the people I grew up with. Even some of the inmates I bunked with before I was isolated thought I was either a lunatic or schizophrenic.

Everyone says it. I'm sick, depraved, wrong, yet she loves me anyway. These assholes who seem to assume to have me figured out are clueless. Always thinking they know me best, asking me things like I'm a helpless child. They wouldn't know the first thing about what goes on in my head. Every corner of my mind is filled with a girl named Olivia.

I blink a few times, the haziness vanishing when my fingers run through her dark strands, bringing them to my nose and inhaling.

That same delicious scent of strawberries fills my senses. It's been the same since we were kids. She has no idea how calming it is to me.

And she's real this time.

Olivia really is in my bed, clinging to me like I'm going to disappear. She's not running from me. No parents are knocking at the door and making us break away and hide. Society isn't keeping us apart and telling us it's wrong to be together. We're just two adults, cuddling, happy, and I'm fucking terrified something bad is going to happen, putting an end to the joy I feel swelling in my chest.

I want to be happy so fucking much, but I don't know how to be.

Her contractual obligation to marry that dickhead Xander still looms over us, but it'll pass. He doesn't even know Olivia and has no reason to expect her to run to him. His family is rich, way richer than the Vizes.

Money—it's all Mom cares about. To the point she'd sell her own daughter for power.

Maybe I should kill her, right after I strangle Xander and leave his body for his family to find, my name carved into his forehead.

With all the security around him, and the fortress of an old orphanage he lives in with his elitist family, I'm nervous for the first time. Because if he does come for her, and if he successfully gets her, I won't know how to get her back.

I might lose her.

"Your heart is beating so fast all of a sudden," Olivia whispers, placing a gentle kiss on my naked chest. "Go back to sleep. It's early."

I half-smile and continue brushing my fingers through her freshly dyed hair. She did it to get rid of the blonde she was forced to have. There are still golden waves throughout since she trusted me to get the back, and, shockingly, I don't know how to use fucking hair dye.

I want to call her bossy, but when I feel overwhelmed, I fall over my words. I'm still learning, and since we've been in bed for nearly a week, I haven't gone to any of my appointments, despite her arguing with me to do so.

We've barely gotten out of bed except to shower, dispose

of the million condoms my sister made me wear, or to eat. She even stood in front of me and made me take my meds then kissed me as if she hadn't done so for years. And there was that random hour she wanted to chase me in the woods yesterday, so I let her.

I even pretended to fight her off as she sucked my cock and bounced all over me.

She's been stuck to my side, and I don't hate the invasion. I love having her here, with me, in our bed, in our house.

Our life.

We're so fucking close to having it all—but there's something stopping us from getting there. There's a weight, so fucking heavy, on my chest, and it's not Olivia's head as she falls back to sleep.

She's worried about me. She woke up last night and found me talking and signing to myself in the middle of the bedroom. It took her ten minutes to get me back into bed by trying to prove she was real.

I don't really remember. It was like an out-of-body experience—I've had it a few times. When I was in prison, when I watched Olivia, and a few times this past week.

Watching her relaxed face, I tuck a lock of hair behind her ear, wondering how she's going to put up with me. I'm a handful, heavy baggage she would be better off without, but the selfish part of me wants her to take it all on with me.

I don't go back to sleep either. I can't. My mind is against me today. Sometimes I can block it out, and other times, I struggle and it's an effort to even drag air into my lungs without needing to make sure I know where Olivia is at all times.

When she wakes again, she blinks her pretty little eyes and watches me. Her fingers trace my jawline, and I press my cheek into her palm, as if I've not been attached to her almost constantly since she chose me.

"Can we talk about us yet?" she asks timidly. Her voice is a little shaky.

She's been asking nearly every day for us to have "the talk" and I'm completely against the pointlessness of it.

Against everything within me telling her to drop it and just go with the flow, I nod once.

"What are we doing?"

I wrap my arms around her, hugging her to my side. Isn't it obvious what we're doing? We're cuddling in bed. But apparently that doesn't mean shit to her given the way she's looking at me.

"You were released from prison after eight years and then you stalked and kidnapped me. You tortured me, and then you let me go. I only came back a week ago. I feel like we need to really talk about what our plan is."

My nostrils flare, my jaw tensing as her fingers trace my skin.

Fine, I sign. *But I don't see the point in discussing it. You're mine now, and there's nothing anyone can do to take you away from me. I'd need to be dead, and I'd still haunt your ass and fuck you.*

"I'm serious," she says with a sigh.

So am I.

"Can we take baby steps with everything?"

No.

Her chest rises and falls on another sigh. "Malachi."

The way she says my name has me gulping.

Her nose wrinkles as she sits up, straddling me. "I'm going to suggest something." Her fingers splay over my chest, over my instantly sore heart. "You aren't allowed to get mad."

Which means I'm going to lose my shit, but I grit my teeth and take a deep breath.

What?

"But it means you need to let me go back to work without arguing with me to stay in bed every morning."

You already said you were going back even though I said no, I sign. *You're lucky I'm not putting you back in the basement.*

"That's technically kidnapping."

Not my first time.

Her eyes narrow on my hands—she's been desperate to hear me talk every second, but sometimes I'm still not comfortable using my voice. "I'm not going anywhere. Whether I live here or not. Why do you keep thinking I'm not going to come home if I go to work or to see our parents?"

I raise a brow as an answer.

She tilts her head, her face softening. "What can I do to prove to you that I won't?"

"Y-You don't exactly have the gr-greatest track record with f-fucking me over." Then I sign, *And I don't trust you.*

I'm trying to be as honest as possible. Yeah, she chose me, but it took her over a decade to do so. It's only natural for me to be unsure and insecure and worry when she'll leave me again.

Even when Abigail or Anna call, I get nervous—they'll want to go out for dinner or to meet up before the latter gives birth.

As much as I want to stop being a paranoid asshole and enjoy having her here with me, the idea of her doing something as simple as going to work makes me itchy. I can't stop her. I won't. But I want to lock the door and throw away the key, to cuff her to the bed and never let her see her friends again.

If I tell her this, she'll say I'm toxic and claim it won't work. And she's not wrong, so I don't say the words flying around in my head—I can't have her running from me again. I have no idea what I'll do this time if she does.

Probably burn her work building down and kidnap her again. This time, I won't let her go. I'll make the world think she died and keep her hidden forever.

She kisses me, her hands on my face, pulling me closer as she sucks on my bottom lip. "Get out of your head," she whispers. "I love you."

Olivia has messed with my head since we were teenagers. I love her, but I don't trust her. So fucking sue me if I want to keep her shackled to my side.

Her lips flatten, and she runs her fingers through my hair. "I'm going to kiss you again, and then I'm going to shower and go to work. I'm not going anywhere else. I promise. You can drive me there and pick me back up if you're worried."

I don't want you to run away from me again.

Her lips thin, and her eyes drop. "I'm sorry."

Was this what you wanted to talk about? You going to work?

"Can you use your words?" she asks. "Please?"

I don't want to use my voice.

"Okay," she whispers. "I just…"

Her eyes travel to the tank in the corner of the room, and she shivers. I know she's thinking about having my pet on her body again and hating the thought.

I've yet to name my pet. Rex and Spikey were no-brainers, but this one… I'm not too sure.

Olivia has fear in her eyes—I'll squash that emotion from her eventually.

When she looks back down at me, worrying her lip, I know I'm going to hate what she wants to talk about. She's nervous, which makes me feel sick, even though she's completely naked and sitting on me.

"I do love you," she starts, and my heart is beating so much faster than what would be considered healthy. I think it might blow through my chest with anxiety—at least my blood will paint her beautiful face and give me one last wonderful view. "I don't remember a time I haven't loved you, but I want to go back to the start."

I stare at her. I'm not following. She wants to… what?

Go back to the start?

What?

Instead of asking what the fuck she means, I just keep my eyes on hers and wait for her to elaborate on her ridiculousness. She either hit her head during one of our rougher sessions, or she's caught my illness and she's more delusional than me.

Her shoulders fall. "You've never taken me on a date before."

My brows furrow further. "What?"

"We've never dated. We've never tested whether we're compatible. What if we're trauma bonding? Two adopted siblings with shitty backgrounds, forced to grow up together. What if you don't really love me and we've just been latching on to one another since we were kids?"

I sit up, keeping Olivia in my lap. "Don't," I force out, holding her hips and shaking my head. "Please don't."

"Can we at least try it?"

I haven't done anything wrong, I sign when words get stuck in my throat.

"I know you haven't. You've been amazing. The fact you're

even entertaining me in your bed means the world to me after what I did to you."

Our bed, I sign.

Her bottom lip wobbles. "Ask me on a date, take me for dinner, make me feel special, and drop me off at my apartment at the end of the night."

Drop her at her apartment? What the fuck is this?

I shake my head. "No."

"Please, Malachi."

Why are you doing this? We've been fine.

Olivia must be trying to ruin my life. Why would we strip everything back? We've been all over each other. She told me she loved me. She's kissed me every morning, and we have an entire life of memories.

Technically we did go for dinner once when we were younger, and we didn't last ten minutes before I told her to run. Doesn't that count?

She flattens her lips and looks away. "Every date I've been on has been arranged by Mom. I've never had any control. If I said no, she threw it in my face that I owed her for saving me. She even forced me to have a boyfriend while you were locked up."

A boyfriend I'd like to remove from existence—I even saved him a burial spot in the yard with the rest, but I continue listening, even as her eyes brim with tears.

"I'm not asking to end things. I just want to go back to the start. Not as Malachi and Olivia Vize, two people who ended up falling for each other. I want to be Malachi and Olivia, two people who have chemistry and compatibility and love and everything we missed growing up."

We have all those things. I don't understand. Is this her excuse to leave me? We've fucked around since she got here— maybe she's bored now?

Why do I feel like I'm going to vomit?

"I never got the chance to do it with you before," she adds, sniffing as her breaths become messy. "I'll even let you kiss me on our first date, and there's a rule against that."

My little sister has always been a product of her environment, and she's trying to take control of her life. I understand why, but what I don't get is why she needs to do this with me.

For one, I don't know how to take someone on a date.

And two, no.

My silence is her answer. We aren't going back to the start. Olivia isn't leaving my side. We live here together. We have a future. We love each other. I even offered her the chance of a family though I despise children.

I've lost count of how many times my cock has been inside her over the last week. I've woken up to blowjobs, and she's woken up to me between her legs. We've cuddled, kissed, and talked for hours.

Going on a date is pointless.

She tries to climb off me, and I tighten my arms around her waist to stop her. "Don't," I say again, but I can see the light leaving the eyes that have been staring at me all week. I'm snuffing out her happiness, and I hate myself for it. "You…" I stop, gulping. "You want to be normal." My arms tighten, and when my lips move and no words come out, I let go of her and sign, *I don't know how to be normal for you.*

"You are exactly how I want you to be," she says, grabbing my face and kissing me, still leaving me more than confused. "Forget I said anything. I was just being stupid."

She's lying. She isn't happy. I'm not making her happy.

What if we watched a movie tonight? Any movie. You choose.

Olivia tries to force a smile as she stands, the loss of contact making me grow cold. "Okay. We can do that. Come shower with me before I go back to work. I've been gone for too long."

I hesitate at her blank tone, but as she glances over her shoulder on the way into the bathroom, she smiles.

My gaze drops to her ass before I jump to my feet and follow her.

CHAPTER SIXTEEN

OLIVIA

Malachi's arms are tight around my waist while I stare into the mirror and apply mascara to my lashes. The side of his face is pressed to my back while I sit between his parted legs. I keep thinking he's fallen asleep, but then he tightens around me some more and groans with moodiness.

His fingers play with the waistband of the sleep shorts I threw on after the shower because apparently sitting in a towel makes him feral. I slap his hand away when he tries to slide it between my legs. He lifts his head to glare at me in the mirror from over my shoulder.

"Learn to be told no."

He sighs and buries his head into my back again. "You don't love me."

Laughing, I try to move forward, but his hold gets tighter. I huff. "Can you let me go so I can get my hairbrush?"

He shakes his head, pulling me into his body more. "Stay."

"You're so clingy," I reply with a laugh, checking the time on my phone. "Shit, I'm late. Mom's already going to flip about me being off all last week. Do you want her to hunt us down and arrest you for kidnapping?"

The silence is deafening. He's thinking about the possibility of her intruding on us, popping our little bubble of happiness. If she appeared, he would probably be arrested for murdering her. Even the thought makes me shiver because it's not like he isn't capable. Malachi may revolve his entire life around me, but he's violent and unpredictable.

I think he'd kill someone for me. I mean, he nearly murdered our father because he caught us at the top of the stairs. What would he do to Mom?

Maybe I should set up a meeting for us to all sit down and talk. Get it over with—rip the Band-Aid off and accept the backlash that will definitely come our way. They already know we're together, so what's the worst that could happen? They don't accept us? We're adults now.

Besides, I could use their help right now.

They know him—they'll have an idea of how to help with the way he is. They adopted him knowing about his troubles and his issues, even helped him get his diagnosis—they'll be able to give me directions on how to help him not spiral and lose himself.

I always knew he struggled, but this last week since coming

back to him… Sometimes he's here but he's not. It's getting worse, and I don't know what to do. I try to make sure he takes his meds, and he's refused to go to his therapy appointments this week because being separated from me is the worst thing to possibly happen to him, so he dismisses everything else to be close to me.

It's the main reason I want to go back to work—I need Malachi to focus on himself.

He's going to fall off the cliff, and I'm not strong enough to catch him.

He's going to hurt someone—I can feel it. Unless he already has. He has an alarming number of weapons in one of the spare rooms.

I think he's hurt people since he was released. It explains why the people Mom has thrown me towards have gone silent.

Images of Malachi throwing our bloody father down the stairs after beating him to a pulp make me inwardly wince. That was a long time ago—he's not like that anymore surely?

Well, if we forget the fact he abducted me, chained me up, then continued to pleasure me against my will while hiding his identity. I had a feeling it was him. I pretended in my mind that it was him. Maybe that makes me ridiculous, but I loved every moment.

He has every reason not to trust me based on the fact I let a stranger ruin my body without knowing completely that it was him the entire time. But my delusional self knew, deep down, that it was Malachi.

It excited me.

It also scared me because I was fully willing to let Malachi take his revenge on my body. I still have his initials burned into my skin. He kisses them when his mouth travels down over my breasts, on his way between my legs to fuck me with his tongue.

He won't apologize for the burns. It's his way of claiming me. A brand that tells everyone who I belong to.

And I belong to Malachi Vize.

I'm not sure how this will work. We have so many hurdles to get over. I want it to work though. I love my brother, and he loves me—that won't ever change.

I blink, staring at myself in the mirror. I should stop calling him that too. We aren't siblings anymore. We're boyfriend and girlfriend. I know he likes it though, and a depraved part of me does too. Does that make us sick to crave such a taboo and forbidden connection?

When he's inside me, and I call his name, he groans and fucks me faster, but when I call him my big brother? He grows within me, thicker, longer, pulsing against my sweet spot while we both find our release.

I'll need to try and explain everything to Abigail and Anna. I've gone into an antisocial bubble ever since I ran from my wedding. Anna told me to keep her updated on everything. I sent Abbi a text saying I was fine, and she told me she was going to punch Xander's big brother.

Apparently, after I ran from the church, his brother and Abbi argued—he told her he was going to kill her, and she slapped him and told him to go fuck himself.

I'm not sure what happened after. Her details are a little vague, and her story has changed three times. She's also now chanting the tune of celibacy. She went on about it for nearly an hour—something about swearing off men forever and becoming increasingly violent with her words before Malachi grabbed the phone and hung up on her.

I try to turn and look at Malachi, but he's too tangled around me. He's always attached to me in some way. If I'm cooking us some food, he's behind me. If I'm in the shower, he's either in with me or sitting on the sink counter. If I'm trying to tidy up, he's helping or forcing me to sit down so he can do it properly.

Ever since I told him I had to go back to work, he's been clingier than ever, as if I'm not going to come back here. I am. I will. I just feel like we need to pump the brakes and slow down, but he's in total refusal.

It hurts me, but I'm also happy. We could hide in this little home for years and I'd be happy, but there would always be the outside. The place that won't accept us. Society. Parents. The fiancé who'll hopefully give up and move on to the next person on his list.

"If our mom and dad came to see us, would you get all angry and aggressive?" Another beat of silence, and I sigh. "You need to accept them if you want them to accept us."

"They hate me," he says quietly, slowly, so carefully I know the words hurt him to admit. His pronunciation is still off, but I can understand most of what he's saying. "Nothing I say will ch-change that."

The corner of my mouth tugs because he has no idea Dad has been tracking him since he was released from prison, making sure he's okay, ensuring Mom gave him enough money to survive until he figured out what to do with his life.

They've loved him from afar. Despite everything, they still raised Malachi since he was eight years old. They still took him under their roof, loved him, made everyone around them learn sign language, and ensured they had him placed in a school that could accommodate his needs.

Everything he ever needed, they gave him. They care about him.

Well, I'd like to think they still care. No one can go that long seeing someone as their child, only to throw them away so easily. Dad tried to visit, but Malachi refused. If I'm correct, Dad paid a prison guard to give him weekly updates on his son and made sure the therapist that visited him was one of the best around town. As a criminal defense attorney, or an ex one, he has a lot of influence given the clients he's had in his career.

I guess it helps to know people in power. Mom being a judge definitely helps.

"Will you drive me to work before you go to your appointment?"

He nods against me. I glance over my shoulder, pressing a soft kiss to his lips when I see the look in his eyes.

Like he's about to lose me.

I chance my luck once more by sucking in a deep breath and turning in his arms, hugging his hips with my thighs. I smile, tilting my head to the side as he narrows his gaze.

"Don't," he warns.

"Ask me on a date," I say, ignoring him, pleading with my eyes. "Wine and dine me and treat me like a princess before dropping me off at my apartment. You can kiss me against the door until we're breathless."

His nostrils flare, his eyes darkening, and I shriek as he flips us over, placing me on my back. "No," he says, smashing his lips down on mine, capturing my bottom lip between his teeth and nipping.

I gasp as he shoves his hand into the front of my shorts and cups my pussy with firm fingers, digging against my entrance with the barrier of my panties while my bottom lip is trapped between his teeth.

He releases it with a snap. "Stop asking."

CHAPTER SEVENTEEN

OLIVIA

My phone dings while I reply to an email about a court hearing for a new adoption. I'm so badly behind, Mom had to ask her other assistant to take some of my workload before she went into her meeting. I'm waiting patiently for her to come for me.

She'll yell. I don't doubt that at all.

I pause my fingers and glance over at the screen to see the text. Since Malachi reconnected his phone, he sends me messages all the time, even when I'm right beside him. Right now, he's obviously just bored.

Malachi

I hate kids.

I roll my eyes and type back a response.

Me

They can be cute sometimes.

Malachi

> They're screaming in the waiting room. Why the fuck do they need to be so loud? What do they have to cry about?

> Please never make me a father.

My smile drops. Even though we already agreed not to have kids when he offered to get me pregnant, it still stings for some reason when he says stuff like that. You'd think someone who never wants to become a parent would use a condom all the time, but he loves the thought of his cum inside me. He does, however, obsess over my birth control pill.

Me

> I won't.

Malachi

> I debated getting you pregnant as a way to keep you with me. Thought you should know. Never for long though. Promise.

Oh…

Wow.

I wonder how I should respond to that. There's a small, lonely part of me that secretly loves the idea of a tiny human by my side, but I'd never force that upon him.

Me

Remember to pick up the rest of your meds after your appointment.

His final reply makes me smile.

Malachi

Such a bossy little sister.

Holding my breath, I switch chat boxes to the one that's been burning a hole in my phone since I received the first message four days ago.

Asshole

I've given you a few days, brat. You signed a contract, remember?

So it's the silent treatment then. Good. It seems you want to make this harder for us both. You embarrassed me in front of everyone. It won't happen a second time.

I know who you're with. Does your family know you're fucking you own brother?

And the most recent one this morning. Malachi nearly saw it while I was doing my makeup in the mirror.

Asshole

I'll be back in a few days. Unless you want my cock to rip apart your insides, don't make me chase you, and don't fucking ignore me again.

The main reason I'm keeping these messages from Malachi is not only because I'm worried about his current state of mind, but also because we've been good. We've been having fun. We've been in our bubble—Xander throwing threats at us will cause him to react, and I don't want that at all.

It's wrong of me to hide this, but Malachi can't control his anger, and he'll either whisk me away where no one can find me, or he'll do something unhinged.

I'm terrified he'll get himself into trouble again. He'll definitely do something to Xander if he finds out, and a huge part of me wants him to.

That part needs to shut up.

In my peripheral vision, I can see someone marching towards my office through the glass of my door. I take a deep breath, tucking my phone into my bag and awaiting the storm that's crashing in three… two… one…

"What do you think you're playing at, young lady?"

My eyes close, and I take another deep breath in through my nose and release it from my mouth. "Morning, Mom."

"I've had the Reznikovs on the phone to me every hour for the last week!" The door slams, and she stands in front of my desk, crossing her arms and tapping her foot. "Where were you?"

"You know where I was," I reply calmly, dragging my eyes to my computer screen and pretending to click on things to calm my nerves. "I have quite a lot of work to do. Can we discuss this later?"

"No," she grits out. "Do you know how much you embarrassed Xander? You left him at the altar in front of his friends and family."

"He's made his embarrassment very clear in all of his threatening messages."

"What do you expect? You left him at the altar!"

She's so deluded that she's completely ignored the fact he's threatening me. I honestly didn't think she'd help me anyway.

"I don't care," I reply, typing nothing. "Did you forward any important emails on to me?"

Her glare makes me want to shrink in my chair, but I roll my shoulders and try to remain calm.

Anxiety bubbles all over my body, and the bad butterflies are going wild—Mom rarely yells at me, so when she does, I always shy away and automatically apologize.

However, I won't give in this time. I won't marry Xander, no matter how much she shouts at me for turning my back on her. It's the first time I've made my own decision, and I'm dreading the backlash. If his family can get over it and move on, maybe my mom will too.

Xander's anger tells me he'll struggle to get over it. But maybe if I keep ignoring him, he'll vanish and go to someone else.

Mom is scowling at me.

She was the perfect mother growing up. The mom I always wanted. Needed. But when she first mentioned to me that it was perfectly normal for rich families to marry other rich families to combine their wealth, she told me I'd be marrying a prince, and I'd be treated like a princess.

Obviously, I was initially excited. I was sixteen and being told I'd be spoiled and loved forever, without needing to go through the process of falling for someone, was so attractive.

Until Mom told me I had to have sex with them—she even talked me through it all and how it would be sore my first time, that I'd bleed, but I couldn't tell a soul, not even Malachi or my dad. She told me that they'd be mad and think I was dirty, a disgrace to the Vize name. I'd be looked at differently, and my brother wouldn't be my friend anymore.

The night I lost my virginity, I lay in bed with Malachi while he held heat packs to my body. I wanted to tell him. I was dying inside having to keep the grooming to myself, but I had no choice.

Parker wasn't gentle. He didn't even look at me while he did it.

But Mom was proud of me when I walked out of the room. She smiled and hugged me, then said she was certain he was the one.

I was already falling for Malachi—though being told I had to marry someone else safeguarded those emotions, because it's not as if I would've ever had the chance to marry him and be happy. Mom and Dad fully adopted us both. They were legally our parents.

At the time, I had no idea how that worked with adopted siblings, but I knew it was wrong on so many levels.

We had no chance from the moment I got my first good butterfly from him. Even when I realized he had an interest in me beyond possessiveness, I did everything I could to hold him as far away from my heart as I could, but it was impossible.

He crashed his way into my love for him, and he's still there.

From the moment he asked me to teach him how to kiss, I was doomed. I knew I wouldn't ever get over him, and the fact I was forced to date just made knowing it worse. Call me selfish, but I jumped at the opportunity to have any closeness with my brother—it was only going to be for a short time anyway.

Those eight years he was locked up, I hated myself. I should've taken Dad to hospital and run with Malachi. Or even better, I should have sat down with him when I overheard the girls in the locker room and got the truth from him.

I shouldn't have silenced him. He's been silenced his entire life. Maybe I deserve Xander's threats. Karma really is a bitch.

Mom's still standing in front of my desk, tapping her foot like I'm some insolent, misbehaved child in trouble for pulling someone's hair. I want to ask her for help—Malachi isn't doing well, and I need her or my dad to tell me what to do, but I can't ask her.

It'll have to be Dad.

I'm scrolling through my emails—one came in five minutes ago from him, asking to arrange dinner since I haven't replied to any of his messages. That could be my opener to get some information about Malachi and how they handled him when he was spiraling.

Plus, I haven't seen my dad since the wedding. He was going to try to get me out of it—maybe he's found a way?

Usually, I help Dad out with Molly. When Mom is too busy, I like to care for him—he needs a lot of help with some things, and he has physiotherapy three times a week. My little sister is learning, so she's been helping while I've been gone.

I glance up at Mom. "Did you take Dad for his appointments last week?"

"He's capable of going himself."

Flattening my lips, I look back to my screen. "How's Molly? Did she do her math test on Tuesday?"

"Don't change the subject. I'll arrange a meeting with Xander and his parents as soon as they get back from their business trip. You will apologize for being immature about the situation, and no legal action will be taken. You will marry Xander by the end of this month. And then you'll move to Canada with him like you're supposed to!"

Sighing, I press my forefingers to my temples, rubbing them

clockwise. "No."

"No?"

"No. I'm not marrying Xander. And I'm not moving to Canada."

Her hands rest on my desk as she leans down and sneers her next words. "You signed an agreement, Olivia. You agreed to marry him. You said yes and put your signature on the dotted line to become Olivia Reznikov by a set date. Don't embarrass me a third time."

My head tilts with confusion. "A third time?"

"The first was when Malachi announced to the world during his trial that you were sleeping together." She looks disgusted. "The second was when you ran away from your own wedding in front of everyone! There won't be a third. You will cut ties with Malachi, and you will fulfill your role in this family."

"You literally nodded at me at the wedding to leave."

Her teeth grit again, the line between her brows getting deeper. "I had a lapse of judgment and forgot the implications of you breaking the agreement."

"No, you remembered for one little second that I'm supposed to be your daughter and you knew forcing me into that family would be suicide. You were human, but then you fell right back into your controlling ways and reminded yourself that you adopted me for money."

She has the audacity to look shocked. "Excuse me?"

"I won't marry him. Have my dad terminate the agreement. Xander has no reason to pursue me. The man made it very clear he had no attraction to me when he told me to go on a diet and dye my hair." I tug at my brown hair, at the flashes of blonde still showing through the box dye. "He can marry someone else who comes from money."

"No."

"He's threatening me." I grab my phone, open his message about ripping me apart, and shove it in her face, but she doesn't look at the screen; instead, anger radiates from every inch of her.

"You're acting like a child."

"You're trying to force me into an abusive marriage," I say, dropping my phone onto my desk when she turns away from me. "I won't do it."

Shaking her head, Mom paces the office. "Why are you fighting me on this? I have trained you since you were young for this exact moment! After everything I've done for you, this is how you repay me? I gave you a life, Olivia!"

Shoving myself to my feet, I glare at her. "You took me from one abusive home and put me into another!"

Her eyes go wide, choking on her next word. "Abusive? The only abuse you went through was from your brother."

"I was sixteen," I say, trying to stay as calm as possible. My body is shaking. I don't want to hurt her feelings. She's done so much for me. Gave me a better life, but this I cannot do. "I was sixteen when you started forcing me to sleep with people who were older than me. You would do my hair and put makeup on me, tell me to shave. When I got my period, you were excited, not because I was becoming a woman, but because you saw dollar signs. You could finally marry me off."

Her face falls, but she stays silent.

"When I was forced to sleep with Parker, I cried to you that I was sore and that I couldn't do it again. You told me I'd get used to it. You forced me to watch videos of blowjobs so I'd know what to do because Parker demanded one. Do you remember telling me to eat less and exercise more to maintain my figure, so I'd stay appealing to men? Will I keep going? There are millions of moments you've destroyed for me. You ruined relationships for me, Mom. I didn't even get to have a normal childhood. Why couldn't you just let me be normal? Malachi was allowed to do whatever he wanted, but I was on a damn leash."

"You know the tradition of being a Vize."

My mouth falls open. She's so damn cold and careless. Not a single tear falls from her eyes, but mine are soaked, and I can't stop.

"It's also tradition for me to be pure, but you cut corners by selling me to Parker because he pretended not to be interested in me, so he could be paid for an easy fuck to mark off his list and go blow it all on drugs. All you had to do was say no, that you had rules to follow."

"Paying him was a mistake," she replies. "My biggest mistake."

"You made me sleep with Adam too." I drop back into my chair and shake my head. "We both begged you not to make us. Was that a mistake too?"

"Stop being difficult about this," she snaps. "It's not like you can be with your brother. Do your duty to this family."

"Why is it a tradition at all, Mom?"

Her shoulders rise. "It's always been one. For generations."

"Were you forced to marry my dad?"

"That was different. I was already dating your father in school before the Vize family came to mine and brought up the marriage agreement. My parents were secretly struggling for money—that contract saved us."

"Would you have married my dad if you hated him? If you didn't know him? If he told you to lose weight and change your hair and style of clothes? If he threatened you? Did your mother force you to sleep with older people the same way you did to me?"

Her silence is my answer. I can't stop the words from spilling out. "And did Dad have a clause that you weren't allowed birth control? Or did you find another loophole when he brought mine and Malachi's cases to you?"

Her head lowers on a sigh, her shoulders dropping. "We had the clause too. But we tried and tried for years, and I couldn't fall pregnant. I'm infertile. We didn't know before we got married. I wanted to adopt because I've always wanted a family. He thought bringing me you and your brother's cases would make me happy even though he hated the idea of having children not biologically his."

My breathing grows heavy, my chest suddenly aching. "Dad didn't want to adopt?"

"Not initially, no," she replies, breaking my heart some more. "But he loved you and your brother regardless. He still does."

A tear slides down my cheek. "You wanted to adopt so you could manipulate me into making you more money? Is that all you see me as? Another income after you marry me off to your highest-earning suitor? Dad didn't even want me, and you just saw me as being able to fulfill another generational tradition."

Adam was an agreement because Malachi attacked him, and Parker was her choice when I was younger, but neither of them have the same wealth as the Reznikovs. Xander's family are borderline billionaires. It makes no sense for them to even want to collaborate with the Vizes. It's like Xander's being told no and he refuses to accept it.

Xander doesn't even think I'm pretty; his reaction when he first saw me was evidence of that. He was unimpressed and said I needed a nose job and that he'd arrange for me to get breast enlargement surgery, then took a picture of me and sent it to his friends. His social-media posts show him and his brother partying with girls who look nothing like me.

As soon as my mother tells him the wedding will no longer be going ahead, he'll send me more threats, but ultimately, he'll move on to the next girl on his list. Mom just needs to accept this isn't happening, but going by the way she's looking at me, she's not going down without a fight.

"What if I ask for some changes to the agreement?"

Huffing, I lean back in my computer chair and cross my ankles. "Why can't you give up on this? I've been forced into this my entire life—why can't I make my own choices now? I'm about to turn twenty-seven."

"Because your choice is to be with your brother! It's sick!"

"The term that I'm not allowed to use birth control will mess everything up for you. I'll fall pregnant, and I won't know who the father is because I won't leave Malachi, and I'm assuming Xander will force himself on me."

I'd rather die than go anywhere near him.

"This is ridiculous. Why can't you see how ridiculous this is? Malachi is your brother. You are siblings. He is my son, and you are my daughter! We raised you both. You were brought up together in the same house, and you acted like brother and sister. You played together. Ran around the house with toys and laughed like all brothers and sisters do! If it wasn't for Malachi manipulating you, you wouldn't even care about him."

I let out a laugh. "Every time you took away one of my choices, I needed him, and he was always there for me. You pushed me closer to him. You're the reason we're together."

As soon as the traitorous words leave my mouth, every drop of blood drains from my body, my veins running ice cold. My heart snaps in two, because although I was just trying to throw it in her face…

It might be true.

I stand, piling my files together and grabbing my bag. "I need to go."

"Don't you dare walk away from me, Olivia." She follows me to the door, and even as I swing it open so everyone in the office can hear, she yells after me, "I'll be arranging a meeting with the Reznikovs regardless!"

Malachi is supposed to pick me up. My shift doesn't finish for another few hours, but I don't stop running until I reach the apartment I've left empty for the last week.

My shoulder hits a few people on the way, but I keep going.

I slam the door shut behind me, throw my things on the ground, and run to my bedroom before I allow the screaming cries to release into my pillow.

CHAPTER EIGHTEEN
MALACHI

I don't want to be here.

I don't want to be here. I don't want to be here. I don't want to be here. I don't want to be here. I don't want to be here. I don't want to be here. I don't want to be here. I don't want to fucking be here.

I should be at home with Olivia. She shouldn't be at work, and I shouldn't be here. What the fuck am I doing? Why am I here?

I don't want to be here.

They're the only words running through my head while Dr. Preston talks me through our last few speech therapy sessions. He's been showing me my progress pyramid, and that I'm halfway from the top. Considering I was near the bottom when I first came to him a few weeks ago, I'm making progress, even if it doesn't always feel like it.

"Okay, so when you first came in, we went through what

you struggled most with and set some small targets, and since we haven't quite reached them, let's take another approach. We've covered shorter sentences and more straightforward pronunciations. Instead of longer sentences, I think we should add in words with more syllables, some trickier words that don't necessarily roll off the tongue, and work on your confidence. I can hear your nerves. Try not to focus on the fact I'm sitting in front of you."

The voice in my head wants to tell him to stop telling me what to do—it's an immature knee-jerk response I won't let out. He's helping me and, in turn, helping my relationship with not only Olivia but the outside world.

Dr. Preston is around my dad's age. His voice is soft, and for some reason, I don't feel the need to strangle him when I fuck up my words. He doesn't laugh, doesn't even seem fazed by my fuck-ups. He takes notes and gets excited when he talks about different approaches we'll be taking.

Yet he sees me as an experiment.

A bit like Olivia. She encourages me every step of the way, but I know she's trying different things. Different routines for my meds, and she even wants us to eat at certain times. I still don't know why she's become so focused on my mental state.

I'm fine.

I stare at the words on the table in front of me. We've been working on five-worded sentences and words with two syllables.

He tries to encourage me to read, to try to sound out the words I know will be difficult, but sometimes I overthink and fall over the way they sound. I can hear them in my fucking head so clearly, but I can never actually speak them clearly.

Frustrated doesn't even describe the way I feel right now.

He types on his laptop then looks at me. Too bad for my short-fused temper and hating the way he stares at me—I kind of need him to fix me. "Can you read the first line?"

My gaze drops to the paper again, and I lick my lips, but I can't. Something is stopping me. Like my voice box has vanished and my mouth forms no sound. I look up at the guy, feeling heat crawl up my cheeks. I shouldn't be embarrassed, but when he hums and types again, I grow anxious.

He's probably writing about how much of an idiot I am—what twenty-eight-year-old struggles to fucking talk? I know how to. I can read, write, and I can fucking speak, but for some reason, sometimes I can't.

"You're more nervous than your last appointment. Has anything changed?"

Yes. Everything. My entire life.

I stare at him—I want to tell him that I fucking won, that I got the girl and she finally chose me, but not only can I not form the damn words, I also don't fully believe them.

Olivia's smile is in my head. Then sadness takes over her eyes and snuffs away the happiness—she's not fully mine. Not yet. I can feel it.

She's biding her time before she can leave again.

My heart is thrashing, and my fingers cramp up, so I drop the paper on the speech therapist's desk and lean back in the chair. The need to call Olivia has me very aware of my phone in my pocket, but I need to try to do this myself.

I did well when I first came in this morning, but it lasted all of ten minutes before things got tricky, and everything within me has crawled under the fucking bed and is staying hidden.

"Do you have someone you could read to?" He puts on his glasses and checks his paperwork. "Any children you could read a bedtime story to?"

Frowning, I stare at him unblinking—he knows I don't have any kids. I shake my head anyway. The poor kid wouldn't last a week if I was their father.

"A partner?"

Pausing my breaths, I stare at him for a long second more before I slowly nod.

"Great. That must be what has you more perked up. What I'd like you to do at home is sit down with your partner and read. Or you can record yourself reading and listen back. You'll know which words are harder, and you can work on those too. Look at it as minor homework."

I nod again and lean my elbow on the arm of the chair, my fist to my temple. He talks me through a few other exercises while printing off sheets of paper, and I sign in response.

"Does your partner sign?" he asks, typing on his laptop again.

For a few beats, I blink, but then I take a deep breath. "Yes," I say quietly.

"She's patient with you?"

My eyes narrow. What kind of question is that? Olivia is one of the only people who has ever been patient with me. Even when we were kids and I was insanely obsessed with everything about her. She learned sign language for me. She struggled so fucking much—half the time, she signed wrong, but since she would say the words, I could correct her hand movements.

Mason's family hired someone to teach him so he could talk to me.

Dad learned easily, but I think he just did that so he could see what I was saying to my little sister. He never liked me near her. Then my mom made sure the entire house was trained so I felt included.

What the fuck went wrong? I had a family who actually cared for me—did they notice the way I was with Olivia and decide I wasn't good enough for them? Did I scare them? Did they only tolerate me because of Olivia? When I was a teenager, I was spoken to on multiple occasions about the way I looked at her, that I was stepping out of line as a big brother.

They wanted me to rein it in. They didn't toss me away like the other families—they kept me regardless of my issues.

If I hadn't nearly killed my dad, would I still be considered their son?

Did I choose my obsession with my sister over a loving family? I made them the way they are. Dad hates me because of me. Mom hates me because of me. We're broken because of me. Olivia is going to leave me because of me.

I shake my head and pinch the bridge of my nose. Stupid thoughts that'll never get an answer. Even if I go to my parents, they'll tell me to fuck off. Olivia wants me to try with them, but I think she forgets how much they despise me and deludes herself into thinking we can all go back to normal.

Mom and Dad will never accept the fact their son is fucking their daughter.

No, not fucking. We're together. Olivia Vize is my girlfriend.

A smile tugs at my lips, and I wipe my hand down my mouth to hide it when I notice Dr. Preston is watching me with curiosity. "How are you finding the medication?"

I raise my shoulder. Everything is new. I feel the exact same.

Lie. I feel an unexplainable heaviness on my chest and a bomb inside me, ready to blow. Our parents won't accept us and Olivia will leave. I'll lose my speech again and she'll leave. I'll fuck something up and she'll leave.

I don't know how to make her stay. Maybe I should put her back in the basement?

"You're on quite a high dosage. Do you have any side effects?"

Olivia might realize she can do way better than me—I'm an ex-convict, jobless, can barely speak, not to mention the backlash from our parents. Has she told her friends about us? Is she embarrassed by me?

Fuck, my head hurts thinking about this constantly.

"Your therapist's notes indicate that he's referred you for further diagnosis, specifically for non-catatonic schizophrenic syndrome. How does this make you feel?"

My eye twitches. He's my speech therapist. That's all. Why the fuck is he trying to talk to me about this shit?

Maybe I can put him in the basement without all the sexual shit—I'll make him shut up by shoving his own dick in his mouth and force *him* to try to talk.

My hands fist. "I can't do that."

Did I just answer myself aloud? Fuck. Maybe I really am losing it.

He hums. "Can you tell me what it's like when you feel yourself slipping away?"

Like I could kill someone without even blinking—I have, and I'll do it again without hesitation.

The world fucked me over. My parents fucked me over. If my mom didn't turn to drugs and my dad didn't kill himself, I might not be the way I am now. I'd be good enough for myself, and for Olivia.

The therapist spoke to me about my childhood. He asked

me when I had my first appointment, "What did they take from you?"

Everything.

They took everything.

My heart is fucking racing, and sweat starts to coat my forehead.

Typing again, he clicks his tongue and takes my silence as an answer. "There's another note here about referring you to group therapy sessions. I'll write down some places. It might be good to be around others with similar struggles. Maybe find a friend."

What? A friend? Is this asshole for real right now?

I don't need a fucking friend. I have Olivia. I used to have friends, and they vanished when I was arrested—they didn't even attempt to stick around, so what the fuck is the point in finding a friend? I'm not some kid with baggage and a need for socialization.

I had someone I considered a best friend. I still haven't found the courage to see where he is or what he's doing out of pure shame for blocking him out of my memory.

"Okay," he says, knowing I'm no longer going to reply to anything. "I think it would be very helpful to do the reading I suggested. Even just for ten minutes a day. I'll see you back here in three days. Go to one of those meetings."

My phone buzzes in my pocket, and I'm itching for this to

be over already so I can message Olivia and take her home. Lying in bed with her is my safe place, and I really fucking need it right now.

Before I dropped her off at work this morning, she asked me again to take her on a date—I said no obviously. There's no need for us to pretend we're teenagers again and act like our worlds don't revolve around one another.

Once our next session is booked, I grab the homework and fold it into my pocket, then pick up my helmet. I unlock my phone and see the message isn't from Olivia; it's an alert that some of my meds are ready. It takes me five minutes to ride to the pharmacy. It's just down the road from the courthouse where Olivia works with Mom.

I'm surprised I've not had any messages from her, complaining about Mom or whatever bullshit she throws her way for not only ditching the wedding she planned but also for being off work for the last week.

Mom won't like that we're together, but fuck her.

If Xander has anything to say, I'll fuck him up too.

I park the bike up outside the pharmacy, open my seat, and hunt for the list of meds I've to pick up. Olivia told me to mark off the ones I have to make sure I don't forget any.

Once inside and waiting, my fingers fidget, alternating between tapping the arms of the chair then twisting together in my lap while I wait for my name to be called by the pharmacist.

It's just after three, and Olivia finishes work in an hour.

An old lady keeps looking at me. Her gaze trails down my arms, grimacing at my ink, then moves to my neck and the red mark from Olivia claiming me last night. She whispers something to her little friend, and both of them stare like I'm some disgusting piece of shit they've never come across before.

Why do they keep looking at me? It's not as if I'm any different from half the population. I don't have ink on my forehead saying "fuck you". I'm not scowling or giving anyone attitude. I'm silent, like I always am, and they're still watching me like I'm going to stab them or steal their purses.

They shake their heads, and I fist my hands.

Would Olivia care if I killed two grandmas? Maybe I can make it look like an accident, or they just disappear altogether without a trace of evidence leading investigators back to me.

"Vize," a voice calls, grabbing my attention. She asks me to confirm my date of birth and address. I struggle to get the words out, and the grandmas behind me huff at how slow I'm being. I want to drive my fist into their faces, but I hold back and take the plastic bag filled with a number of different pill bottles.

I don't know what half of them are, but Olivia does. She has a contraption with the days of the week on it, each section filled with different tablets. Certain ones need to be taken at certain times of the day, and she has a whiteboard in one of our side rooms that she marks off whenever I swallow a pill.

She's organized and obsessed, and me being the big brother who wants to please his sister, I do as I'm told and take the damn things.

Olivia hasn't responded to my last message. I stare down at my phone as I toss the pills into the storage under the seat.

Me

Such a bossy little sister.

I type out another.

Me

I'm driving over for you now.

She'll argue with me that she isn't getting on my bike, but I'll force her on, even if I need to knock her out and sit her in front of me, my hand traveling between her legs while she's unconscious to feel her bare pussy.

I shake my head—I don't need to do that anymore.

Shoving my phone into my pocket, I make my way to the courthouse. She hasn't finished yet, but I always used to wait to get a glimpse of her face, even though she didn't know I was there. We'd walk to work together, home together, and then I'd sneak into her house at night and…

I sigh to myself. I enjoyed doing all those things. They gave me a thrill, mixing with control and fucking power. I kind of miss hiding and hunting and watching her when she didn't know I was there. But having her by my side is way better. The lost part of me isn't lost anymore when I'm with my little sister.

I pull out a smoke then settle my helmet between my legs while balancing my bike. I light it up and take a draw. The sun beats down on me while I wait across the street.

Ten minutes pass, and the sun sets behind the buildings.

Thirty minutes.

An hour. She should be out by now.

Two hours, and it's night—the moon settles between rooftops in the far distance, and the clouds open to a little rainfall. It soaks my hair, my clothes, but I keep waiting.

I frown when most of the workers leave. She usually walks out with two older women, smiles at them, then heads to her apartment. Yet, the two older women have left, and there's no sign of my sister. She wouldn't go to her apartment either—she lives with me now.

Lighting another smoke and sheltering it from the rain by angling my hand, I impatiently tap my finger on my handle, checking my phone for any new messages. I try to call, but all I'm met with is her voicemail.

I drop my helmet and cigarette on the ground and walk across the street, nearly getting struck by a car, but they sound their horn and swerve just in time while I fully focus on the main door.

There's no reason for her to be late, unless she's trying to catch up on emails. But what if that asshole she was supposed to marry is there?

What if he took her?

I thought he was still in Canada on a business trip? I've tried to keep tabs on him without Olivia noticing my newest obsessive trait of following his every move. He's still fucking around despite waiting to get married.

Palpitations push me forward until I reach the entrance, but before I can yank the door open, it nearly smacks me in the face, and my mom freezes like a deer in headlights, eyes wide and in total shock.

She's as tall as me in her heeled shoes, her lips parting, her graying hair flying around her face. Her glasses hold her bangs off her forehead.

The woman who raised me.

CHAPTER NINETEEN
MALACHI

Mom steps back, her mouth open. Then rage takes over. "You have some nerve," she sneers, "to show your face around here."

She's mad. I fully expected her to hate me, but I'm not a fan of the way she's looking at me like I'm a monster.

My brows knit together; I'm confused by the slight twinge of pain in my chest. I knew I'd lost her as a mother the second I laid my fists on Dad, but this has just set it in stone for me.

I lost my father the day I was arrested.

I've lost her too.

As angry as Mom is, she also looks terrified of me. And that's all my fault. But why send me money? Why give me enough funds to survive so I didn't need to try finding work as an ex-convict with a terrible track record with communication and behavior?

"You..." She stops and shakes her head. "It's your fault.

Every hurdle in Olivia's life is because of you. You're the reason she ran out of work crying. Why won't you leave her the fuck alone?"

She slaps me across the face, making my head turn to the side, my cheek burning. She fixes her bag on her shoulder and marches away without waiting for a response, her heels clicking until she climbs into the car picking her up. It drives off.

My mom just hit me.

So did my bio-mom.

Why do they keep fucking hitting me?

My confusion vanishes the second her words register with me. Did she just say Olivia was crying because of me?

I pull my phone out and try to call her again, but there's no reply. The security guard walks out of the building and locks the door, so I know she's not in there—the lights are all out too.

Fuck.

Checking the cameras in our house while I cross the road, I don't see her, and no movement has been detected. Then I open my other app—the one I haven't used since she came back to me—and check her old place, then stop when I reach my bike.

She's there. In her apartment. Not ours.

I only have one camera left in there. It's facing the front door, just above a picture of the family, hidden, so she'll never know it's there.

Her bag is by the door.

Fuck. What did I do?

I pocket my phone, throw my leg over the bike, shove my head in the helmet, and set off to her apartment. I still own the one across from her. It has too much shit in it for me to give up right now. If she knew about all the pictures, TV screens, lists of names I hunted—people who even as much as looked at her— she would lose her shit with me. I managed to take the ones I still need to the house, but not the rest. She'd faint if she knew just how much I was buried in her privacy.

The cops would pull me over if they saw how fast I'm going, especially in the pouring rain—I zip between cars, squeezing the throttle to gain even more speed until I reach our street.

I pause at the main entranceway, glancing over my shoulder to see a black car stationary outside. The window slides up, hiding whoever it is behind blacked-out glass.

I unlock her apartment with the spare key I had made months ago, then close the door quietly and pause when I hear soft sobs traveling down the hallway from her bedroom.

Despite it only being weeks, the place feels different. I used to come here all the time when she was drugged and passed out. It was like a second home. But Xander came in, changed her wardrobe, made her dye her hair, and the place feels more poisoned than the bottles of wine still in her fridge.

The closer I get to her cries, the more my nerves shatter at the thought of my Olivia being hurt. If it wasn't me that hurt her, then who is making her cry like this? Who the fuck do I need to kill this time? Everyone else Mom set her up with while I was in prison is buried in my backyard with no trace back to me. The only reason Xander is still standing is because he's literally untouchable given how much protection he has.

When I reach the room, the cries are louder, and she's face down on her bed, her body shaking with sobs. My breath halts at the sight.

I want to say her name, but my mouth moves, and no sound comes out. My heart is fucking racing, and all I can do is slowly walk to the side of her bed, lower to my knees beside it, and place my hand on her shoulder.

She flinches, growing silent, except for the sniffs she can't control from hyperventilating.

"I can't lose you," she cries, not looking at me. "I can't."

She won't. Olivia is stuck with me until one of us dies, and even then, we're still bonded—sealed together by our undying love. Even if she tells me to leave, I won't. I'm hers and only hers, even if she doesn't fucking want me.

I'll take a thousand slaps from Mom. I'm staying.

I kick off my boots, strip my wet clothes to my boxers, and climb into bed beside her. I freeze when I see how red her eyes are—she's looking at me like she's in pain. She's been crying for hours by the looks of her face.

"Why can't I be in control of my own life? Why did Mom

make me like this?" Her entire body wracks with how much she's trembling in my hold. "I hate who I am because I just want to please her. She saved me, only to put me back in danger. I won't marry him. I promise I won't leave you again. She's setting up a meeting with them, but I won't do it. I won't. I promise I won't."

My chest swells at the same time my hands fist. Mom made her sad. I should do something about that. Maybe a threat, or maybe I completely ruin her fucking life like she's trying to do to Olivia.

"I can't breathe," she says, gasping and shaking again. "I need you. And that's what scares me. It scares me how much I need you."

Holding her tightly through her sobs, I bury my hand into her hair and massage her scalp, placing kisses on her temple and tear-streaked cheek until she falls asleep. I stay here, still as a statue, and wait until she's completely out cold before I slip away from under her.

I rise from the bed, watching her for a long minute while I try to plan my next move.

I need to deal with Mom. It's her fault Olivia is upset. It's her fault she was forced into this life. It's her fault Xander wants her, and it'll be her fucking fault when I bury her next to everyone else who becomes an obstacle between me and Olivia. I have two more left to deal with before we can move on.

The image of Mom's lifeless eyes on me as I rob her of her last breath doesn't make me excited or want to jump at the opportunity of revenge, but if I have to do it, I will.

She and my dad will be sitting down for their dinner—made by the manor's chef—about now. They'll discuss work, Olivia's marriage, and how ridiculous it is that me and her are together.

Two eliminations.

I can do it discreetly too.

Olivia groans and reaches for my hand. "Hold me," she whispers. "Please."

My plan can wait until tomorrow.

"Make it stop," she says, more tears spilling down her cheeks like she hadn't just fallen asleep. Her body trembles as I come back down beside her, pulling her into my arms.

She's sobbing again, and I'm clueless—surely I should know how to calm her down? I'm supposed to be her boyfriend.

Do I make her a coffee? Run her a bath? Maybe play some music?

Trembling, she's uncontrollably crying against me, and I'm frozen. Whenever she was upset when we were younger, I'd cuddle her until she fell asleep. Twice, I held her up in my arms and swayed around my bedroom while she passed out with her head on my shoulder.

This feels different—those moments were me being a good big brother. I'm not the same guy I was then, and Olivia is different too.

I want to ask her what I can do to help, but words aren't coming to me, and she's curled up against me, so I can't sign. I stroke her hair, feeling how hot she is.

I drag my hand down her back and up inside her shirt to feel her bare skin, and she's sweating. Her entire body is hot. My girl is so fucking emotional, she's going to make herself ill. I need to distract her.

Pressing a kiss to her temple, I try massaging her shoulder, her hip and ribs, as she hikes her leg, but she's still crying, still clinging to me like I'll disappear.

Then an idea comes to me, and I fist Olivia's hair and hold her there as I sit up against the headboard and tug down my pants and boxers, freeing my cock. She doesn't seem fazed by the fact I'm pulling off my clothes—she even moves herself so I can kick my pants from being trapped around my feet.

I'm not hard. But this isn't about me—this is me trying to calm down my little sister. "Open," I force out as I tighten my grip on her hair and rest her head in my lap, using my other hand to press the tip of my dick to her lips. "Put me in your mouth."

Just when I think she's going to scowl at me and tell me to get fucked, she relaxes a little and parts her lips, taking most of my softness and closing her eyes with a hum.

Fuck.

Tears are still streaming down her face, but she's not in

hysterics anymore—her tongue is wet against my cock, keeping it nice and warm as she heavily breathes through her nose.

Just sitting in her mouth.

It's somewhat calming her.

Slowly, I grow inside her mouth—I can't fucking help it. Even as she hums again, her body shaking from her hyperventilating, I can't stop myself from reacting. Heat crawls up my spine, and the soft way I stroke her hair is the total opposite of how I'm feeling inside.

Her tongue glides along me as she swallows, and I tense my jaw at how her mouth tightens around my cock. Her head stays in my lap as I thicken and stretch against her tongue until she can't help but suck, making my balls tingle, my own layer of sweat sticking to my forehead as I stare down at an angel—her mouth stuffed with my dick.

It's like her anxiety is lessening, replaced with a calm that spreads to me—I want to sink into the mattress with us connected. I want to touch her too. I want to feel her heat against my tongue while my cock stays settled in her mouth.

"Shhh. No more sad tears." Then I stop stroking her hair as her eyes open to look at me. "You're my good little sister, aren't you?"

She nods, her head still resting on my lap as she sucks, not moving, just sucking and humming, and the sadness starts to vanish from her eyes.

Swallowing again, her throat contracts around the head of my dick, and my hips absently push against her, encouraging her to take more of me, and I bite my lip as I hear her gag.

Fuck. I can't handle this. What was supposed to be me calming her down and distracting her from whatever had given her anxiety has now turned into me wanting to fuck her.

I won't.

I can't.

Keeping my dick in her mouth, I shift so I'm on my back, readjusting her so we're in the sixty-nine position. I tug down her shorts, her panties, and my hands shake as I grasp at her inner thighs. Pausing, I look down at Olivia to see her eyes wide, mouth filled with cock, watching, waiting, the need for me to taste her in her hungry gaze.

I rest my head on her inner thigh, the tip of my nose touching just below her entrance, and she whimpers as I lightly breathe against her pussy. I'm trembling more than she is, but I hold back, keeping my hand gripping her skin while I settle, relaxing into our position as Olivia's tongue glides up the underside of my dick.

She pops me from her mouth. "Please," she begs.

I make a dismissive sound and shake my head, inhaling deeply, feeling the heat of her radiating against my mouth. So fucking close. I could stick my tongue out and taste her, push it in deep and make her come, but when I hear that she's still hyperventilating, a sign she's still deep in her emotions, I stay still.

I want to rock my hips—her mouth is so fucking perfect.

I want to tense my ass cheeks and empty deep in her throat—hear her choke and gag and sputter for air while I rob her of it.

Closing my eyes, I focus on everything else but the way she always moans my name. Hugging her hips to my chest, I rest my face between her legs, desperate to taste her but having enough control not to stick my tongue in her pussy.

Then my eyes ping open as she palms my balls and sucks me all the way into the back of her throat. It contracts around my cock—she's sucking and licking, bobbing her head as her tongue strokes my flesh.

The groan I let out vibrates against her pussy, and she sobs loud enough to echo off the walls as she arches her back, forcing herself against my mouth.

Instead of going wild with her cunt, I keep the side of my head resting on her inner thigh, opening my mouth, and pushing my tongue out, allowing her to ride me as she swallows each inch of me.

Olivia grinds that perfect pussy against my wet tongue until she finds her release, and the way she cries around me, that soft hand strangling the base of my thickness, makes me latch my lips around her needy clit and suck her into a diabolic mess as she comes.

It only takes me a few of my own hard thrusts into her crying mouth to send a shockwave of pleasure down my spine to my balls. I empty down her throat, loving the way she struggles to breathe—she tries to push me back, but I wait a few seconds before I grant her oxygen.

I sit up and wipe the back of my hand across my mouth. "Why were you crying?" I ask clearly.

Barely lucid, she slides her palms down her face and keeps her fingers over her eyes. "It was just a bad day."

"Liar."

Her hands drop before she shifts on the bed, crossing her legs to face me on the mattress. "Mom gave me crap about you and my role in the family, that's all. I'll deal with it."

"Xander?"

Her shoulder lifts. "I haven't heard from him."

I fist my hands and run my tongue across my teeth. When I struggle to find my words, I sign, *Do you want to leave town? We'll leave everyone behind. Fuck them.*

She smiles, then it turns into a non-humorous laugh as she shakes her head. "Dad is here, and so is Molly. My friends are nearby too."

I stare at her, silently telling her they mean nothing and we can easily leave. What's stopping her? We have money, we have a bike for transport, and we can buy somewhere to live. All these assholes are extra baggage she can drop. All they're doing is taking up her time—time that should be spent with me.

Olivia sighs and pulls her panties back on, and then she's climbing up beside me in bed and pulling me to lie down. "I'm tired."

It takes her minutes to fall asleep, and all I can do is stare at her while I try to imagine what the fuck she dreams about.

CHAPTER TWENTY

MALACHI

Mom smiles at the cashier as she hands over the credit card, thanking her as she takes her lunch and heads to the table in the corner of the small cafe.

She comes here on her work breaks. At first, she was always in her office during her hour off, but her routine changed soon after Olivia came back to me—like she knew she'd lost her daughter to her son and needed to stay away from the constant reminder of that fact. Olivia used to sit with her, listen to her controlling ways, then they'd continue with their day.

Taking a draw of my cigarette, I remain hidden across the street—hood up, cap hiding my face—while she eats her lunch and chats on the phone. It won't be Dad—he's in a meeting about going back to work.

My foster sister Molly, who's like a hyperactive puppy, is always with our father—I think she misses Olivia since I've taken all of her attention.

She can fuck off if she thinks she's getting her back. She's mine, no one else's. Olivia wants me to go out with them tomorrow, and although I want to say no and leave it at that, I'm trying to be a better person for her, so I agreed.

Plus, Molly is technically family. I need to meet her eventually, being the black sheep and estranged brother and all.

My phone vibrates in my pocket, but I ignore it as I lean against the wall and keep my eyes on the woman who not only raised me but who's also still trying to ruin my life by insisting that my girlfriend marries Xander.

I can see her emails—she wants the Reznikovs to meet up after their business trip. She wants the entire family there. Mom, Dad, Molly, and Olivia. But not me. No. I'm technically no longer part of the Vize family. I'm shunned. Shamed. An embarrassment to the name.

I'm the black sheep once more.

Adryx Reznikov is the older brother, and he's a bit of a dick from what I can see online. The brains of the family business. Xander is the face, the spoiled child, the golden child, the one handed everything on a plate while his brother needs to fight for a sprinkle of what Xander gets.

They'll land soon. I still need to formulate a plan, a threat to Xander so he'll stay the fuck away from my sister. I'll try to kidnap him maybe. I still have the chains in the basement from when I had Olivia. I'll make him suffer, but not in the same way

I did her.

I won't feed him for days. I'll make him drink his own piss until he vomits everywhere, then I'll force that down his throat too. Possibly, depending on how my mood is, I could pull Olivia in, and she can hurt him too for even thinking about marrying her. The fact he made her dye her hair and commented on her looks makes me fucking mad.

She's sensitive, my little sister, and this asshole made her think otherwise.

Olivia is perfect, in every goddamn way.

I'm going to destroy his face, so all the girls I've seen him partying with online will be terrified of him. I'll carve my initials into his skin, stick his cock in acid, and then I'll feed his brother his half-melted balls and slap him across the face with Xander's liver.

My phone buzzes again, and I sigh, glancing down to see a notification that my therapy appointment is this afternoon. Olivia makes me set reminders, multiple alarms, and even has my appointments written all over the whiteboard.

I kind of don't want to do this therapy stuff, but I know in the long run, it'll be worth it—it also makes Olivia happy to see me getting help, for telling her that I know I need help. I do. I'm a mess, and I need direction.

Being in prison for eight years has well and truly fucked me up. Some days, I'm okay. On the bad days, I think of how Olivia screwed me over, and then other days, I regret everything and wish I'd never been adopted by the Vize family—but I always banish that thought because then I wouldn't have met my sister.

I took her home the other night after I calmed her down with my cock—I woke her up and rode us on my bike all the way to the farmhouse in the middle of nowhere. I stripped her so she was naked, set her into the bed, kissed her perfect fucking body until she moaned loud enough to wake the dead, ringing my ears, fucked her, then I cleaned out my pet's tank while Olivia came back to reality and asked me to bathe with her.

She's seemed sad the last few days, and it makes me uneasy. But she still kisses me, lets me fuck her, and sends me messages saying she misses me while she's at work, so the paranoia is just my mind fucking with me.

I can never get enough of her. Sex is everything for us— the missed time, the missed days and nights and orgasms. We missed nearly a decade, but we have time now. The fact she wants me to take her on a date too is ridiculous. What would be the point? I get it, I really do, but that doesn't mean I'm going to start serenading her, treating her like a princess, then acting like I don't want to fuck her into a coma every second of every day.

I'm not a romantic guy. I can't do all this soft bullshit. I can barely make love to Olivia without it turning rough because it's all I know—my life has been driven by anger since I was a kid. Being with Olivia is the only time my mind is kind to me.

With her, the voices fuck off. She smiles at me, and for fuck's sake, what else could I want? There's nothing wrong with us. We're active. Really active. Kissing turns sexual. Cuddling gets me hard. Even seeing her blush at me makes me want to stuff my cock into her mouth until her eyes are filled with tears.

How the hell am I supposed to take her on a date and pretend none of that stuff happens?

"You could be a little more discreet," comes a voice to my left.

My already shitty mood sours.

I glance up to see Olivia's friend Abigail. She still has colorful hair, and her eyeliner is a little atrocious. How the fuck she's been friends with my girl since they were young still baffles me to this day.

I ignore her.

She crosses her arms, leans against the wall beside me, and pulls out a cigarette. "I'm guessing the reason for her short replies and not answering my calls is because of you. You can't take my friend from me."

Looking up at her once more, I calculate how long it will take before my silence makes her uncomfortable. She's never spoken to me before. Ever.

Annoyingly, she doesn't fuck off. She takes a draw of her cigarette and blows a cloud above her head. "You don't want her getting married to that jackass, and neither do I. Xander isn't backing down. Him and his father have made that perfectly clear. Please keep this between the two of us."

I want to question her, but I can't. I only feel comfortable talking in front of Olivia. Other than my therapist, she's the only person in the world who will ever hear my voice. I won't let Abigail hear me, and she doesn't know sign language, so all I can do is stare at her.

She huffs, steps on her finished cigarette, and pops her hip out.

Does Olivia know this? That Xander isn't backing down? Is that why I've to keep it to myself—because Olivia doesn't want me to know?

Or maybe Olivia doesn't know yet.

Wait. How would this dipshit even know?

"If Xander gets Olivia, we'll never see her again."

I know that. I don't need the reminder that the only person I'm struggling to keep her from is looming around the corner, waiting to ruin my life.

"If you plan on removing Xander from the equation, make sure you deal with his brother too. He'll become more of a problem. Their father is the one who controls them both though. But he'll be impossible to reach."

I'm at a loss as to why she's standing here conversing with me like we know each other. Or why she's telling me shit I'm not aware of.

"I'll never understand you and Olivia. I always knew there was something going on—Mason told me. And you couldn't have made it more obvious you were in love with your sister, and she was just as obsessed with you. If you break her heart, I'll kick you so hard in the balls, you'll never walk properly again."

And then she strides across the street, smiles at my mom as she leaves the cafe, and they both walk back to the courthouse to meet with my sister.

I'm confused and pissed off.

Did she just fucking threaten me?

I watch them walk around the corner, waiting a few moments before I follow. Keeping my cap low, and staying out of their line of sight, I tail them all the way to the courthouse.

The warmth in my chest appears when my sister walks out, grinning at her friend and ignoring our mom, and then they climb into a car and head to her friend Anna's house.

Annoyingly, she gave birth yesterday. Two newborn babies screamed down the phone while I tried to sleep on Olivia's chest this morning, and she acted as if our eardrums weren't ringing and my patience wasn't thin. I was very fucking close to throwing her phone against the wall and making sure none of her friends could ever contact her again.

She tried to show me a picture, but I didn't even attempt to lift my head to look. Who cares? Anna is a bitch, and so is Abigail. I mean, who the fuck does she think she is to speak to me the way she just did?

I want to choke her, but not the same way I choke Olivia. The thought alone makes me shiver in disgust. I've never even as much as thought about having anyone except my sister beneath me—yeah, I fucked with her head a little by going on a date with Anna, but I did that out of maliciousness.

Olivia needs new friends. They're all idiots. Or maybe she doesn't need any? Not having to deal with them disturbing our bubble sounds fucking perfect. I'm her friend. That's enough.

She's my only friend too.

I get on my bike and follow the car to Anna's, parking it up the hill—far enough away that they won't be able to see me, but I still have the perfect view of all the windows at the front of the house.

My mom hugs Anna, hands her a gift, and then beams at the baby the husband places into Olivia's arms. The other baby goes to Abigail.

Something strange rushes through me. I can't quite put my finger on the feeling. I'm not jealous of any of it. I'm not staring at Olivia baby-talking and picturing her holding my kid, and I'm not planning in my head what it would be like if I was ever going to be good enough to have all of that.

It's impossible.

But maybe it's a bucket full of annoyance that's in my veins. Because my sister is smiling. Grinning at a baby. She's never smiled at me like that—or anyone. It makes my insides twist at the thought of her wanting that—a family, kids, with me. It's not something I can give her.

Fuck.

She's beaming ear to ear, her cheeks rosy red. She sidesteps the husband, and I lose sight of her from the window—I might scratch his car and slash his tires for ruining my view.

She reappears in front of another window and pulls her phone out of her back pocket, the baby in her other arm, as if she's a natural at holding something so damn fragile.

She's typing while her smile grows, and I make a mental note to check her phone while she's asleep to see who it is. I've been good recently. Before, I'd hack her phone and read her messages, look at her pictures and videos, and it became obsessive, but I'm trying to do better.

I haven't checked her phone since she came back to me. Maybe I should, just once?

The thought vanishes as my own phone dings in my pocket.

Olivia

> You're quite clingy, big brother.

I huff a soft laugh, looking up to see her watching me. She tilts her arm to give me a better view of the newborn in her hold while she sways softly, side to side, still smiling.

I sigh as I type out a reply.

I want to ask her if she's getting some sort of baby fever and if I should restock as many condoms as possible, but I settle by asking:

Me

How long will you be in there?

Mom takes the baby from her arms, then she's chatting away to her friends, leaving me waiting for about five minutes before she moves away from them and chews her lip while reading my message.

Olivia

Do you want to come in and meet the twins? It would be great to have my friends used to us being together.

I frown, looking up at the window to see Olivia waiting patiently for my reply. What kind of question is that? In what fucking world would Anna and her husband allow me to be anywhere near their newborn babies? Plus Mom is there—she'll slam the door in my face.

I have no reason to go in.

Me

Why would I?

I know the moment I hit send that I've made a mistake, but I can't take it back now. Her smile drops, and so do my teeth on my bottom lip as I await the attitude. Or maybe the middle finger.

But I don't get either—she stares at her screen for a long minute. I adjust my bike, my ass getting numb. Her smile drops further, then she's moving away from the window and out of view once more.

My phone vibrates in my hand.

Olivia

I'll be out in a minute.

I pocket my phone and turn the key in my bike, making it vibrate beneath me. Revving, I catch the attention of Olivia's friend—that fucking Abigail—and she scowls at me before shutting the blind.

What's her deal?

Part of me wants to get her out of the picture, but she knows things. Her saying that Xander won't back down, even though Olivia hasn't once mentioned it to me, means either my girl is lying, or her friend is fucking one of the Reznikovs, maybe to get intel?

The front door opens, but only Olivia leaves. She's hugging herself as she walks across the street and up to me. She doesn't seem happy to see me.

I gulp and smile at her. "Hi."

"You couldn't give me some time with my friends? Anna just had twins."

I frown in confusion—she just spent time with them and now I'm taking her home.

Her phone buzzes in her hand, and she glances down before stuffing it into her purse. "Abigail," she says, seeing my silent question about who's messaging her.

My gaze flicks to the house then back to her.

Chewing her lip, her eyes glaze over. I try to take her hand, but she pretends to rub her arms to heat them up. She shakes her head and takes my helmet when I pull it off. I still need to get her one, and I refuse to drive with her on my bike without her being protected.

I grab the helmet and drag her to my chest. "Look at me," I demand, keeping the visor up to see her red eyes. *Tell me what's wrong.*

Her silence kills me. She's hurting, and I'm the reason why.

"I'm sorry," I say, wetting my dry lips. "I'm trying."

She nods. "I know. So am I."

"Do you still love me?"

She lets out a breath. "Of course I do."

Good. That's good. If she didn't love me anymore, I don't know what I'd do. Maybe keep her tied up in our bed until she fell back in love with me.

When she slides behind me and wraps her arms around my waist, I pull off with a feeling of unease encasing me tighter than Olivia's hold as I speed up.

I feel… not nice.

Does she still have the ridiculous idea of me taking her on

a date and going back to the start, and that's why she's being so cold?

What if seeing her friend and her new, happy family made her realize I'm the wrong person for her and she's thinking of ways to leave me?

So many thoughts are rushing in my head as I speed down the road faster than intended, causing Olivia to tighten her arms around me.

Maybe I should go faster.

Olivia doesn't say a word when we reach home, or when she hands me my helmet and walks into the house. I follow behind with my brows knitted together. I want to ask her what's wrong, but words fail me, and she won't look at me so I can sign to her. She goes straight into the bathroom, shuts the door, and slides over the latch to lock it.

My jaw tenses as I press my forehead to the door, eyes closing as I hear her soft sobs. She's crying. Because of me. I'm doing it again—making her unhappy. She's going to leave me because all I do is upset her.

I can't call her name. I can't unlock the door and communicate with her. I can't do anything but wait outside the door with one question on my mind.

What should I do?

Olivia is far too excited as we wait for Molly to finish school—her classes end in twenty minutes, and we're taking her dress shopping for homecoming. I had no choice but to join them—I have to meet my little sister, be nice, and also be patient.

I'm also not to smoke a cigarette or joint in front of her, scare her, or do anything violent.

So, in turn, I do fucking nothing but stand and be a damn shadow.

I've been inside Olivia, in every goddamn hole, and I've also claimed her with my initials on her body, yet she thinks I've got a nice, patient bone in my body for someone who isn't her?

Has she fucking met me?

"She's coming now," Olivia says, nudging me with her shoulder to get my attention. "Remember what I said."

The girl is fragile and sensitive and I've to go easy on her—basically, I've to stay silent around her. She probably doesn't sign, and I don't like kids, nor do they like me, so it looks like today is going to be a quiet day.

I already asked Olivia ten times this morning why she was upset last night, but instead of giving me an answer, she kissed me and avoided it—my paranoia at this point is close to mass destruction because what the fuck?

Abigail's words are hanging in my brain like a disease. Xander isn't giving up. Will he force her? What if he tries to take her?

What will I do if Olivia agrees again, and I lose her?

A whole lot of death, that's for sure.

"And don't call me your sister, especially if you're flirting with me or holding my hand."

I frown at her. *But I'm your brother?*

"No, you're my boyfriend."

I'm both.

She sighs, her shoulders dropping. "You need to choose, Malachi. Am I your sister or your girlfriend?"

Without hesitation, I sign, *Both.*

"You're insufferable."

My eyes narrow, but before I can argue my ground and demand that she still call me both, a pink, sparkly presence appears in the distance. The young girl waves at us excitedly, looking over her shoulder to say goodbye to her friends before rushing to us. She hugs Olivia then looks at me.

If she even thinks about trying to hug me, I'll sidestep and watch her fall flat on her face.

"Hi," she says with a huge grin. "I'm Molly."

I blink.

Olivia nudges me.

I blink again.

I flatten my lips and tip my head a touch, and it seems to be enough because the energetic teenager goes into a full blown description of her week so far—she's so fucking dramatic, even with the way she moves her hands as she talks, her tone too enthusiastic as she explains why her friends want her to hang out at some day club for teens, and then shows Olivia a bracelet she made with one of the house workers at the Vize manor.

Drowning her out, I shove my hands into my pockets and fall behind a little as we walk through the park—it's only a short way to the mall, although both girls complain that their feet hurt ten minutes in.

I end up carrying a pink bag on my back because apparently it's too heavy for the girl who's been carrying it all fucking day, and I'm not exactly going to say no to Olivia when she hands it to me.

Molly's dark hair swings as she turns to me. "You're way taller than I thought."

I don't reply.

What would I even say anyway? *Thanks, kid, I got my height from my dead bio-dad?* Or do I try some bonding by saying, *I heard yours was a dick and left you at home for three days while your addict mother lay dead on the bathroom floor. Want to bond over trauma? I can partially relate.*

Instead, I stay silent. Olivia would most likely kick my balls, and I quite like my balls.

Despite the rules thrown at me, I light a cigarette and try to ignore them both while they talk about what Olivia wore to her homecoming dance. I never attended ours. But I did stand outside, waiting for my sister to come out. I was going to ask her to dance with me in the parking lot, just the two of us, but Dad appeared and told me to get in the damn car and took me home.

He knew.

He always knew how I felt about her.

Molly slows down to walk beside me. She moves her hands to make a few signs, but they're wrong. Olivia corrects her, and she turns back to me again. *I'm happy,* she signs then takes a few seconds to figure out the next movements. *You're out of prison.*

And just like that, my heart rate picks up, and I want to go home.

Olivia always cried about you, she adds while Olivia isn't looking.

Swallowing a lump threatening to strangle the shit out of me, I inhale my smoke deep and make sure I blow the poison in the opposite direction from the kid.

"Dad's been teaching me a little. I'll try harder."

"You're doing great," Olivia says. "It took me a long time to figure it out. Dad and Malachi taught me."

Her eyes move to me, and she smiles. I remember growing up, I'd write down the words and sign them to her. Dad was teaching her, but she always came to my room to ask to teach her some more.

I taught her how to sign my name—and hers.

It's a shame she never got the chance to teach me how to say my name like we planned when we were eighteen and nineteen.

I taught myself how to say hers in my cell. And even then, I was terrible at it.

"Did Dad teach you?" she asks me. "To sign?"

Why is this kid giving me anxiety? My heart is racing, and I feel sick all of a sudden.

My jaw ticks, and I focus on the entrance of the mall, my teeth crushing together, not because she's annoying me or because she won't stop talking. No. I'm caught off guard because she didn't say "my dad". She said it in a way that suggests Jamieson is still my father, despite everything I've done. Meaning she still views me as his son and her brother.

I gulp and look away, an intense heaviness pressing into my chest. Like it's trying to crush my soul and remind me I'm an empty shell and useless.

When I got arrested, I accepted I was alone again. My bio-parents left me, and I ruined my relationship with the Vizes because I fell in love with their daughter. Until Olivia came back to me, the only person I could talk to was myself. My inner voice is a dick and thinks he's funny one minute and suicidal the next, so it's good to drown that side out and replace it with Olivia and this kid who's still talking.

We cross the street and head towards the mall—I'm counting down the hours until we can go home so I can forget this day exists.

"Can I come and stay over one night?" Molly asks me, and my right eye twitches. "Our big sis said we could watch movies and you'd show me your spider! What kind is it? Does it bite? Do spiders make noises? Has it ever bitten you?"

Fucking hell.

"Olivia," I say, gesturing to the hyperactive teen, silently begging her to take over before I pretend to have an aneurysm and pass the fuck out. She's on the phone, leaving me to deal with this fucking child and her incessant voice.

Molly's eyes widen. "Oh my God. You just said her name! Can you say mine? It's easier than Olivia's. Moll-ee. It rolls right off the tongue! Are you even listening to me?"

I want to die.

While Olivia still talks on the phone—to Abigail I think—I push Molly from my left to my right when I realize she's walking on the curb side. It's an automatic thing I always do with Olivia. For some reason, I feel uncomfortable having Molly close to the busy road. One swerving car could hurt her.

I toss my cigarette and open the glass door, letting Molly and Olivia walk in first. Olivia takes my hand, and some of the tension lifts from my shoulders. "Be nice. Please. She's trying so hard, and you won't acknowledge her," she whispers. "Please.

She was so excited to meet you."

I nod and huff. There's no point in me trying to build any sort of relationship with the kid—she'll hate me when she's old enough to understand everything that's gone down with the family and why I've been kicked out of the Vize unit. And the fact I fuck Olivia on the regular and how it's technically wrong.

Molly's gaze drops to our clasped hands, and she attempts to hide a smile.

Does she know I'm *with* with our sister?

"Oh, this is the store!" Olivia pulls us towards a shop filled with dresses and shoes, and I inwardly sigh when they both squeal in excitement.

This is going to be the worst day of my life.

CHAPTER TWENTY-ONE

OLIVIA

My eyes slide open at the sound of the floorboards creaking.

It's early morning, the sun starting to rise and brighten the sky—birds are chirping, and a little rain drizzles against the window.

But when I sit up, I see Malachi standing in the middle of the room with his back to me. The tattoos of snakes and doves and web-coated thorns stare back at me.

He's not signing with his hands or muttering words like the other times I've woken to see him like this—he's swaying side to side ever so slightly, his hands fisted, and he's covered in sweat so badly that his hair is wet at his nape.

I pull off the covers and walk to him, resting my hand against his back. "Malachi?"

His eyes are open, glued to the wall—he doesn't acknowledge me.

I chew my lip and look around the room—he's been taking his meds, and he gets plenty of sleep, which were factors in why he was spiraling. Dad told me that, as a kid, when Malachi was deprived of sleep, his mental health worsened.

What's causing it now?

"Do you want to come back to bed?"

Although he's silent and he barely looks lucid as his eyes find me, he lowers his head to give a gentle nod, his breathing heavy. He's slow in his movements as I take his hand, fighting with his fingers to loosen them so I can interlace them with mine as I lead us back to the bed.

He wraps around me, cocoons me, burying his nose into my nape and inhaling my strawberry-scented strands. His body relaxes, and his next words stab me right in the heart.

"I'm sorry," he whispers shakily. "It won't stop."

"What won't?" I ask after a long few seconds, but he's already fallen asleep.

But I can't. My mind is in overdrive—stuck on the messages sitting in my phone that I've yet to delete. They came through while I was visiting Anna and her babies. Xander, reaching out with his usual threat. That I have no idea what his father is like and the lengths he'd go to have me marry Xander.

I ignored him. Then another message came through, stating that it was in the contract I signed that I've got to communicate with him.

Thanks, Mom. Thanks a lot.

I won't respond. I can't and won't do that to Malachi—I made a promise when I came back to him, and I'm keeping it. It's a secret I need to keep for as long as possible—he'll eventually find out, but I can cross that bridge when I come to it.

But telling him right now would be detrimental to his current state. I will. I really will tell him, but not right now. I have everything under control, and when I go to the meeting— whenever it is—I'll point-blank refuse, tell them all to go fuck themselves, even my mother, and I'll hand in my resignation.

I have no need to work with my mother. I can get a job somewhere else and actually be happy, and not bossed around like I'm her damn slave.

Maybe I'll ask Malachi if Molly can come stay with us? Once I'm free of my obligations, Mom will try to put my sister in my shoes, and that's something else I'll refuse. I know Malachi likes her—he doesn't scowl at her the way he does with everyone else, even though he hasn't spoken to, or signed to her, once. But he does listen—he took in every single word that fell from her lips while we were dress shopping earlier, even if it was drama at school.

He wouldn't even blow his cigarette smoke near her, yet I always get a face full, whether it's to annoy me or to make me come for him.

Deep down, he tolerates her, which means something.

Maybe she'll be the little sister I couldn't be growing up? He needed a sibling when he came to the Vizes, and instead, he got a twisted heart and fell for someone with a ball and chain attached to her ankle.

My eyes finally close, and I wake a few hours later to the alarm on my phone reminding me to get up for work, sitting up quickly when I feel the bed empty beside me.

Getting off the bed, I spot him lying on the floor, and my heart ricochets in panic as I rush to him, then stop when I realize he's on his back with his spider crawling around his hand, and he's in deep thought.

"Have you slept?" I ask.

His chin lowers in a quiet yes as the eight-legged monster shuffles off his hand and onto his chest.

I inwardly shiver.

He shifts, putting his arm up above his head and resting against it while the other hand rests at his side—he's not even trying to stop the spider crawling over his chest, my body stiffening when it stops at his shoulder.

"Have you figured out what you're going to name him?"

His lip pulls at the corner, and he leaves his pet on his chest as he signs, *She's a female.*

"How can you tell?"

I thought she was a male, but when she shed, I examined the molt, he signs then says aloud, "for spermathecae."

For being a complicated word, Malachi says it surprisingly clear.

I honestly have no idea what he's talking about though. He did a lot of research when he was younger—he's like a genius when it comes to eight-legged creatures.

"You like spiders," I state the obvious. "They creep me out."

He laughs silently. *Red-knees are docile. She's harmless to you. Do you want to name her?*

"You name her."

He tips his head, staring at the animal as if she's going to look like a name. He shrugs then looks at me again. "Cordelia."

"I like that," I say.

Although I need to get showered and ready for work, I sit down beside him, still keeping enough distance as Cordelia crawls over the top of his hand slowly—Malachi rotates his hand as she moves. I've always known he's loved spiders. Cats, dogs, rabbits, parrots, all the other household pets, you name it, he loves them, but spiders—or more so tarantulas—hold a special place in his heart.

He even has a spider tattooed on his hand and some webs across his chest and the backs of his calves. The aesthetic is beautiful, mixing with all his other designs too. I trace the tip of my finger across the ink on his shoulder, down his bicep, while he keeps his attention on his pet. "Cordelia is the same breed as Spikey," I say, watching him. "Is the red-knee your favorite then?"

All he does is nod once.

I want to ask so many questions. I know he had a tarantula as a kid and that it died. Mom said when he was brought into the hospital, it was dead in his pocket. All of its legs were ripped off, and it took four nurses to take it from him.

The brave side of me peeks through, and I get closer, reaching my hand out and hovering my fingertips over her. Malachi looks at me questioningly, his brow raised.

I've always been afraid of spiders—anything small and monstrous looking makes me shiver and want to run in the opposite direction, but if I'm going to live under the same roof as this one, then I need to try to squash this fear.

My arachnophobia is screaming at me as I feel the furriness of her coat, and when one of her legs lifts, I flinch my hand back.

"I can't," I say, holding my hand as if the spider hurt me.

He laughs, half-smiling, and takes her back to the tank. *You'll like her one day*, he signs.

"When I'm dead," I reply, accepting his hand as he helps me to my feet. "Can you take me to work?"

He nods, grabbing my face with both hands, dragging me towards him, and planting a kiss on my lips.

CHAPTER TWENTY-TWO

OLIVIA

For some reason, being at work has me feeling on edge.

Abigail has insisted I don't go in at all this week and tells me I'll understand, and Molly has been calling me all morning, but I'm too busy.

I'll get back to them both on my break. I have fifteen emails to respond to, and Mom needs me to take her coffee at midday.

My phone dings, and the message that pops up has me pausing.

Molly

Why is Malachi standing outside our house?

She attaches a video, and the five-second clip, which has been taken from Molly's window, shows Malachi across the street from the Vize manor, smoking, while sitting on his bike.

I open my chat with Malachi and type. All my messages have been ignored since I came to work earlier. He's not speaking to me for some reason, and I hate it.

> Molly said you're outside the
> manor. Is everything okay?

He reads it, but no dots appear to tell me he's typing back a reply. Ten minutes pass, and I accept he's not going to respond. I try to call, but he hangs up on the second ring.

With my heart beating hard in my chest, confused and terrified, I shake my head and type one last message.

> Tell   me   what's   wrong.
> If   we're   going   to   make
> this   work,   we   need   to
> communicate, Malachi.

How hypocritical of me—I'm keeping secrets from him, yet I'm demanding he reply to a text message and throw words like that at him.

An hour later, the door of my office opens without the person announcing themselves, and the prickling sensation at the back of my neck spreads all over me, mixing with the anticipation of the silence and footsteps that pull my flat lips into a smile.

Everything was fine when he dropped me off. He kissed me then went off to do his normal morning exercise. A run in the woods, boxing in the garage, and some other workouts he does in the yard.

For some reason, I'm not allowed in the backyard. And if I

do go out there, he's in a rush to get me either into the woodland or back into the house.

I type away on my computer, pretending I'm not paying attention and that my body doesn't instantly become alive and aware of Malachi closing the door behind him. Feigning indifference, I act as though I'm not in the least bit affected by him—I keep my eyes on the screen, my fingers moving over the keyboard.

His quiet is always so loud to me.

I love it.

My breathing grows heavy as he walks to the glass panel that gives me a view of everyone else in the office—they're all at their desks, working, none the wiser as Malachi pulls the string to snap the blinds shut, hiding us from their potential attention.

Still feeling his lips on me from this morning, I shift in my seat, swallow, and trap my bottom lip between my teeth.

"Are you here to kidnap me again, big brother?"

He doesn't look at me as he turns and walks towards me, to my desk, and snatches up my letter opener. He flips it in his hand a few times as he stalks the room, changing the energy around us as he circles my desk until he's behind me.

Just when I think he's going to kiss me or speak or break this tension, I gasp as the cold, sharp edge of the letter opener presses to my throat.

His other hand fists at my hair, yanking my head back so I'm staring at the ceiling, his hard face glaring down at me.

No words pass between us; only our breaths can be heard in the room. I want to ask him what's wrong—even when he's quiet, he's the loudest.

My mouth parts to ask him, but he grits his teeth and yanks me to my feet, the blade nicking at my skin but not enough to hurt—the sting follows me as he bends me over the wooden desk, removing the sharpness from my throat and stabbing it through the desk.

My eyes widen as I look forward—he's stabbed through my sleeves, trapping me in place as he pushes off me and starts unbuckling his belt.

"Tell me why you kept it from me," he demands, the leather of his belt snapping as he pulls it from the loops of his pants.

"If you want me to fuck this," he says, slapping my pussy from behind and making me flinch, "then you'll tell me, Olivia."

Gasping, I ask, "Tell you what? What did I keep from you?"

He spanks me so hard, the pain vibrates through me.

"Mason is dead."

I bite my lip, refusing to speak.

He kicks my legs together then wraps his belt around my thighs and fastens it tight to keep them shut.

"He died nearly ten years ago." His voice is shaky. His emotions are beating him up. "The same night I was arrested, he fucking crashed his bike and died."

I flinch as he spreads my cheeks and a ball of spit hits my back hole. I shiver, expecting a finger or a thumb, but I pause when I feel the pierced head of his cock. He doesn't give me a chance to ready myself before he pushes it into my ass, fully sheathing himself.

My nails dig into the wood of my desk, my body on fire from the sudden fullness. I gasp, pain following as he grabs my hair and pulls out, only to slam back in again.

"He's dead," he grits, thrusting hard once more, fucking my ass with so much hatred, my pussy begs for attention.

All I can do is chew on my bottom lip to stop the entire office hearing me cry as my brother fucks me over my desk.

I let out an accidental scream as he pulls out and thrusts hard, hitting my hips into the desk. He tuts and leans over me further, which only draws him deeper, then takes the metal ruler from my stationery holder.

Malachi forces it into my mouth and closes my jaw with a firm grip.

"If someone hears," he says slowly, moving in and out and making me cry around the metal, "I won't stop. I'll fuck your ass in front of them."

Malachi has a bit of an obsession with anal—my butt is like his safe place recently, but he also uses it as punishment. He knows I want my pussy fucked. My entire body is screaming for it as he pounds into my back hole, knocking things from my desk and shaking my computer so much, I think the screen might snap from the stand and smash on the floor.

There's a knock at the door, the shadow of someone on the other side, but Malachi ignores them and keeps fucking me, stretching me, bruising my hips against the desk and yanking my hair so hard, I think I might lose a few strands.

I'm panting through my nose, breathing heavily, my eyes watering—if he just reaches his hand down and touches me, it'll be everything. I'm throbbing and needy and seconds from exploding.

Just one touch. I'm silently begging.

"Olivia? The stupid door is locked."

Abigail.

She knows how to—

The door opens after she messes with the handle, making us both freeze.

Malachi doesn't pull out when he sees it's my best friend; he just huffs and presses his forehead into my back.

Meanwhile, Abbi closes the door, only noticing us when she turns around. Her eyes widen, and she drops her bag to cover her eyes. She parts her fingers to make sure what she's seeing is real—me, bent over my desk with a letter opener stabbed through my sleeves to keep me in place, a ruler in my mouth keeping me gagged, and my brother's cock in my ass.

She's not in a hurry to leave either. She crosses her arms.

"We need to talk," she says. "I'd appreciate it if I had your full attention."

I try to budge, but Malachi takes his forehead off my back, his hand snatching my nape, and I gasp as he pulls out to the tip and hammers back in so hard, the desk creaks.

"Hey!" Abigail grabs a pen and throws it at him but misses. "Stop fucking your sister! This is important!"

Malachi grunts, lying his front on my back as he thrusts again, turning his head away from Abigail and snatching my lobe between his teeth, filling my ass with every inch of him.

Another pen flies towards Malachi, smacking him in the head this time.

It annoys him enough to stop, his pissed-off gaze lifting to her.

I spit the ruler out. "What is it?"

"The Reznikovs are coming tomorrow morning," she says, not taking her eyes off Malachi as he still doesn't pull out of me. "I'll come as moral support since your mom is psycho about it all."

"How do you know it's tomorrow?"

Her eyes flicker to me with a touch of hesitation. She lets out a forced laugh, shaking her head. "I don't know."

My brow raises. "You don't know how you know?"

"I can't focus. Please tell him to get out of your ass and leave," she says. "Anyone could just walk in and see the two of you. The entire office thinks you're siblings."

Malachi isn't going to leave—I can already feel the rage building around him. He was interrupted once before, and it nearly cost our father's life. Who's to say he won't hurt Abigail?

Despite my contracting pussy, desperate for attention, and the way my ass grips Malachi's cock, I pull my sleeves free of the letter opener and try to stand.

Malachi doesn't budge.

"Can you please leave?" I don't know who I'm talking to, but both are offended—Malachi because I move in a way that means he has to pull out; Abigail because she's offended by his entire existence.

Malachi hides himself as he tucks his dick away, scowling at Abbi like she's crashed his party and stolen his favorite present.

She raises her brow and pops her hip. "Don't let the door hit you on the way out."

His jaw tenses, eyes burning into her.

I grab his wrist when he takes a step forward. "Wait for me," I tell him. "I'll finish up my last email and meet you outside."

This isn't finished, he signs.

I smile because I absolutely hope it's not.

Abigail raises her brow when he closes the door behind him. "What the fuck?"

I groan. "He found out about Mason."

Her face drops. "Oh."

"Dad didn't think it would be good for him to know. Even when he was in prison, he said it was detrimental to Malachi's mental health and he'd know eventually, just not yet. It's been eight years. We thought the danger had passed."

Her eyes flash. "Eight years or not, he was his best friend. Of course he's going to be upset that everyone kept it from him." She crosses her arms. "What are you going to do about tomorrow's meeting?"

"Refuse and run."

CHAPTER TWENTY-THREE
OLIVIA

Abigail was telling the truth about the Reznikov meeting being this morning. As soon as I woke up, Mom had sent me messages telling me to look my best and wear makeup. Her driver picked me up, much to Malachi's dismay— he wanted to drive me and wait outside until after the meeting. He's still mad about Mason. He's quiet. More quiet than usual, but I understand he needs time.

He did make sure he fucked me before I left.

I'm currently sitting in the meeting room, my mom and Abigail present, with my brother's cum leaking onto my panties every time I cough.

The door flies open to a hyperactive teen.

Molly helps our dad by holding the door and kicking aside Mom's bag, earning herself a glare, then sits down beside me. She just got her hair cut and colored with some blonde flashes, and her nails are all pretty and pink after the manicure Dad bought her.

"Did you pick up the files I told you about?" Mom asks my dad, who merely nods with a hum.

They're not getting along. Ever since the wedding—and now that my father is trying to call everything off—they've argued every day and barely spend time together. She's not even trying with him, and he's given up too.

They've been together for over thirty years, and it's sad to see their relationship go up in flames because of me. I've never felt guiltier than I do now about their situation. If I just married Xander like the obedient daughter I was raised to be, this wouldn't be an issue.

But I can't.

"I finally got to meet Malachi!" Molly announces, stealing everyone's attention. "He's taller in person."

Mom glares at me. "What is she talking about?"

My shoulder lifts. "I don't see the issue. He's her big brother."

She grimaces then her gaze drops back to her phone. Molly glances at me, confused and unsure, but then Dad breaks the awkwardness.

"Did you try out some of the sign language I showed you?"

"Yes!" She's beaming, a huge smile across her face. "And oh my God, Dad, he said Olivia's name."

Dad looks at me, a small, invisible smile playing on his lips, but it's hidden with a hint of wariness. He doesn't trust our relationship, and I can't blame him. Abigail crosses her arms and says nothing.

She's also wary about my new relationship.

Molly seems to be the only one who's happy that I'm happy.

Mom taps her fingers on the meeting-room table impatiently while we wait for the Reznikovs to arrive.

"Malachi found out about Mason," I tell Dad.

His shoulders drop. "I know. He was at the cemetery along from the manor yesterday. He found out by searching his name, and the news article about the crash came up."

"How do you know?"

He taps his nose and winks.

He must still have PIs on Malachi.

Ten minutes pass, and all I can do is stare at the door while everyone works.

Dad is typing on his laptop—he hasn't broken a breath to Mom. He doesn't even want this meeting to happen. He's been working with lawyers to figure out a way to have the agreement voided, but so far, it's impossible. And for some stupid reason, the termination clause only comes into play if both parties agree to not go ahead with the marriage.

Since Xander is adamant about proceeding, I'm so far screwed.

Regardless, I won't do it.

Abigail shifts beside me, checking her phone every two

seconds, her knee bouncing in anticipation. She's not supposed to be here—she doesn't work in this building, and Mom said she has no place in the meeting, but apparently the Reznikov brothers were happy for her to be here despite their parents' refusal.

Adryx is the one who calls the shots on this stuff—he said she could be here, and no one could overpower him. He's the brains and the muscle behind the Reznikovs' fortune and empire, but not the heir as some may assume. Something happened within the family and future ownership was passed to Xander.

The door opens, and my nerves plummet into a pit of lava.

First to walk in is Adryx and Xander's father, Igor Reznikov, with his wife Angelina. They're way older, both with gray hair, yet they've aged like fine wine. They look rich—Angelina gives me a warm smile as she sits in front of me, her husband beside her.

Adryx is next—he's tall with dark hair, and his fitted suit shows he works out. He greets us and sits beside my father, directly across from Abigail. He's watching her, no one else, and she keeps her eyes down as if she has no desire to be here anymore.

Xander clears his throat at the door—he's just a wanker with an ego problem who doesn't deserve a description.

My eyes narrow when the final person enters. He's just as tall as Adryx, with brown hair, and he isn't wearing a fitted suit like the others but a white shirt and dress pants, sleeves rolled up to flash an expensive watch.

However, they all look similar, definitely from the same family.

"Howdy," the last one says as he closes the door and sits.

Is he… Scottish? And a bit Russian? Is that even possible?

"This is my nephew Sebastian," Igor says. "He'll be acting as a bonder during this period until he returns home to Russia to deal with my father. He'll be the contact between families after this meeting is over."

Sebastian grins at everyone, folding his arms and leaning his elbows forward on the table. His knees are bouncing—I can tell from the way his body is moving. He's nearly as hyper as Molly. I think he might be the same age as me.

"Just pretend I'm not here," he says, popping gum in his mouth. "I know that'll be hard, considering I'm the good-looking one of the family."

Adryx rolls his eyes. "Shut the fuck up, Base."

"Nope."

Igor slams his hand down on the table. "Can we begin?"

Abigail still hasn't looked up, and Molly now looks nervous. She asks if she can leave, so I tell her to go to my office and I'll get her once we're done. She silently walks out.

Xander is quiet. His eyes are on the wall above my head. He looks pissed. And nervous.

The father and Adryx do all the talking.

Making arrangements for me to sign official documents.

Marriage certificates, as if I'm not sitting right here. Igor addresses me as his son's wife on multiple occasions, and then talks over my mother numerous times when she tries to explain that I'll stay in line and do what I agreed to do.

Whenever I try to talk, they ignore me.

Sebastian is drawing a face on a bit of paper, his legs still bouncing under the desk—he keeps popping bubbles with his gum.

Dad is growing annoyed. He's quiet. Probably waiting for them to finish so he can hit them with the legality of all this. He isn't a famous attorney for nothing.

Adryx and Xander keep looking at my best friend. Maybe she's rolling her eyes or huffing, that resting bitch face I've warned her about a million times putting a target on her back.

"We have all the documentation with us," Igor says in his accented drawl. "She may sign, and we will leave so our children can begin their new life together. There is no argument here, Mrs. Vize. Olivia will be leaving with us as soon as she signs on the dotted line."

I bark out a laugh. "Yeah right."

Mom grits her teeth. "Olivia," she reprimands. "Shut up."

My dad shakes his head. "Why don't we discuss this properly? I've worked on many, many cases in my life, so I have plenty of experience. Yes, my daughter signed an agreement but not the marriage certificate, and things can be altered. I already have a lot of issues with the contract." His eyes move to Xander. "What exactly is it you're getting from marrying Olivia? You have power and wealth. And going by your social media, you can have any woman or man you want, so why her?"

He smirks. "Maybe I'm in love with her."

Adryx pinches the bridge of his nose, and their cousin snorts.

Abigail clears her throat but says nothing.

"There is no solid deadline detailed in the contract. Olivia can marry you when you're ninety if she chooses to."

"You're going to get on my bad side, Mr. Vize."

Dad looks at Igor, silently telling him that he doesn't give a fuck if he gets on his bad side.

My father then glares at Xander. "Listen, you little fucking punk. You're not marrying my daughter. You'll stand up, take your brother and cousin and parents, and get the fuck out of my wife's building."

Igor tuts. "That's not very generous of you, Jamieson."

"Please," my mom begs, grabbing my father's arm. "This has been in agreement for months now."

"Behind me and our daughter's backs," he hisses then looks back at the Reznikovs. "Olivia isn't going with you. She's my daughter and will stay by my side."

Xander tilts his head. "You allow your son to fuck your daughter, so I think your view is a little distorted. If Olivia doesn't come willingly, force will be used."

My entire body sags, and my heart seizes on a final beat. "Is that a threat?" I spit.

"It's a promise, sweetheart."

"Get out," Dad warns. "All agreements are void, and if I need to, I'll take you to court for a harassment order to keep your family away from mine."

Igor glares at my mother. "We honored our side of the deal. We'll come back tomorrow to collect what belongs to my son."

She nods. "Yes, sir."

Dad leans forward. "Honored what?"

The Reznikovs take that as their cue to leave. The hyperactive one gets up first, opening the door for the older woman, winks at me, then vanishes. Adryx glances at Abbi before leaving, and then Xander and Igor exit, leaving the four of us in awkward silence.

"What the fuck was that about?"

Mom scowls at my dad. "None of your business, Jamieson."

"What did they already honor?"

"Nothing." She stands. "I'm going to take Molly out for food. Do you want me to drop you off at home?"

Dad tightens his jaw. "I want to know everything."

Sighing, she nods. "On the way."

He grabs my hand and squeezes. "I'll fix this."

I try to smile but fail. They all leave, and Abigail tells me she'll catch up with me later then jumps out to grab lunch from across the street.

The walk to my office somehow takes forever. I'm numb. Dizzy. Scared. I want Malachi. I need him.

I bristle when I get to my office and find Xander with his back to the door, staring out the window. "What do you want?" I ask.

"Close the door."

"No," I respond, opening the door wider as he turns to look at me. "You can leave."

"Despite all this messing around and arguing with my father, you are aware of the contract you already signed. For someone who works in a courthouse, you're pretty dense."

"I'm not marrying you. Now get the fuck out of my office before I call security."

He smirks, staring at me for far too long, then huffs out a laugh. "You've completely misjudged me, dear Olivia. No one will be throwing me out of my wife's office. In fact, I could drag you out kicking and screaming and no one would help you."

"I'm not your wife; nor will I ever be. You need to—"

"I could fuck you over your desk and no one would save you."

I pause, stepping back. "Like I'd ever go near you."

"We'll see."

"You can leave now." I keep my voice firm and controlled, though my hand is shaking as I tighten it around the doorknob.

And then his entire demeanor changes as his hands fist at his sides. "Don't get on my bad side, you little brat." He forces me to let go of the door, closing it with a click. "You will end your thing with your brother and sign the fucking marriage certificate."

Staring, I refuse to grace him with a response or question how he knows about my relationship with Malachi. If I show I'm scared, my fear will feed into his power. Men like him thrive on control—unlucky for him, I've had plenty of practice dealing with my mother, which has left me thicker skinned.

But deep down, fear is wrapping around all of my organs and strangling them, even as I tip my chin up. "I'd rather die than be your wife."

"You won't even deny that you're fucking your own sibling?" He narrows his eyes and shoves his hands into the pockets of his dress pants. "It's disgusting. Do you know what people will say about you when they find out? The Vize case went public, or do you forget? As soon as Malachi comes out of hiding, and the press catches on to what you two are doing, it'll be plastered everywhere."

My eyes sting, but I still stay silent. That was nearly a decade ago—people won't care what we do; they've probably forgotten all about the case by now.

He comes closer. "I wonder if he'll beg you to stay when you inevitably end things? Will he use his voice? Will he struggle for his words? My father will likely cut off his hands, so he'll have no way of communicating with you ever again."

I flinch as he comes even closer, leaning down so we're at eye level. "You put your brother behind bars, and now you're opening your legs for him. You're a fucking whore."

Despite my insides spiraling into a deep hole, the panic rising, my heart thumping in my chest, I manage to smack him across the face with a heavy palm, laugh lightly, and back away. "It's no wonder you need to pay someone to marry you given that you won't stop talking. How much did you offer my mother? One million? Two?"

He smirks and rubs his cheek. "My father paid her eleven million. Now do you understand why I need to do this?"

My stomach twists, this new betrayal burning at my insides. "You're an asshole, and no one would willingly give themself to you. Leave, or I'll make you."

Not that I could do a thing—he's six foot something and a wall of muscles. Thankfully it isn't his brother here taunting me; he's with his cousin waiting outside.

He glares at me—then smirks again. "Unless you want my father to send his men over to deal with your brother, stop fighting this."

Xander is tucking a lock of hair behind my ear while I stay as still as a statue, wondering if kneeing him in the balls will be more trouble than it's worth.

The door opens. Abigail pauses in the threshold, her eyes zoned into where Xander has my hair between his fingers.

He snatches himself away like it burned him then takes more steps back.

Confusion and a hint of something else takes over my friend's gaze before she turns around and runs out of the office.

Xander swears under his breath and goes after her.

I stand in solid silence, the pounding of my heart heavy in my ears, trying to make sense of what just happened, then hunch forward, trying to breathe. I had no idea I was holding my breath for so long—my eyes burn as they water, and I can feel my pulse hammering throughout my body.

I'm sweating, and I feel dizzy as I grab a bottle of water from the minifridge and down half of it in one. I reach for my phone, and then I pause.

I should tell Malachi—I should warn him that Xander isn't backing down and we should make a plan—we should run. I'm sure this need to marry me will vanish as soon as his father finds someone else to torment. They don't even know me—I'm a stranger to them.

But I sit back and dig my fingers into the leather of the chair. If I tell my brother, there's no doubt in my mind that Malachi will go into full-blown attack mode. He'll hunt Xander, and since he's a one-man army, Xander's father only needs to send one order out and he'll be dead within the hour.

My stomach twists, and I chew my bottom lip. It's too dangerous. He isn't the type to sit down and talk and then react. He shoved a bat down someone's throat and snapped Parker's legs when we were teenagers without thinking about the consequences. He attacked Adam. Dad.

What would he do to Xander? Or at least try to do? Xander is Russian, has tight security, and I think Adryx would rain hell on us both if something happened to his little brother.

Oh God.

I can't risk Malachi's life. I need to lie to him—again. Or withhold information. But he knows the meeting was today. What should I do? He's supposed to pick me up from work in a few hours.

I grab my bag, lock my office, and head to my mother's office to hunt for her spare keys. She always keeps a car here, just in case of emergency.

Right now, I guess it's an emergency for me to get home and start working with my dad on how to stop all of this. Then I can sit Malachi down, explain things, and how it'll be fixed. He won't need to react and hurt people.

It'll be fine.

I shoot Dad a message saying I'm heading over to talk.

As soon as I get out back, rain soaks my hair. I unlock Mom's car door, toss my bag into the passenger side, and close the door, then run around the front to get to the driver's side while trying to get my phone out of my pocket.

But a fist in my hair and a hand over my mouth snatches me

from my feet and drags me, kicking and screaming into a heavy palm, to a black car.

CHAPTER TWENTY-FOUR
MALACHI

Before I was arrested, me and the guys always hung out at Mason's place.

We'd be in the converted garage, getting high, gaming, fighting. It was our go-to when we weren't riding or at some sort of party.

I remember the first time he invited me over—his mom and dad were kind, loving people, and I hadn't a clue how they ended up with someone like Mason as a son. He wasn't even allowed to cuss in front of them, yet he was sneaking out, taking drugs, smoking weed, and fucking girls in their kitchen while everyone was asleep.

His mom tried to ask me if I wanted any lunch with faltering sign language. They were learning… For me.

A few months later, they were all fluent.

When I wasn't obsessing over my sister and her whereabouts, I'd be there, pretending I was normal, that people tolerated me because they chose to, not because they had to.

The same place that's all boarded up now.

Some of the windows are smashed, the grass long, bottles all over the yard. Despite being in an expensive neighborhood, the place looks like a wreck.

It's been vacant for eight years, despite the house still being owned by Mason's family—they left it here to rot along with the memory of their son.

It didn't take me long to find him. One single search for his name and town, and article after article flashed before me. My friend died the same night I was arrested. He was hit by a truck at high speed and died on impact.

Ever since my speech therapist brought up having a friend, I kept wondering what he was up to. I thought maybe he was married with kids, that he'd won that scholarship he was trying to get, or maybe he'd moved Down Under, living it up with the Australians and surfing and bathing in the sun.

Learning about his death made me wish I was numb—that I felt anything other than the raw pain of how much I'd hated him all these years, thinking he'd just left me in there to rot. He hadn't ever tried to see me, not that I would've accepted, but all along, Mason was dead.

Olivia has had multiple opportunities to tell me what happened—she could have, at any point, told me that Mason was gone. I hadn't mentioned him. I hadn't mentioned any of my friends to her since she came back to me, but surely, fucking surely, I deserved to know?

When I went to her office, I wanted to confront her—I wanted her to have a good reason for not telling me—but my anger, the terrified look in her eyes and tone of her voice, turned me on. I was going to spank her over her desk, but I ended up with my dick buried in her ass.

Her punishment was not being able to come, but I fucked myself with that when Abigail walked in. I would've kept going if Olivia let me—I would have screwed her right there, in front of an audience, to prove how much I owned her.

Abigail is lucky I didn't break her neck and throw her out of the fucking window.

I chew my lip and get back into my car—the drive back is about an hour. I need to pick Olivia up from work in a few hours, and I'm setting up a date.

She's desperate for it, so I've finally given in.

According to Google and online forums, most date nights consist of seeing a movie or going for dinner in a restaurant. At the start of relationships and getting to know someone, there are nerves, blushes, and, most of the time, they never see each other again.

They can sometimes lead to a second date, third, fourth, where they end up screwing each other's brains out then one ghosts the other. Or, on rare occasions, they end with the couple in a relationship, married, having a family, and all that bullshit.

My eyes were sore by the time I stopped my research.

By the time I reach home, the sun is setting. Still a few hours until I pick Olivia up. I hunt for candles, set them up on the coffee table, set out bowls of chips and various dips, and make sure the bottle of wine is in some ice.

See? I can be romantic when I'm not on a warpath of revenge. Thanks to Google and reading too many forums, I've taken notes on this shit.

I pause when an idea comes to me, and then I smirk to myself and head to my locked side room. It's filled with pictures and footage and TV screens. I took them out of my apartment while Olivia was at work and set them up here, making sure the cameras were on each route Olivia takes in life, including to and from the courthouse.

I've even hacked the security cameras of the coffee shop she goes to on the way to work.

I scan through the files on my computer and spot the one from years ago, from when we were teenagers and she was "teaching me" how to kiss and touch her. I watch it all, shaking my head at how ridiculous and shy I look while she's talking me through everything like I hadn't drugged her and fucked with her body already.

Back then, I thought I was muscular and inked—now I'm larger, my hair is longer, my ears are stretched, and I'm covered in tattoos. I think the old me would be terrified of who I've become, since I'm still as hung up on the same girl, obsessed to the point of danger, all these years later.

I was a bit of a dick back then—pretending I had no idea what I was doing despite practicing on her while she wasn't conscious. Should I even tell her about those times, or will she get mad that I lied about the whole "I have no idea what I'm doing" thing?

Technically, I was still clueless and needing lessons from her. But sticking my fingers in her holes while she was unaware and me not understanding the way her body reacted didn't exactly teach me.

Although she still got wet, moaned in her sleep, and she still tasted like fucking heaven when I sucked my fingers and licked her pussy.

The real thing is way better.

I land on a file labeled "Halloween" and click through different clips until I find one I know she'll love.

I freeze as one of the screens draws my attention. Olivia is rushing out the back of the courthouse, stopping at our mom's car. She looks like she's been panicking.

My spine straightens, my brow furrowing at her posture and worried look.

I narrow my eyes. Where the fuck is she going?

A car pulls up at one side, the driver jumping out and

grabbing her.

It takes a long second to realize this is real and some asshole is dragging my girl into their car with their hand over her mouth. She's kicking her legs out, trying to slap her attacker, but I'm on my feet and grabbing my keys as she vanishes into the car.

Rushing to my car, I pull my phone out to see where she is. I have a tracker in her phone, something I was worried about her discovering, but now I'm grateful for my paranoia.

The red dot is moving. Fast.

I set my phone in the holder, press the gas, and speed out of the drive, the car tilting onto two wheels from the tight turn before I straighten it up and accelerate down the dirt road.

Fuck.

I could lose her.

I refuse to lose her.

I can't. I fucking can't.

I grit my teeth as I follow the dot, trying to remain calm. Leaning over, keeping the car steady, I empty the glovebox to get my small toolkit and grab the screwdriver.

It's not the one I used on Olivia.

Someone is trying to take my girl from me, and the faster I catch up to the blip on the screen—which is turning onto a road that will take them into the forest—the louder my heart beats in my ears.

I don't have anyone's number to contact them. The only

person I have in my new phone is Olivia. Why don't I have my dad's number?

The dot stops in the middle of the woodland—I'm close, so I slow down until the car comes to a halt. If they hear me or see me coming, they'll drive off and it'll be another chase. Plus, they might be hurting her.

I grab my gas mask from the backseat, slide it on, and take a deep breath before making my way quietly out of the car, gripping the screwdriver in my hand. Each footstep draws me closer, my breathing heavy within the confines of the mask.

I hide behind a tree when I see the black car. They're still inside it, the window of the driver's side down. I can hear Olivia screaming. It's muffled, as if she's got tape on her mouth.

Tensing my jaw and taking another deep breath, I go straight towards the car. The driver is on the phone, Olivia lying on the backseat with her wrists bound and rope around her face and in her mouth.

Without hesitation, as soon as I reach the driver's side, I tighten my hand around the screwdriver and stab it into the asshole's neck over and over again, blood splattering all over me as he chokes, each thrust sending more blood over my mask and coating the steering wheel and windows. Warm liquid spits at me as he tries to breathe, gasping like a slaughtered animal.

I jab the screwdriver into his jugular and yank it out then drive it into his fucking eye.

He's dead already.

His head is hanging off, the flesh and butchered muscle keeping him from decapitation.

Motherfucker deserved worse. I should have taken him to the house and tortured him for even thinking he could take my girl.

Leaving him to slouch on the steering wheel while the soul drains from his body and soaks his leather seats in blood, I pull open the back door to find Olivia crying around the rope, screaming, a red mark under her eye.

That piece of shit hit her.

I'm too angry and losing it to speak. I can't give her any comforting words. I tuck the screwdriver into my back pocket and go to her. She doesn't question who I am. She knows. She saw this mask before when I took her and fucked her. A time I wish I'd dealt with differently, now that I know she could've eventually picked me, but I can't take any of it back.

I untie her and pull her into my arms tight, holding her, never wanting to let go as my heart ricochets all over my damn body. Without her, there wouldn't be any point in taking one more breath.

She cries into my shoulder—alive, here, with me. She's with me. She doesn't care that I'm covered in blood as she pushes the mask up and off my face and grabs my cheeks and kisses me.

Desperate. Each press of her lips is desperation—as if she's trying to tell herself that this is all real and I'm here, in front of her, and she's not being taken.

"Oh God," she sobs. "He works for the Reznikov family. They… they tried to kidnap me. They'll… they'll try again."

I shake my head, unable to talk or get my words out given how much adrenaline is rushing through me.

I won't let them take her.

I can already feel the crimson staining my skin starting to dry. His blood is all over the car. Evidence of his murder. Fuck. I just killed him and haven't got a single plan. I usually do this carefully. I make sure they can't be found. I create a story. I have files upon files in my locked room of different strategies to remove someone from existence. But this… this is bad.

"Someone is coming," she tells me. "He was on the phone to a man. I couldn't hear what he was saying. We need to go."

I glance over at my car, hidden behind bushes, then at the body in the driver's seat.

Help me put him in the trunk, I sign. *I have a plan.*

"Okay," she replies quietly, wiping tears from her cheeks.

Olivia is barely any help. She drops his head on the ground while I hold his feet, shrugging when I glare at her. Then she stands aside, shaking, with a dead man's blood on her hands as she hugs herself.

She covers her mouth. "I think I'm going to be sick." Then turns and vomits all over the ground.

I shove him in the trunk, slam it shut, and go to Olivia, who's hunched over still. Pushing her hair behind her ears and grabbing it all in a fist, I hold it back until she finishes bringing up her lunch.

She wipes the back of her hand across her mouth. "Oh God. What do we do? We're going to get into so much trouble and they'll send you back to prison. Malachi... I can't lose you again. I'd rather be dead than lose you again."

No one is dying, I sign. *I have a plan.* Then while sliding my thumb over the mark under her eye, my nostrils flare. *What did he do to you?*

"I managed to knee him in the balls, so he punched me."

I grit my teeth and glare at the trunk, wishing I could bring him back to life so I can kick his ass before killing him again.

"Look at me. I'm fine." She rubs my cheek, running her thumb across my lips, coating them in red. "Tell me your plan."

Nervously, I stand at the entrance of Vize Manor.

Olivia is beside me, holding my hand tight, rubbing her thumb over my skin to reassure me that everything will be okay. I can't go back to prison. Especially for murder. I refuse.

The door opens.

Mom frowns, her face growing paler by the second when she sees Olivia, and how we're both covered in blood.

"We need help," Olivia tells her. "Someone tried to kidnap me."

"Oh. What happened?"

Why isn't she more concerned?

Dad appears at the door, tilting his head and pausing when he notices the mess on both his children. "What's the meaning of this?"

Our fingers slip apart as Olivia runs for our father, burying her head in his chest as she sobs and cries and shakes. He's confused yet holds her back anyway, lifting his gaze to me. Given the look in his eye, he thinks I did something.

My shoulders slump as her words fail and all we're left with is silence beyond my little sister's crying.

I need your help.

Mom laughs. "You must be joking. Why in the world would we help you?" she sneers, looking at me in disgust. "You're not welcome here. Get the hell away from our house before I call the cops."

Dad stops the door with his walking stick as my mom tries to close it in my face, shutting me out from Olivia.

She points at me, stepping right into my face yet speaking to my dad. "He tried to kill you and now he's hurt Olivia! We aren't entertaining him. He's no longer our son." Then her eyes burn into my soul. "You were my biggest mistake. You should have stayed in the system and messed up someone else's family. Or better yet, you should have died with your mother."

I can't hit her. But fuck do I want to.

"How dare you," Olivia snaps, stepping away from Dad. She takes my hand again, showing she's with me. "Don't ever speak to him like that again."

"I've heard enough." Dad glances between us then at Mom. "Leave us be."

"Excuse me?"

When he doesn't respond, only glares, she scowls at me, then huffs and walks away.

I want to rip her apart.

When she goes to work tomorrow, I hope she gets hit by a damn truck and dies slowly.

"What happened?" Dad asks.

"Someone tried to kidnap me, and Malachi killed them. The man's body is in the trunk, and we don't know what to do."

Dad looks at me, and I don't blink, waiting for his lecture, waiting for him to call the cops or tell me how much of a headcase I am, but doesn't do any of that.

He's quiet for far too long, and I grow anxious. My hand sweats in Olivia's, and I break eye contact and stare at the ground.

"We'll need to dispose of the body and destroy any evidence."

I look up with wide eyes.

Olivia covers her mouth on a sob and throws herself into him once more. She hugs him, thanking him over and over again while he rubs her back. His eyes lift to me, but I lower my gaze again so it's fixed on my boots—which are covered in a dead man's blood.

I have no right to ask for his help. I don't deserve any of it. He's the way he is because of me. I attacked him. I put him in a coma, gave him brain damage, and, ultimately, ruined his entire life.

I gulp and fist my hands.

Maybe Mom was right? Maybe if they didn't adopt me, their life would be way easier. If fate was real, I would've found Olivia regardless of which family took me in, if any did at all.

"Do you have anywhere to hide him for now?"

I nod, but I don't lift my eyes.

He follows behind me on the way home. Him and Olivia in his car while she drives, and I take the car filled with enough evidence to lock me up for the rest of my life back to the farmhouse. I have the guy's phone, his wallet, and a random set of keys with a keyring of him and someone I assume is his wife.

I don't feel bad.

He tried to take what belonged to me.

I pull in and reverse the car as far back as I can to the backyard—it's dark now, and it's starting to rain, but I have flashlights we can use.

Dad doesn't blink at the home me and Olivia have been living in—as if he already knows. Olivia helps him out of the car and gives him his stick, then the three of us hunt for a flashlight while everyone stays quiet.

Olivia is about to find out a huge secret I've kept from her.

That I have bodies buried in the backyard.

Fuck, why am I nervous?

Dad being here doesn't help. If I dig in the right place, they might not notice the other body bags. I've made more than enough bags to last a lifetime, and when I pull one out, Dad watches me in silence.

While Olivia showers, I lift the body from the trunk, stuff it into the bag, and tape it up. Rigor mortis is already setting in, so the guy is a bit stiff and heavy as I carry him to the yard and drop him.

Still, Dad doesn't say a word as I start digging a hole. He doesn't need to be out here with me. He could sit inside, sheltered from the storm, instead of all this awkward silence.

Rain is soaking my skin, saturating the blood and making it slide down my body. After twenty minutes, I have to remove my shirt from how hot I am—sweat coats my skin, mixing with the rain, and still, Dad watches me without saying a word.

It's better if we don't talk. We don't like each other. There wouldn't be anything to say, other than him asking me to leave Olivia and me telling him to fuck off.

My shovel hits something hard, and I swear when I notice the body I forgot to bag. It's decomposed—been hidden in the dirt for about two months now, so it's mostly bone.

I pause and stare, my lips flattening as I lift my gaze to my father.

He's staring at his killer son, the murderer, the abusive asshole, yet he isn't being judgmental or giving me shit.

"We won't tell Olivia, but this is the last one."

I roll my jaw. Who the fuck is he to tell me who to kill and not to kill? If someone gets in my way, they deserve a shallow grave in my yard.

Despite wanting to tell him to mind his business, I toss the shovel, climb up to the surface, and roll the body into the hole.

Even though he can barely walk without his stick, Dad helps me fill the hole with dirt. He's only doing this for my sister. He can't stand me. I'm the reason he can't walk properly.

"I don't know if I can ever forgive you," he tells me. "But I'll try."

I flinch as his hand lands on my shoulder. He pats me twice, then slides his hand off me and goes to turn around.

"Dad," I say, my nerves taking over when he pauses. I rub my fist against my chest with more meaning than ever. *I'm sorry.*

"I know, son."

Walking back to the house, I stand in the middle of the kitchen while Olivia talks to Dad—they're discussing our next steps and how he's going to protect her, possibly send her to a safe house.

I pull the phone from my pocket. The screen is cracked at the corner, but it still works. There's a preview of a message from hours ago that has me frowning.

Unknown

> Igor will meet you at the destination in exactly one hour.

There's no passkey or fingerprint scanner, so I unlock the phone with a swipe of my thumb, open the chat box with the unsaved number, and see they're discussing an exchange with Igor Reznikov for a fee of five thousand dollars for delivery of the "package".

My dad comes up beside me, staring at the screen too. "Motherfuckers," he mutters. "This has gotten out of hand!"

I call the number and place it on speaker for everyone to hear.

"What happened? I told you not to call this number," a voice says.

The voice of Jennifer Vize.

The woman who raised us.

CHAPTER TWENTY-FIVE
OLIVIA

I t feels like déjà vu, watching Malachi wash blood from his body.

We're teenagers again, and he's just saved me from Parker. Except this time, he saved me from our own mother.

I can still hear the man's strangled choking as Malachi drove a screwdriver into his throat repeatedly. I can hear the blood splattering on the windows, how he fought to stay alive, even though his head was nearly hanging off.

I can still see the way Malachi looked at me when I slid his mask off—his eyes were a void, like he was close to drowning in his own mind from panic, but the tether we have between us kept him above the surface.

Dirt and blood slips down his muscles, and I stretch onto my tiptoes, pressing my lips to his. "Thank you."

He frowns, signing, *Why are you thanking me?*

"You saved me."

Malachi chuckles deeply, audibly, clearly, as he walks me into the tiles of the shower wall. His head tilts, causing his black hair to fall over his forehead, a smile playing on the lips I can't stop staring at.

Clear as day, he speaks. "I'm your partner. Your lover. Your brother. Your everything, Olivia." Then he lifts his slightly stained hands to sign, *But what you are to me is something more than any words can explain. If someone found a way to remove you from existence, I would burn the world before making sure my soul found yours in the afterlife.*

"How poetic of you, Malachi." I smile at him. "You're my boyfriend, not my brother."

His eyes pinch at the corners as he narrows them, his hands lowering to my ass, grasping each cheek as he closes the distance between us—his body presses mine up against the tiled wall, his cock stabbing into me.

"And we're going to stop referring to each other as siblings," I add.

He shakes his head, looking like I've suggested we break up given the way he's glaring at me. He's so easily annoyed. A man with a short fuse.

To annoy him further, I slide my hands up his chest, wrap my arms around his shoulders, and fist his hair. "Tell me I'm your girlfriend. Tell me you aren't my brother."

He shakes his head again, this time with a firm jaw. Despite the anger in his eyes, his cock jerks against my navel, and I rub myself against it, needing him to touch me, to take away the memory of someone trying to kidnap me. I need him to replace the hand over my mouth with his lips, to make me feel anything but the paranoia and sickness in my gut.

"You need to choose, Malachi." I lick my lips, arching my back. "I'm either your sister, or I'm your girlfriend."

I've mentioned this before, but he really does need to choose because we can't go around labeling each other as partners *and* siblings.

His eyes flash, his jaw so tense I think his bones might break as his hand slips up to my neck, grasping my throat. "Both," he grits then slams his mouth against mine, his thumb pressing into my pulse as his tongue delves past my lips, tasting the moan leaving my lungs.

"I need you." I take him in my hand, feeling him grow in my grip. "Please."

This isn't slow and romantic. It never is with Malachi. He lifts me into his arms and wraps my legs around his waist, fisting my hair to tip my head, kissing me deeper as he pushes into me.

Hard. Fast. Abrupt. He fucks me against the wall, dragging whimpers from my lips as he kisses me the total opposite from the way he's thrusting into my pussy. He drags his mouth to the corner of my lips, my jaw, along to the sensitive area below my ear and nips the skin, making me flinch and clench around his cock.

"I love you," I whisper into his ear.

He lifts his head, still buried deep, then groans as he shuts off the water and carries me into the bedroom. He slides out, throws me onto the bed, and shuts off the light so only the moon shining through the window glows on his face.

"I love you too," he replies firmly, as if the words were hard to say instead of signing. He's trying so hard for me and for himself.

I smile as he climbs on top of me, parting my legs around him.

"Put my legs on your shoulders."

He hesitates as he takes one of my legs, and I can see it all over his face. He doesn't have a clue what he's doing. This man has tied me up, fucked me in chains, fucked me unconscious, fucked me against walls and on all fours, even over our dying father's body, and this is what he struggles with?

It's not even the position. There's something else there. His entire posture stiffens.

"You haven't done it that way before?" I ask.

He looks away from me, but I force him to give me his eyes as I grab his jaw. "Hey. Talk to me."

I've only ever fucked you, remember? His signing is angry, his eyes even worse, and my mouth closes.

"I'm sorry."

A silent beat passes, his grip tightening on my leg, and he gulps deeply.

Show me, he signs.

I don't want him to feel embarrassed. His cheeks are going bright red and he's closing off on me.

I nod slightly, chewing my bottom lip as I lift my other leg, resting both on his shoulders. "Wrap your arms around them and hold the sides of my thighs with the opposite hands."

Tentatively, Malachi does as I tell him, and his fingers dig into my flesh, his cock twitching against my slit. I reach down between my legs and take him in my palm, pumping him in the fist while rubbing his precum-soaked head against me.

His chest is rising and falling, the grip on my thighs growing harsher, especially when I position him right where he wants to be.

Like he wasn't inside me minutes ago, I'm desperate for him, but I want him to take his time. I want him to be comfortable.

I know what he's like. He's going to be in his head right now, thinking about how this is obviously a position I've done before. And I hate myself. I hate that he's not the only man I've been with, that I didn't fight harder for him.

I truly believe I'm the only person Malachi has even as much as looked at in a sexual way—it makes me feel special.

"Push your hips forward," I say. "Slowly."

I gasp as he eases the head of his cock into me, his piercings rubbing against my glistening pussy. Each inch that pushes into me, from this position, feels deeper than every other position.

I'm open for him as he slides in to the hilt, keeping himself buried as he closes his eyes and groans.

He's not even wearing a condom—I've been trying to tell him to, considering where we both stand in terms of having children. I'm starting to hate the idea that I'll never become a mother, but I'd never put something like that on him when he doesn't want it. Ever. He's more important to me than anything else in the world.

I arch my back as he fucks into me faster, a spiraling heat coiling in my spine as he sucks his bottom lip into his mouth, watching himself slide in and out of me.

"Fuck," he groans. "Fuck, Olivia."

My hands fist the sheets as he goes harder, my moan probably waking the dead for miles while the headboard smacks the wall.

He releases my legs and covers my body with his to kiss me. His hands fist my hair, tugging harshly as he devours my lips and groans and grunts into my mouth.

My eyes start to roll as he hits the spot that has me seeing stars. My body tenses, my arms wrapping around him, my heels digging into his ass to draw him deeper. "Keep going," I cry, sinking my teeth into his lip and releasing it with a painful snap. "K-Keep going."

Malachi buries his head into my shoulder and lets out a deep moan as my orgasm has my inner walls clenching around the thickness of his cock. I tense all over, my nails ripping into the skin of his back as I shake beneath him.

He pauses, his cock pulsing inside me, filling me with every drop of his cum until we're both breathless.

My eyes suddenly start to water, and after a few moments, he straightens his arms to look down at me. I blink away the tears, refusing to think about the last twelve hours.

He grabs my jaw to stop me from looking away, drawing his face near.

"Stop crying," he tells me, whispering the words against my lips as we both pant from our highs.

The betrayal is lodged deep in my bones. I always knew my mom wasn't a good person, but to do what she did…

I can't describe the way I truly feel.

Dad had his driver pick him up and take him straight home. He was going to confront our mother and put an end to all of this. She's been the catalyst to this arranged marriage from the beginning.

First, she accepts millions from Xander's family for my hand in marriage, then she fights every step of the way when I beg her not to make me do it, then she arranges for me to be kidnapped and taken to the Reznikov family to be used and abused and wedded to an asshole who'll do nothing but bring me hell.

I hate her.

I'm done with that woman.

Dad is desperate to hide us. He wants us to run. To stay away until he fixes everything. Malachi is in total denial about running. He wants to fight for me. I could see the calculating look in his eyes. He's never going to run. He's going to stay and fight for my freedom with every ounce of his being, and that terrifies me.

Malachi kisses my cheeks. "Please. Stop crying."

I nod, sighing as he drops his head to my chest and hugs me.

When we eventually sit up, Malachi gazes over at me with his back against the headboard, watching as I run my fingers through my hair. I give him a questioning look when he doesn't do anything but stare at me.

"What?"

I don't know if I've ever really told you, but you're beautiful.

The blush running over my cheeks and down my chest has me trying to hide my nervous smile. I don't know why that melted my insides and made me a puddle on the floor. Malachi has always been expressive with me, but being told by someone like him that I'm beautiful is something I wish I'd recorded to watch over and over again.

I go to him, and he flips us so he's above me, grabs my face, and lowers his to mine. His lips press to the tip of my nose, my forehead, each eye to soak up the tears, then he kisses me on the mouth.

For some reason, I feel safe. I know that we'll be okay.

Malachi's struggles with his mental health and me being targeted by the Reznikov family will only be stepping stones for us. I'll help him adjust to his new life—he'll help me adjust to mine. We'll be fine because we love each other to death.

"You're… mine," he says, falling over his words.

"And you're mine."

I don't know how to beat them, he signs, his nostrils flaring, angry at his own words. *I'm one man. But I'll fight. For you, I'd do anything.*

"We'll fight them together. No matter how dangerous it gets." I tilt my head, giving a slight smile. "I'd die for you—do you know that?"

He frowns. *I wouldn't let you die for anyone. Not even me.*

Wrapped in each other's arms, we lie in a warm embrace. He buries his head into my shoulder, and I brush my fingers through the hair at his nape, feeling him go heavy on top of me as sleep starts to pull him under.

Then he flinches and sits up, glancing over his shoulder at the sound of footsteps. Turning to me, he presses his finger to his lips before getting off the bed and grabbing his bat.

Oh God. Please tell me they haven't come for me?

"Olivia?" our dad calls, and my shoulders slump in relief.

Malachi's body relaxes, then he tosses the bat to the floor. He runs his hands through his hair and shakes his head at the second voice.

"Are they home?" I hear Molly ask. "Can I see the spider?"

CHAPTER TWENTY-SIX
MALACHI

I f this girl keeps trying to open Cordelia's tank, I might need
to put a padlock on it and set some boundaries. She's in my
room, touching all my shit while she asks me far too many
questions that go unanswered.

Olivia sits on the bed I just fucked her on, trying not to
laugh at the look on my face when she knocks her fist on the
glass and asks to hold her.

I glare at Olivia, silently begging her to help.

"She's asleep," she tells her. "Maybe Malachi can show her
to you when she's awake?"

Absolutely fucking not.

Molly grins. "Okay! I'm going to ask Dad when we're
ordering pizza!" Then she skips out of the room.

Ordering pizza? To my damn house?

What is this?

Olivia hugs me from behind. "I think you're starting to

like her."

I grunt and pull her arms from me, spinning her round to my front. Her eyes are still glazed from her orgasm, her cheeks flushed, and her eyes are red and puffy. I'm surprised Molly didn't ask her why she'd been crying, since it's very obvious. I think the teenager was more interested in seeing my pet than anything else.

"You look worried," she says.

Flattening my lips, I shake my head, tucking strands of hair behind her ears. *Come on,* I sign. *Before she breaks something.*

Olivia fixes her clothes to make sure Dad isn't going to know we just fucked around, then kisses my cheek and takes the lead. I watch her ass like I used to do when I was a teenager. This time, I can lean forward and grab it, making her muffle a scream and slap my hand away.

Dad is sitting at the dining table, his head in his hand, while Molly texts on her phone and chews on her gum. She blows a bubble, pops it, then continues to tell our father that she's going to the mall with friends tomorrow.

"What's the plan?"

"Your mother is gone," Dad says.

Olivia frowns. "Gone as in… she left?"

"I told her to leave. She won't be an issue any longer. I've sent documentation to the Reznikovs to inform them we'll be pursuing harassment and attempted kidnapping charges if they continue to push my buttons. In the meantime," he says, looking up at us, "you're both leaving."

"Leaving?" Olivia replies while I sit down, spreading my legs and crossing my arms. There's no point in me having any input. He'll want her to leave for her protection—nothing to do with me.

"Both you and Malachi aren't safe here. I'm going to get you out of town without Igor finding out."

"What about you and Molly?"

Molly pops another bubble and looks up from her phone. She probably wants to know too.

Before Dad can reply, there are three knocks on the front door.

Getting to my feet instantly, I give Olivia a look that tells her to stay where she is as I make my way to the door.

I swing it open, frowning at the random guy I've seen hanging around Adryx and Xander. His eyebrows rise, then he smiles like we're best friends. "You must be Malachi. Can I call you Kai?" He reaches his hand out, but someone grabs his wrist and drags him away.

"There's no time for this shit. If my father finds out we're here, it'll be my fucking head next."

Adryx Reznikov is standing beside Abigail, both of them staring right through me. He speaks again. "Malachi, this is Sebastian—my idiot cousin who just killed one of my father's closest allies and the main reason why he's in a bad-enough mood to send about forty people here to collect Olivia. They've been ordered to kill everyone else on sight."

I blink, staring at them, unsure if I should try to kill them or to question whether or not I'm high, because why is there a Russian Scot at my front door with the brother of the man who's trying to steal my girl? And why the fuck is Abigail here?

"So you all need to leave," Abigail says as she pushes past me and goes straight to Olivia. "Igor is sending people here. Right now. You need to run. We have somewhere you can go."

Adryx takes up the entire doorway as he walks in, his cousin in tow with a goofy grin as he tries to defend himself.

Olivia frowns, looking over at me, Dad holding Molly close to him. He's unsure of their presence, as am I.

"We can't be caught here," Adryx says, pulling out his phone and going to stand by my father. "Go to this location. My father doesn't know it exists and won't think to check there. Take the girl too. They'll kill all of you and take Olivia."

I don't trust them, I sign to my dad.

"It doesn't matter if you trust me or not. If you don't leave in the next twenty minutes, you're as good as dead."

His cousin, Sebastian, crosses his arms with a frown. "How did you know what he said?"

"I know sign language." Adryx doesn't look at him as he sends my father the location. When he glances up to see

Sebastian scowling in confusion, he sighs. "Someone close to me is deaf. Do I need to explain more, or can we fucking leave before my father's men storm the place and finds us conspiring against him?"

"There's no one deaf in our family. You don't have friends either."

"Shut up, Base."

The other guy shuts his mouth and rolls his eyes. "This is too dramatic for a Tuesday." He narrows his eyes on me. "So you really can't talk?" he asks, and I imagine slicing him into pieces—slowly. "Or do you prefer being mute and mysterious to attract your little sister?"

Adryx shoves him. "I'd be careful speaking to him like that. He's more the act now, think later type." His eyes shift to my dad momentarily—he must know what I did to him and why he struggles to walk.

A pang of guilt hits me again. I never felt bad before—he made me snap. He made me react the way I did. If he hadn't hated me my entire time in the Vize house, then I wouldn't have lost my head and attacked him.

I think.

Adryx clears his throat, grabbing my attention. *I apologize for my cousin's ill manners*, he signs. *He's a dick.*

I think I like this guy, but I hate Base—he's like an insane little puppy who won't fucking stop. Images of me kicking him off a cliff keep springing to mind, and I might need to do just that.

"I think I could take him," Base stupidly says.

I narrow my eyes, silently telling him to fucking try it.

"I think he'd fight me if I tried to fuck his girl."

"That's my goddamn daughter," Dad snaps.

"Please just ignore him," Adryx says. "Your cars are all bugged. You need to take mine, and we'll have my driver pick us up at the end of the forest."

"I'm going with them," Abigail adds, hooking her arm into Olivia's.

"The fuck you are," Adryx retorts. "I'll drag you out of here kicking and screaming."

Why are you helping us?

He shrugs. "I hate my father, and he's using my little brother for power. I want to wipe him out and his empire. You have no idea what it's like being a Reznikov child. We're untouchable, but at a price."

Base whistles. "As I said, dramatic. Can we leave? I think Kai might kill me if I stand in his vicinity any longer."

I mentally kill him, chopping the little asshole into cubes of flesh and feeding him to a wild dog. His mouth annoys me, his accent is giving me a headache, and I think if he keeps giving me that goofy look, I might hit him.

The older Reznikov brother turns to me. *If you don't trust me, trust that I won't do anything to risk my girl losing her best friend.*

Both Olivia and I glance at Abigail.

They'll kill the young girl too. Keep her safe. They're animals.

No one is getting anywhere near Molly. Over my dead fucking body. She's a pest, but she's my little sister.

Checking his phone, his lips flatten. "You have fourteen minutes."

With that, Adryx gives Abigail a firm look until she huffs and goes with him, and Sebastian grins at me as they leave through the back door.

Olivia covers her mouth. "Oh God."

Dad shoves his phone into his pocket and grabs his walking stick. "My driver won't make it here in time. Molly, grab your bag. You two don't have time to pack."

I chew my lip, deciding whether to go with them or stay and fight. I've never been one to shy away from a threat, and I'm not a runner. I didn't even run from the officers when they came to arrest me.

"You're leaving with us." Olivia takes my hand tight, squeezing it. "I won't leave without you. Like you said, he has an army and you're one man. It's suicide, and I need you. We all need you."

Dad steps forward. "This isn't up for debate, Malachi. Move."

For once, I don't want to hit my dad or tell him to go fuck himself. The worried look in his eyes means he fears for me.

Which is insane and confusing because the guy should hate me more than anything.

Molly is watching me. Her eyes are glazing over, and she's terrified. A part of me, maybe the big brother in me, wants to keep her safe the most. She's my little sister, and it's my job to protect her. I already failed at being a brother to Olivia. I'm not going to do that a second time.

My nostrils flare at the thought of someone hurting either of my sisters.

I can't leave Cordelia here either.

What the fuck do I do?

When I give in, I go to the front door first to check if the area is still clear and safe for us to run into the woods.

As soon as I open the door, pain lashes at the side of my head—someone's swung a metal pole at me, knocking me into the door frame. Then a foot connects with my chest, and I'm thrown back as air rushes painfully from my lungs.

"Malachi!" Olivia yells as I try to get up. Someone grabs a fistful of my hair when I get to my knees, but I shove my elbow into their face to get them off me.

I get to my feet and back myself into the kitchen, where Molly and Olivia are hiding behind Dad as loads of suited-up men in white masks flood the house.

Some have guns, some have blades, and some have bats and poles and other weapons.

Fuck.

"Grab her," I hear someone say in a Russian accent. "Kill the rest."

"Run!" I yell at Olivia.

A gunshot goes off, and I see my dad go down.

It's the only warning I get before I grab Molly and run with her. They'll shoot her, and I refuse to let anyone hurt this hyperactive teenage kid. She's crying as I pull her into the washroom, pulling the washer out the way to open the small hatch and pushing her in.

Stay here, I sign, but the lost look on her face tells me she hasn't a clue what I've said. "Stay," I force out, and she nods.

But when I turn round, someone grabs me by the throat and a fist jabs into my side. It burns, and the gasp I let out has me glancing down to see a blade plunged into my side.

Gritting my teeth through the inferno ripping through me where the metal is lodged, I grab the asshole by the shoulders and drive my head into his nose, breaking it instantly. He lets out a painful groan, silenced by my head driving into his again, knocking him to the ground.

I hold my side, the warm liquid seeping through my clothes, and yank out the blade, hunching over at the pain. Fuck. It's like I've been punched with fire and it's lashing all around me, my breaths coming out as pants. I screw my eyes shut, grip the handle of the blade, and slice it across the guy's throat.

Leaving him there to bleed to death, I drag the washer back in front of the hatch to keep Molly hidden, then go into the front room to find Olivia.

I freeze when I see her and Dad on their knees with guns pointed at their heads. Dad has blood coming from his leg, his nose bleeding, but Olivia is untouched. No one has hurt her.

Molly is safe. No one will find her where she is. At least I managed to keep one of my sisters safe.

Igor Reznikov chuckles, pulling a toothpick from his mouth and tossing it. "Kill him."

The first thing I hear is Olivia's screams—then the sound of a gunshot right in front of me. There's a second smack of pain to my chest that knocks me right back. My ears ring instantly, yet I can hear Olivia screaming louder, even though it's like she's growing further away.

I try to sit up, to get to Olivia, but I fall back down.

"Leave them. We got what we came for."

"You motherfucker!"

A second gunshot goes off, but I'm unable to move as I stare at the ceiling. It's morphing into different shapes, like a kaleidoscope.

Get up. I need to get up.

My dad is grabbing at my face, his palm pressing to my chest—it burns, as if I've been punched with a fiery fist.

"No, no, no. Please, son. Please open your eyes. Malachi!"

Someone's begging for me to stay—then another, softer voice is there. Younger. It's not Molly. It's a memory.

Behind my gaze, flashing in and out of images, I see Olivia grinning at me and holding up seven fingers in her princess dress.

The image distorts, and I'm being pushed on a swing.

"Will we go for some ice cream?" I hear as the world darkens around me.

"You're such a good kid, Malachi," the darkness says, echoing and falling into the distance as my mind goes silent.

CHAPTER TWENTY-SEVEN

OLIVIA

The wallpaper is curling at the corner. My fingertips glide over it, tearing it a little as I continue walking the length of the bedroom I've been trapped in for the last three weeks. Round and round I go. Over and over again. Like a toy race car on one of those tracks kids get at Christmas—as basic as they come. That's me. One foot in front of the other, as my fingers guide me where I need to go. My eyes are closed. I won't walk into anything—there's only a bed in here, and the small bathroom with no window for me to escape through.

One step. Two steps. Three steps. Four.

If I focus on my breaths and the sound of my feet shuffling on the carpet, I can make up a song in my head. An imaginary drum, a bass, a singing voice mixed with a guitar that's actually someone using a drill nearby in the manor.

Manor.

It's not a manor at all. It's a prison. My prison. An old

asylum bought over by the Reznikovs nearly a hundred years ago that's been refurbished into a fancy fortress with too much security and non-stop parties. A home that will be passed down for many generations.

They need an heir—Igor demands one. Xander hates the idea of being in my vicinity despite the war he caused to get me here, and Adryx has disappeared. He was caught helping us, and now he and his cousin have been in hiding. So it's safe to say Igor has so far gotten nowhere in his plan after kidnapping me and shooting my father and brother.

Dad took a bullet to the leg, and while I was being dragged out by the hair, Malachi was shot. He was already bleeding heavily from his side—but he must be alive.

He can't be dead. I would know. Igor or Xander would throw it in my face if they'd murdered him—they'd make a party of it.

Malachi is alive. I refuse to believe otherwise.

I only know about Adryx from Xander's secret phone calls to his banished brother through the night when he thinks I'm unconscious. They don't think I know, after the first night, that they crush pills into my night-time glass of water.

I pretend to drink it. There's a section of the carpet under the bed that's soaked with drug-laced water. The first night, Igor forced Xander into the room and locked it—he warned him to get the job done while I was struggling to stay awake, and I'm certain I heard him telling me to breathe and to stop panicking, that I was safe.

I swayed, fell on my ass, and woke up the next morning.

I didn't feel violated. He hadn't touched me. Xander was threatened again because there was no proof he had, and my mother suggested Igor send in a witness with him—that I'd crack under pressure, though Xander refused.

She's a dirty traitor.

I hope she dies. I hope Malachi kills her, and Dad forgives him for it.

I hate Xander too, but the longer I'm here, the more I realize he's a product of his environment and only trying to please his father—he's controlled greatly, hates the idea of being forced to be with me, and spends a long time staring at himself in the bathroom mirror with a drained look on his face.

He gets to take over Reznikov Industries if he finds a wife and has her push out the first grandchild. His reward. The only thing he seems to think he needs to focus on.

He's failed for years, and Adryx wasn't given a second look for some reason, so Igor paid my mother millions because he heard she used to sell her daughter.

My fingers pause on the wall, my head tilting to listen. I never know if it's real. There are voices. Sounds. Music. Laughter. I can't make out words, as if I'm trapped down in the basement or up in the attic, far away from life.

Xander throws a lot of parties. One night, when I was bored, I watched him scroll through pictures while he sat on the bed beside me. He's a womanizer, that much is obvious, but he has a touchy spot when it comes to Abigail. I asked him a few days ago if I could see her, and he went deathly pale and could barely get his words out before shouting at me to stop trying to be his friend.

He only comes here to sleep—or yell at me to walk down the aisle since I keep refusing. When I only refuse more, he tells me I'm making his life harder then leaves me here, all alone, with only the voices in my head and in the walls keeping me sane.

I won't marry him. I've stood my ground on that. Igor has tried to blackmail me. If I don't marry his son and combine our wealth and power, he'll hurt my mom. When that didn't work, because fuck my mom, he said that if he ever finds my father, he'll make me watch him being murdered.

All I got from that is my father is hiding too. Maybe with Malachi?

Xander's father is a powerful man. It makes sense for my dad and Malachi to hide. Would Molly be with them since Mom is here, in the manor?

They might be working on a plan to save me. And maybe Malachi needs more time to recover. It's only been three weeks.

I'm terrified of Igor. I was always scared of Xander, but his father is a monster compared to him.

He slapped me across the face and ordered Xander to take me to his bedroom and deal with his future wife. I've been here ever since. Within these four walls with peeling wallpaper, no window to see what time of day it is, and the only time I eat is when a little old lady brings me my meals.

I pause walking again when the door opens, inwardly begging the world that it isn't Igor. He recently told Xander that if he doesn't get the job done, then he'll do it himself.

When I first got here, I used to jump and go into defense mode. I'd shy away into the corner while Xander took all the good energy in the room and tainted it with his presence until I realized he wasn't the real enemy. I mean, he was, still is, but it's not the same now I know he's being forced. Like I was when I was a kid.

I glance over my shoulder to see a tall Reznikov running his hands through his hair. I look to the side of him, to see out into the hallway, the faraway window showing me it's night-time.

Xander sighs and shuts the door, locking it, then removes his tie and tosses it on the bed we're made to share.

My shoulders slump as I relax. I'm not hiding or begging him to let me go like the first week—I simply turn my head away again and continue walking along the edge of the room, tracing my fingers over the wallpaper.

He says something, but I block him out, counting my steps, humming to myself as I focus on the way the wallpaper feels under my fingertips.

"Has my father broken you already?"

I freeze, dragging my gaze to him. I say silent, but anger runs through me, probably obvious in my expression.

"Good. Being mad means you can still feel, so you aren't a complete shell. He wants us to attend a charity event this weekend," he says, unfastening the buttons of his shirt. "I'm sure you miss being outside of this room. Will you attend with me and behave? You are supposed to be marrying me, so we can't have you being a nuisance in public."

My teeth grind. "I'm not marrying you."

He pinches the bridge of his nose. "Making this more difficult helps neither of us." Then he pulls off his belt and drops it on the ground. "You look like shit. Go shower and wash your hair."

When I don't move, he takes a step towards me. "Unless you want me to drag you in there and do it myself? We still have loads of areas to explore with our new relationship."

"We have no relationship, and you're not going to touch me. We both know that."

He glares at me, his jaw tensing. "My father already said he would allow you to leave the room and have access to the manor, with your own free will, if you just let this happen."

I raise an unplucked brow. "I'm not marrying you. I'm not fucking you and birthing your heir. I'm not going anywhere near you, regardless of who your dad threatens. Take no for an answer, Xander."

Despite the threats from Igor making me itch, Xander's threats mean nothing, considering I've been here for weeks and he hasn't even attempted to touch me.

Which is still a shock. He was very vocal about what he wanted from me before I was kidnapped. I can still remember how sore my throat was from screaming so loud as the bullet lodged in Malachi's chest. They had to knock me out in the yard to shut me up and stop me from fighting them. I kicked and screamed and begged, but I woke up in here, and I've been here ever since.

Xander comes closer, pinching a strand of my hair and rubbing it between his fingers. It usually smells of coconuts now, from the shampoo Igor makes me use. The same as his wife—Xander's mother.

If he comes any closer, I'll kick him in the balls.

Three hard raps interrupt whatever he was going to do.

Xander huffs. "What?" he snaps, gritting his teeth while glaring down at me as he waits for a reply.

When none comes, he releases my hair and goes to the door, swinging it open to reveal one of his father's men—suited in black—standing with his lips pressed together.

"What?"

"I understand it's late, sir, but we have a potential sighting of Miss Hempill."

I narrow my brows. "Abigail?"

"Shut up," Xander snaps at me then turns to the man. "Adryx?"

"No. Only her. Do you want us to go for her?"

"I'll go," he says, rushing to his jacket and throwing it on. "I don't want anyone going near her without my permission. And make sure Olivia stays in this room."

The guard nods, and then the door is closed in my face, leaving me alone within these four walls once more, wondering why Xander is trying to find my best friend and why he looked deathly pale again.

CHAPTER TWENTY-EIGHT
OLIVIA

T he dress drags on the ground as I walk through the main entrance to the party I'm being forced to attend. Violins and other instruments play, a sing-song voice echoing in the air as Xander holds me to his side, then pulls me through the crowds to find his parents and their friends.

My head hurts—I've had a headache since I was escorted from the bedroom to a dressing room, where a red dress waited for me. It's too big for me. There's a clip at my chest to hold the fabric together because the stylist didn't want to tell Igor I'd lost too much weight to wear it.

Igor told me to keep my head down the entire party, but since I have nothing else to do, I sometimes lift it and look around, hunting for familiar faces—potentially someone with black hair, tattoos, and a bat to hand. He'd bounce through the crowd and smack everyone on the head, throw me over his shoulder, and get me the hell out of this nightmare.

My reality is that I don't recognize a single soul.

Igor and Xander converse in Russian then laugh together. I'm led to a booth, and I flinch as Xander rests his hand on my thigh, grips it, then squeezes tighter when I try to pull it off.

"Is she behaving yet?" Igor asks. "Or do we need to take harsher measures?"

"She's getting there. She's following orders and knows how to get on her knees when told."

I gulp at his lie. Why is he lying to his father?

Igor hums. "And you still haven't fucked her?"

"Not yet. Like I said, we're getting there."

"That's an issue. But then again, we still need her to marry you."

If there's a window nearby, I might throw myself out of it—what could be worse than this? Nothing. Nothing is worse than this situation.

"Maybe I should be the one to put another heir in her. You could pretend the child is yours," Igor offers, and every drop of my blood runs cold.

"No need," Xander grits out. "I'm capable of doing it myself."

Igor hums in disapproval. Then he starts speaking in Russian again. I don't know what they're saying, but Xander's hold on my thigh softens—and then vanishes as he checks his phone discreetly.

His father goes to talk to someone else, drawing his attention away from us, and I feel Xander's lips against my ear. "Tell me you need to use the bathroom. Make sure he can hear you."

"Why?"

"Trust me," he whispers.

"I have no reason to trust you," I hiss.

He rolls his eyes then looks at his father, who's still in deep conversation. "Just fucking ask me, unless you enjoy being manacled to my family?"

My lips part as I search for any dishonesty on his face.

Then I clear my throat and say loud enough for Igor to hear, "I need to pee."

Igor chuckles as he glances over. "Take your future wife to the bathroom, son."

He nods, and I walk with him through the crowd, his fingers wrapped around my wrist. We go downstairs, following the signs for the bathrooms, but take a sharp right down a narrow cold corridor.

"Where are we going?" I ask, my voice shaking as my steps falter.

"I made a promise to someone that I'd get you out." He pulls open a door to the back alley, where two shadows are waiting. "I kept my promise," he says to one of them.

I frown. I'm about to ask him what he means when he shoves me outside. Right into someone's arms.

Abigail's arms.

"Olivia!" she cries, hugging me tightly as the door slams behind me. She buries her head into my shoulder and sobs. "Oh my God. I was so worried. Xan said he was going to make sure you were okay, but I didn't believe him. I'm sorry it took so long."

Disbelief runs through me. My friend isn't here, hugging me, is she? Am I dreaming? Did they drug my drink? Is this all a hallucination? I blink a few times, but my best friend is still holding me. She feels warm against my cold skin, comfortable, and I fold my arms around her to embrace her back.

The rock is still in my chest, but it's lighter.

I won't feel relief until I'm with them. My family.

"Did they hurt you?" she questions.

"Isolated me more than anything," I respond, no tears falling as I unravel my arms from her. "I'm fine."

"This is a lovely reunion."

I turn, freezing when I see Xander's cousin. The other Russian who doesn't really sound Russian. Sebastian Prince stands with his foot against the wall, smoking what I assume is a joint.

"Howdy, little Vize. You look like shit."

I rub my arms in the bitter cold. "What's going on?"

He throws his hands out. "Xander arranged with Adryx to get you out here. It's my job to get you to your father. This one wanted to tag along." He gestures to Abigail. "A car will be here any moment."

I want to cry—tears are building behind my eyes, but they don't fall. I won't feel safe until I'm in my father's or Malachi's arms.

"Is Malachi alive?"

"Kind of."

My heart crashes. "What does that mean?"

"You'll know when you see him. Don't want to traumatize you any further. Did any of my dear family members hurt you?" he asks even though Abbi already did, tipping his head and blowing out poisonous smoke into the air. "You're a lot thinner than before. Did they not feed you?"

I crush my teeth together, a tear finally slipping free. "Is my brother okay?"

Sebastian flicks the joint away and blows the last cloud of smoke out. "Why do you call him that?"

"Answer the question."

"It's likely he'll live. He's in a coma."

I cover my mouth. "Oh my God."

"Give her more than that, for fuck's sake, Base." Abigail shakes her head. "He's not in critical condition anymore."

Sebastian glares at her for a long second then shifts his gaze to me. "He punctured a lung when he was stabbed and was shot in the chest. The bullet missed his heart by two inches. But he lost a lot of blood and had some complications."

Oh God. Malachi.

I swallow hard. "My dad?"

"He hasn't left Malachi's side."

I take a deep breath. "And my sister?"

"Is that the chatty one? She's fine. She tried to put a damn spider on my face while I was asleep on the sofa. I wanted to beat the shit out of her, but I didn't think my father-in-law would've approved." He then beams. "I'm trying to convince him I'm enough for his daughter by being a good guy."

"You're married to someone else," Abbi adds.

"That's irrelevant."

I'm starting to think he fits in well with how psychotic the Reznikov family are. He's a bit unhinged, and that's putting it mildly.

"Is my brother in hospital then?"

"No, we have a safe house with private doctors. And please stop calling him your brother. That's like my best friend fucking my girlfriend."

"Are they siblings?"

"Twins," he confirms.

"Me and Malachi aren't related. We just grew up together."

He raises a brow. "Do you call him your brother while he's fucking you?"

I close my mouth, crossing my arms to look away.

I hear him fake a gag.

Abigail huffs. "Stop being dramatic," she scolds him. "They aren't really brother and sister, so there's nothing wrong with them being together."

That's the first time she's ever defended our relationship. I want to hug her.

"Well, despite his choice of fuck buddy, he's a good-looking guy."

I chew my lip in annoyance. This guy is insufferable. "He's my boyfriend, not a fuck buddy."

"Does he swing both ways?"

I turn back to stare at him, confused. "What?"

"Hmm." He laughs, thinking to himself, then checks his watch and huffs that they're still not here. "If I didn't have a girlfriend, I reckon I'd fuck him."

My stare turns deadly.

He laughs again. "Possessive? Or are you genuinely scared I could steal your brother from you?" Then he grimaces. "Fuck, now you even have me calling him that. Change the damn subject."

"Leave her alone," Abigail snaps. "I think if you—"

The door flies open to reveal Xander, looking worried. "They know. We have a rat. Get back inside, Olivia." His gaze lifts to Sebastian. "Your driver was shot five minutes ago. They don't know who's working on the outside." Xander looks at Abbi. "Get her fucking out of here, Base."

He swears to himself and grabs Abigail. "Sorry, little Vize."

"Why can't we take her with us now?"

"It's too risky," Xander tells Abbi. "They'll hunt for her, and the place is crawling with guards. Leave before they catch you."

She bites her lip, looking desperately at me as she mouths, "I'm sorry."

They rush out of the alleyway without looking back at me.

And there goes my escape.

"If she runs, it will detonate. She'll be dead within half a second."

I pause, my eyes widening as Xander and his father discuss inserting a tracker into my arm. The attempt at getting me out last night proved that someone on the inside isn't loyal, and Igor refuses to lose me.

Which makes no sense. I'm no one compared to all these assholes.

Today, although it's terrible that I'm still here, it has been a little easier to know that Malachi is definitely alive, that he's healing, and my father, Molly, and Abigail are all okay. A weight's been lifted from my shoulders, but that rock still sits in my chest, suffocating me with every breath because I'm not there, waiting for Malachi to wake up.

"Get this over with," Igor says, crossing his arms and ankles, and leaning against the kitchen counter. "We have a meeting in an hour, and I need your plaything back in her room."

"You're not putting a damn tracker inside me," I snap, trying to step away, my back hitting one of his immovable guards. "I won't run," I lie.

Xander steps in front of me. "This isn't up for debate, Olivia. Give me your fucking arm."

My eyes desperately search around us—but all I see are his men and Igor, waiting, staring, some chuckling to themselves as tears start to slide down my cheeks.

"Pl-Please don't do this."

Xander is putting on a show. He doesn't want anyone to know he was the one who arranged for me to get picked up outside the party—that Sebastian was there and about to save me from all of this. He could easily run too. If he really does have a thing going on with Abigail, then why not hide with her?

The look on her face when he barged through the doors and told me to get inside told a thousand stories. Something is going on between them. If she was smart, she'd run in the opposite direction, and definitely not into the arms of another Reznikov like Adryx.

What is she thinking?

"Do as you're told, or this will get ugly. Give me. Your

fucking. Arm."

"I hope when Malachi gets you, he makes it slow and painful."

Igor huffs and shoves Xander aside, grabbing my wrist and yanking me to him. I can smell his foul breath and the cigar smoke on his clothes—both scents infiltrate my senses, and I try not to vomit as he pulls something long and sharp from his son's hand.

"How hard is it to discipline her?" he sneers at Xander. "You have a lot to learn, boy." Turning to me, he tightens his grip until I flinch with the pain. "If you squirm or try to pull away, it'll hurt much more."

I grit my teeth and look away as he slowly, so damn slowly, inserts the needle into my skin—it tears at the flesh, and warm liquid drips to the ground.

"There," he says, grinning as he pushes the needle in further, cutting through the muscle and depositing the tracker. "Now you have no way of running from us."

It burns. It feels like he's pressing nails into my flesh, but I revel in it.

If I feel this pain, even for a few minutes, I can ignore the pain and panic in my heart. Because now, no one can save me.

CHAPTER TWENTY-NINE
MALACHI

The beeping won't fucking stop.

It only grows louder the more awake I become.

There are voices. Two voices. I think. Unless there's only one and it's echoing. I can't zone in on it enough to figure it out.

Did Olivia sneak into my room again and not turn her damn phone alarm off? Why is it still beeping? What is she saying to me?

She better go back to sleep. I'm too tired to wake up just yet—her cheer practice doesn't start until the afternoon, so we could have a lazy morning with a movie. Maybe she'll let me go down on her again like I did a few nights ago?

Parker has been silenced, and although Mom is now hellbent on Adam being her chosen suitor, I plan on taking her far, far away from all of this.

"Malachi."

She sounds different—maybe she's been up crying all night so her voice is a little hoarse. Did she have another nightmare? They rarely happen when she's with me, but maybe they're getting worse? I'll need to do some research to figure out how to stop them from plaguing her mind.

There's a heaviness on my chest, and I want to stroke my fingers through her hair. I can't smell it like I usually do. I mentally frown because I can barely move my face.

Then there's a second voice. It's distinctly different. Fuck. Did our parents just walk in and see us in bed together? We aren't doing anything.

Did they find out I've been fucking around with Olivia while she's passed out. Are they about to ruin this entire thing for me? I said I hadn't touched a girl before. I hadn't kissed one. I hadn't fucking tasted her.

What would she do if she knew I was nothing but a little liar?

She's saying my name again.

My brain short-circuits because none of the voices around me belong to Olivia.

One is soft, the other harsh, but I can't focus enough to recognize who they belong to.

Trying to open my eyes, I groan, or attempt to—there's something in my throat. I try to swallow, but I end up choking, sending whatever's beeping erratically to up its tempo. My hand lifts to feel what's in my mouth, but I hear a gasp, and someone grabs my wrist.

"Dad! Get the nurse! He's awake!"

There's a scuttle of shoes, a hand coming to rest on my face—not soft and gentle like my Olivia's. No, this is a rough hand. Large. Their fingers grip my cheek. A firm tap that has me trying to open my eyes, but I'm so fucking weak, and my body aches.

"Come on, son. Come back to us. You need to wake up now. Please."

Is that my dad? Why is he here, begging me to wake up?

Wait.

Hold the fuck on.

I'm not in my bed at home.

I'm not lying with Olivia in my arms. She's gone. She's not here. She… No.

They took her. They have her. They fucking stole her from me.

Fuck, everything hurts. What the fuck happened?

"You should go for something to eat, sir. He's not fully awake," I hear someone say. "Give him a little time."

"A little time? My son has been in a coma for three weeks after being shot in the goddamn chest! This is the first sign of life he's had and you're telling us to leave the room?"

Eight years ago, he was the one in a hospital bed. I wasn't with him; I was behind bars for putting him there. I hurt him, and he shouldn't be here with me now, trying to make me wake up.

Yet here he is, his hand still on my face, refusing to leave my side.

Did I wake up in a different body? Does he know I'm Malachi?

My entire body screams at me as I try to sit up, but I can't.

"Let's go, Dad."

I try to move again at the sound of Molly's voice.

None of this is happening. I'm in a fucking nightmare, and Olivia is waiting for me. She's not gone. They don't have her. I refuse to believe it.

Where is she? Why isn't she here? Did they not manage to save her?

Fuck. Where is my fucking sister?

I manage to crack one eye open and instantly wince at the sensitivity overload, a bright light blinding me, burning into the back of my eye socket.

I might be dead already. It would make sense. I always knew I was going to hell, so they shoved me in a room with my father, and he's about to start getting revenge on my unmoving body.

"I'm not leaving my son," I hear him snap. "I haven't left his side for three fucking weeks, and I don't plan to leave him when he's about to wake up. You'll need to drag me out."

"You've barely slept, Mr. Vize."

"I'll sleep when my son is awake and well and my daughter

361

is back with us."

Back with us.

Olivia really isn't here.

My eyes burn behind my lids—I'm so fucking useless because my girl is gone and I can't even open my goddamn eyes, never mind try to save her.

But then everything goes silent, the world stops turning, my heart starts beating, my lungs no longer controlled by a machine as I hear her echoing scream; see the horror in my eyes as she's dragged away from me while a force knocks me on my back, a burning sensation spreading across my chest.

All I can see is how scared she was when I was numb, dead, unblinking with a stab wound in my side and a bullet in my chest.

I shouldn't be here.

They have Olivia.

My fucking sister.

A pain I can't describe tightens my chest even worse as both eyes ping open to the burning lights and I force myself to sit up.

Dad says something I can't understand given the panic going through me. Someone is holding my shoulders, pushing me back down. A cold sensation rushes up my arm as they inject something into a line connected to me.

Against everything in me, I stop fighting, and the last voice I hear is my dad yelling about getting someone in here now.

My eyes open slowly. I feel disorientated but more in control than the last few times I've tried to wake up.

There's a lump in my throat. Constantly there, strangling me every time I hear voices beside me but am unable to tell them I'm awake.

My body aches, yet I can't move. My fingers barely jitter as I close my eyes and try to focus.

Molly is talking about school, and Dad is explaining something about mathematical calculations. I think she's doing homework.

"The answer is fourteen," I hear someone say in a Russian accent.

My eyes slide open. This time I find a darkened room, a lamp to the side lighting up the small table in the corner, where Molly is scribbling on paper with a calculator in front of her.

"How did you know that without doing the calculations?" she asks, and my eyes follow her gaze to the large form in the chair beside her.

The beeping of the machines starts increasing as I stare at Adryx Reznikov.

His gaze lifts and clashes with mine.

I throw myself up despite the pain lashing at my chest,

 363

something pulling on my arm and tearing the skin. Before I can collide my weak fist with the brother of the man trying to marry my girl, Dad grabs me, putting himself between us.

"Calm down. He's on our side, remember? Calm down, Malachi."

"It's normal to react this way. You went through a lot," Adryx says, crossing his arms and bouncing his knees. "And don't worry—you're in one of my safe houses. No one will find us."

Olivia, I sign to my dad.

"She's with my brother. She hasn't been harmed, and we're working on getting her back."

My eyes snap back to him. *I want her back now.*

"Not gonna happen," he replies, and I feel like slicing his throat with one of the needles in a tray beside the bed. "She's in one of the most secure buildings my father has. The Reznikov manor."

Go get her, I sign, my hands shaking the more I think about her being stuck in there.

"I no longer have access. You see, myself and Sebastian were caught intercepting their mission, and now we're also in hiding. Mainly because my cousin is a fucking useless idiot and had your address in his GPS tracker on his phone, and my father traced it." He shrugs. "He already had an idea that I was working against him though, so my dear cousin is alive—for now."

Dad pats my shoulder. "He's helping us."

I grit my teeth. Why?

"I have my reasons," Adryx adds, pulling a box from his pocket and slipping a pair of glasses onto his face before taking his phone out too. "We tried to get Olivia out a few days ago and failed. She's got a tracker in her arm now."

My eyes widen, and I drop back on the bed, my entire body aching from being out of action for weeks. My legs are already tingling, my toes hurt, and I have spasms in my arms. But nothing compares to the twist in my heart at Olivia's position.

"We can't just break in and take her either," Dad tells me, running his hand through messy hair, his face coated in a beard he's never grown in his life. It's three weeks of no shaving, barely sleeping, and worrying.

Why? I sign before my hands drop into my lap.

"There's a proximity trigger. If she leaves the manor, it'll kill her."

My eyes slide shut, my lungs shriveling to nothing as my heart rate accelerates. The tingling sensation in my legs worsens, spreading to my arms and fingers, and I drop my face into my hands because I don't have a clue what to do.

This is a bad dream, a nightmare. None of this is real. I'm hallucinating again. I must be. All I've been doing recently is losing my mind—this is just the result of it. Olivia is trying to wake me up in bed now, or I'm standing in the woods, the sitting room, the bathroom, and I'm blank and stuck in my head.

Stuck in this fucked-up dream.

I lift my head, the room spinning, but I manage to sign one more question despite how exhausted I am, how fucking dizzy I am.

Is she hurt?

"She's safe," he replies, not really responding to what I asked. "Xander, believe it or not, is on our side. Our father isn't exactly the easiest to go against. He has my brother under strict orders and is hell-bent on them finally marrying and having his next heir."

I feel sick. *Has he fucked her?*

"No." He shakes his head. "Xander has no interest in her, and she's made it perfectly clear she has no interest in him. It's you she keeps asking about."

Why can't I just cut it out of her arm and save her?

"The tracker is attached to her nerve. It will kill her instantly if she tries to remove it or run."

I grit my teeth, trying to get to my feet and wincing. I need to get up. I need to be active. I need to save her.

To add salt to my wounds, he adds, "If Xander doesn't impregnate her soon, my father will do it. She's already been off her birth control pill since going to the manor three weeks ago."

"Like hell he will," Dad snarls. "We need to hurry up with this plan."

I look between them, waiting for someone to elaborate on this big plan that's not in fucking motion.

"We have some aid," he clarifies. "My cousin is acquainted with people who can help us. As long as we help them keep someone hidden, they'll help us."

He checks his phone then sighs. "They're arriving in the morning. I suggest you get as much rest as you can because we need to make a plan and get Olivia away from Igor as soon as possible."

The day after, I feel a little more alive. I could barely sleep with worry and anxiety and fucking zaps of pain, so the nurse came in and gave me something to numb the thoughts and everything else—my dad slept in the spare bed beside me, while Molly slept upstairs with Abigail.

It's just great that she's here. Just fucking great. One more person to remind me why I'm not good enough for Olivia.

Dad said she managed to get away when Base and Adryx were caught. They beat up the guards and killed them, but their names were already flagged with Igor Reznikov. But Abigail was already gone. It took that asshole Xander a week to find her and have one of his trusted guards bring her here.

Something tells me she's here against her will though. She's definitely got something going on with the brothers.

"Where's the purple-haired one?" Base asks as I follow them down a narrow corridor.

"She's asleep," Adryx says.

His cousin chuckles. "You would know that, wouldn't you? I wonder which brother she'll choose?"

"Shut your fucking mouth. Your best friend isn't here to save you from me strangling the shit out of you."

"Kade will defend my honor when he's home."

Dad shakes his head beside me, his walking stick holding his weight. He was shot in the leg; nothing fatal or worse than what I did to him, but he's struggling to walk again.

We make our way into a meeting room. There's a long table in the middle and a whiteboard on the wall, with one single bright light hanging from the low ceiling.

I can smell fresh paint.

I focus on that as Sebastian gestures to the blonde beside him. "This is my wife, Luciella."

She grimaces. "I'm not your wife."

He fists his hand and closes his eyes.

"Nikita is your wife," she snaps, shoving her chair out and getting to her feet, then rearranging her large shawl around her body. "I'm going back to the room."

He tips his head back and mutters something in Russian,

staring at the ceiling as the door slams behind her—then sighs and continues with his introduction, nodding to the older man sitting with his arms crossed.

"This is Tobes. He's a little evil."

He glares at him. "Don't test my patience."

"And a little touchy," Base adds. "He doesn't like me very much because I've made both his daughter and his son come."

"One more fucking word, Sebastian, and I'll put you in the ground."

Dad tilts his head at the older man. "You should be dead."

The man he's speaking to raises a brow. "I'm surprised you aren't, Jamieson."

I give him a confused look, and Dad clarifies, "I was his lawyer years ago."

Base puts his hands on his hips. "And you didn't think to mention that you knew the Vize family earlier?"

The man shrugs. "I don't need to tell you shit."

Base tuts. "Fucking family."

"We aren't family and never will be."

He moves on to the next man as I shove aside a chair for my dad. He accidentally drops his walking stick, and I lean down, ignoring the burning in my side and chest and nearly ripping my stitches as I pick it back up for him.

There's an awkwardness in the way he thanks me, then he clears his throat, and we turn our attention back to our company.

"This is Barry. My assistant."

The guy cocks a brow. "I'm not his assistant."

"Technically, you're my best friend's assistant, so you kind of are."

"Fuck off, Base."

The older one tuts, leaning back in his chair.

Adryx gestures to him. "Since my cousin has no idea how to introduce people, this is Tobias Mitchell. But I guess you already know him."

Shit.

The entire world has heard of him—and his son.

He's psychotic—probably worse than me, and I know that's saying something. I'm surprised he's here and not hunting for the woman who technically put him in jail.

I guess we have something in common. We'd ruin our lives for the people we love and have no regrets.

What's the plan?

"If Olivia doesn't agree to marry Xander by this weekend, my father plans on taking her that night," Adryx says.

My jaw tics. *Meaning?*

His lips press together. "He wants an heir who isn't a fuck-up like me and my brother. He told Xander they'd pretend the child was his."

I stand, but Dad grabs my arm. "Acting on impulsive anger won't get her back, Malachi. They're powerful people, and we need to be smart. If you barge in there, we could lose her forever."

You expect me to sit around and do nothing?

"We aren't doing nothing," Adryx says. "We have a plan. My father is hosting an event in the manor next week. Masked. Olivia will be forced to attend. The tracker forces her to remain in the manor at all times." He drops into his seat and sighs. "But Barry is working on a way to disable their entire system. Long enough to get her back here and remove the tracker. Safely."

My spine straightens. Could that work? Could I get her back? Fuck. There's a rush of hope.

"Xander can get two of us inside. But we need to wear masks too to hide who we are. Olivia will be wearing a gas mask—it's what she requested through Xander. It'll help to identify her."

My lip twitches.

My good girl.

Not that I need to know what mask she'll be in. I don't even need to see her to know she's nearby. I'll be going. I'll wear my gas mask too.

"What do you get from all of this?" Dad asks. "I know you aren't doing this out of the goodness of your heart or for that girl sleeping in your bed."

Adryx smirks. "I get to kill my father."

CHAPTER THIRTY
MALACHI

A fter having my stitches cleaned and my wounds checked over, I go for a shower and get dressed, despising myself every second of it all.

I shouldn't be standing here, staring at myself in the bathroom mirror, at my chest. At the scar that will definitely look like an explosion went off in my chest. I shouldn't be wondering if Olivia will find it ugly, or what she'll think of the impending scar on my side, or the fact I failed to protect her.

She might never want to see me again. I was supposed to keep her safe.

I always seem to fail.

I'm surprised Dad and Molly even entertain me. I'm the reason Olivia is gone—I didn't get her away from all of this when I had a chance. When Dad said to run, I should've dragged Olivia onto my bike and taken her to the other side of the world.

That's exactly what I'll do when I get her back. I'll make Molly and Dad move too. They won't be safe here, and I need them now.

Dad's by my side at all times. Give it five minutes and he'll be done with his physio and hunting the building for me, then telling me to take my meds and watching me swallow each one to make sure I don't skip any.

Who would've thought that the man I nearly killed would become my crutch?

I stop outside one of the bedrooms upstairs at the sound of two voices.

Not that I want to listen in to whatever the fuck Base talks about in his free time, but I'm curious about his drive. Why the hell is he working with us, and what does he get out of it? He was forced to work with his cousins through his grandfather, and he's… what? Married to someone at the same time as having a girlfriend?

A girlfriend who's the daughter of Tobias Mitchell. The asshole must have a death wish.

I can see them clearly.

Base is holding her face, wiping under her eyes, and gently kissing her forehead. She's upset—maybe because she's being comforted by someone who's the equivalent of a wet towel wrapped around a fucking tree with no personality.

Wait. Is she… is she pregnant? I can see the bump. It's huge.

Like she could pop any moment, though she has a slim face.

Please tell me she didn't procreate with this douchebag.

Then he's leaning down and pressing his forehead to her bump, and when he starts speaking to his unborn kids, the twins, I take that as my sign to stop watching them through the ajar door.

I think, if Olivia wants one, I'm going to do that one day. I've witnessed her smiles when holding a baby, and the way she looks at them when nearby. I've no idea when or how or if I'll ever be good enough to take on the role of a father, but if Olivia wants a family, I'll give her one. I'd give her the fucking world if she asked.

I'll ask my dad for help. He'll keep me right. However, telling him his son wants to put a kid in his daughter doesn't seem like a conversation for anytime soon.

One day, he'll see me as Olivia's partner, or Olivia as mine. Will he choose which one of us remains his child? I couldn't imagine him not being my father.

I stop outside Molly's room, knock twice, and push the door open, peeking in to see she's leaning over a shoebox that's pierced with holes.

"Oh, hey. She's been moving around a lot. I think she needs a bigger box."

Did you feed her?

"Yeah. Please don't ever make me touch a maggot again."

I silently laugh as I crouch down to look in the box. I need to get her a tank. Apparently my farmhouse is obliterated. Molly managed to get my pet out before the flames engulfed it.

So, technically, I'm homeless.

Dad said I could stay at his place since Mom is gone. He's filing for a divorce and said she's no longer welcome in his life. I hope she gets hit by a bus or contracts a deadly disease.

Molly sighs and sits on her bed, and I tilt my head at her, silently asking her what's wrong.

"I miss Olivia. I'm worried about her."

I know, I sign, standing tall. For being close to fifteen, she's kinda short. Way shorter than Olivia, and she seems sheltered, probably due to the trauma of her life before she came to the Vize family. I wonder how dark her story really is though? Only some people know mine. I don't like discussing it, but maybe if I tell her what happened to me as a kid, she'd open up and feel comfortable enough to talk and feel better for having someone close to her, able to understand.

She'll be fine. She has me.

"Kai," a voice comes from behind me. "There you are."

I'm going to kill him.

Base pushes the door open, his hair ruffled at the top, his lip swollen from, I'm guessing, that blonde girl biting him. "My assistant is about to go over everything for tonight. You coming, Kai?"

He's trying to push my buttons. I might need to push him out of a fucking window, head first.

I groan inwardly. I need to hold myself back from hitting this asshole. He's been calling me Kai all fucking day, and I might actually kill him.

"His name is Malachi," Molly snaps. "My dad already told you to stop calling him that."

Thanks, kiddo. She might be my favorite now.

I crouch down to check on my Cordelia one last time while Molly watches the way I handle her—she watches everything I do. Copies me. I sat with her all morning showing her some signing movements and how to change the box.

She's not afraid of my pet. If anything, Cordelia's been keeping Molly busy during all this. Maybe, just fucking maybe, if we get out of this, I'll let her have sleepovers at me and Olivia's house.

Teaching her things about Cordelia and even signing makes me feel important, like I have some sort of purpose. And then there's the way she smiles at me, like I'm the best person in the world. She gets excited to see me like a...

Like a little sister.

She says my name as I go towards the door.

I turn, waiting for her next words, but she lifts her hands and thinks for a long second, making sure she gets the movements correct.

You saved me, she signs perfectly. *Now you need to save my sister.*

When I get to the meeting room, Dad is there. The blonde girl stuck with Base—who I now know as Luciella—is eating a sandwich while her father glares at her partner from across the table.

Abigail walks in, Adryx behind her, looking pissed off too. Why is everyone moody today?

Barry stands when everyone is seated then lifts a small drone for us to see. "We need this as close to the manor as possible. Preferably their comms room. I can use an electromagnetic radiation blocker to disable their entire system. So far, I can only do that for one hour. But it should be enough time to get Olivia out and back to this building for me to cut out the tracker."

He lifts what look like grenades. "These release the same thing, but they need to be dropped in the north and west side of the manor. They'll basically remove the first defense barrier for me to then use the drone to infiltrate."

"The party is on the south side of the manor," Adryx adds. "Someone needs to be in the middle of the room. And the other person needs to be in the pool room."

I'll go, I sign, and Adryx repeats it in words.

"Base will go too. He's the worst driver, but he can get you here quicker. Xander will distract everyone so you can all escape without detection, but I can't go. My father will notice me from a mile away."

"I'll tail you. If anyone follows, I'll kill them," Tobias says. He seems bored and fed up, but he glances at Adryx. "You keep your end of the deal. Nothing happens to my daughter. You know more than anyone how important she is to me."

Adryx nods. "Right."

"What does he mean?" Abbi asks. "Do you have a daughter?"

"Of course not," Adryx replies. "Can we move on with this plan? What happens when we get Olivia here?"

Barry goes into detail about needing Olivia in the medical room so he can cut the tracker out safely, without damaging her nerves. He tells us it'll hurt, and he can administer some pain relief, but not if we get her here with little time to spare.

When the system is temporarily disabled, no one can use their radios. Phones will be cut off. Signals blocked. And if we're caught, we need to fight our way out of the manor without Olivia getting hurt.

Tobias is happy to go, even though he's free now, after escaping prison and faking his own death. The story was reported on by news outlets for weeks.

"Can you shoot?" Adryx asks me, and I shake my head.

"I'll teach him."

Base must be insane if he thinks I'll let him teach me anything.

"You're going to fire guns here and draw attention to us?" Luciella asks, mortified.

"We're in the middle of nowhere, princess."

Tobias narrows his eyes. I have a feeling he hates this guy, and I completely understand why.

She glares and leaves again, and Base rolls his eyes. "She acts like she hates me, even though she was all over my dick last night."

Tobias jumps out of his chair and punches him across the face.

CHAPTER THIRTY-ONE

MALACHI

Getting into the Reznikov manor was easy. With my mask on—thankfully saved from my car—I'm wearing a fitted black suit for the first time ever, so no one can recognize me.

Base is wearing a Batman mask, because he's an idiot.

Tobias is in a suit too, heading towards the pool room with a black skull mask on.

I can hear violins, and I want to roll my eyes so fucking hard at how pretentious this family is. Bunch of fucking rich mutated cretins thinking they're classy, but they're all just idiots trying to impress each other and failing.

My feet stop moving when I spot Igor. For being an old man, he's puffing that cigar and downing whisky like he's not going to be on his deathbed within the next year.

Xander is there. Like his father, he's in a white mask that only covers his eyes. As much as I know he's on our side, I want to fucking snap his neck for threatening Olivia in the first place. Whether it was all fake and forced, if he even as much as looks in her direction again, I'll poke his eyes out with nails and hammer his cock to his leg.

Abigail can then choose Adryx. He's the decent one anyway. Then she doesn't need to be stuck in a damn triangle.

"We're here," Tobias says in my ear. The earpiece is covered by my mask and dark hair. "Base will run out back as soon as we drop these and get the car. Can you see her?"

I stay silent, my eyes scanning the hall—I'd know if she was here. Everyone has their face covered, but I'd be able to spot Olivia even by a strand of her hair. She's not here yet. Where the fuck is she? Xander told Adryx she'd be attending.

Maybe she's in the room they've locked her in?

I glance at the main exit, wondering if I should just hunt for her anyway.

"The asshole doesn't speak, remember? Hey, do you think he'd yell at me if I try to flirt with her?"

I'd kill him. Simple as that.

"Fuck off, Base," Adryx snaps, and I can hear Molly and Abigail in the background at the safe house.

"Fucking rude," he replies. "Your brother is here, so she must be somewhere. And hey, Baz, what's the point in you having all these fancy gadgets if you can't follow her tracker?"

Barry huffs. "There's no point explaining it to an idiot

like you."

I roll my eyes and shove my hands into my pockets while they keep arguing back and forth, Tobias telling them all to shut the fuck up and focus on the plan.

Stepping around a group of men with cigars, I search the place some more. The music is growing more ridiculous, the decorations are ridiculous, the people are ridiculous, and the—

I turn and stop breathing at the sight before me.

My fucking soul shivers.

Fuck. I'm stunned into a place where I can't even fill my lungs or blink.

The black satin dress hugs her frame so perfectly, her long hair falling down her back. She's slimmer than before. And I can't see her beautiful face.

She's wearing a gas mask, just like mine, but with glitter around the chambers on each side.

I'm looking at a fucking angel.

My angel.

My anchor.

Mine.

I love her more than life. She once told me she would never be loved the way I love her because it comes so naturally to people who are neurotypical, and for me to feel anything like that, I'd need to try extra hard and fall deeper than any typical love. She told me it was more than enough for her.

There's fucking concrete around my black heart like a shield, and she's trapped inside it. That's the only version of love I have, and I'll make sure it's always enough for Olivia to choose me, to never leave me, to love me until we grow old, die, and find each other in the void beyond.

Igor gestures to her to come to him, resting his hand on her hip when she complies. She stiffens, her spine straight, as her eyes burn into Xander's, searching for some sort of help.

She's asking him to help when I'm right here.

"Don't do anything stupid," someone says in my ear, but my blood is pumping, roaring around their voice as I grit my teeth and step forward.

"Stop," my dad snaps in my ear. "Do not risk your sister's life."

"Shit. Even the dad sees them as siblings."

I pause my steps, my heart pounding in my chest, needing to get to her—I need to remove his hand from her body and snuff out his life force while everyone watches. They need to see what a useless piece of shit he is.

My girl flinches as he leans down to whisper in her ear, and then she nods. He squeezes her side and taps it before going to talk to a group of women who keep smiling at him and his son.

She rubs her arm, and I check our surroundings before I start to approach her.

"Malachi!" Dad yells. "Stop!"

"He's going to screw up the goddamn plan."

 383

"Tobes, if you stand on my foot again, we're gonna have a—"

Base's voice vanishes, and I hope Tobias is kicking his ass.

But I'm more focused on the way Olivia turns around and freezes as I stand before her with my hands in my pockets—because if I don't hold them there, I'll grab her and drag her away, or worse, kiss her in front of everyone and ruin the rescue.

Olivia can't see my face, but she doesn't have to. The gas mask still has dried blood on it, not that anyone can smell the dead copper or can tell between it being fake or not.

She'll remember being my little stranger and running from this mask.

Xander is talking to his father, his eyes straying to me every few minutes.

She's looking up at me, and I can see the fear in her eyes through the glass of the eyeholes. "Please save me," she says shakily, loud enough for only me to hear.

My heart splits in two.

I tilt my head, my gaze flicking over to see what Igor is doing—talking like he's the star of the night, the center of attention, oblivious, while his team keeps us surrounded and his sons plan his demise.

So close. She's so fucking close.

She lifts her mask, her eyes tearstained already. "Malachi."

I can't sign, not when I have this grenade in my hand, and honestly, I don't know what to say. Forgive me? Don't leave me? I'll do better? I promise to protect you even though I already failed?

I won't let anything happen to her ever again. Even if a bullet goes in my head, I'll find a way to protect her.

Fuck. I want to go to her. Now. I need to. She's staring at me, and I'm not doing anything, but my entire body is fucking rattling to go to her.

"Ready?"

I nod, knowing Barry can see us through the CCTV.

"I won't be reachable as soon as this starts. You have one hour. Get her to me as fast as you can. Try not to die in the process."

"Aw," Base coos. "Knew you loved me. Sorry, I already have a best friend, despite sucking his dick too many times—" He starts making an abrupt choking sound, and Tobias tells him to shut the fuck up.

"Drop them now."

I pull my hand from my pocket and let go of the grenade, praying this fucking works. The lights flicker, my eyes drifting to Igor and his men as they try to use their radios.

It worked.

Xander comes towards us. He knows it's about to happen, yet I can't help but hate him.

I draw my attention back to a confused Olivia. She drops the mask on the ground, and her eyes are watering. Xander reaches her, grabs the mask, and tries to put it back on her. "Mal—"

"Now."

It's the only word I need. I drive my fist into Xander's face and grab Olivia, then drag her through the crowd, gripping her hand tight enough that I can't lose her again. People bang into us, Olivia slips and falls, but I lift her weight and push partygoers out of the way, knocking over someone and making them fall onto a table filled with food.

The hallways are empty—it's a straight route to the backyard where Base will be waiting with the car. Tobias will follow and catch anyone trying to get to us.

Looking behind me, I don't spot anyone following us. I hold Olivia's hand tighter and drag her into the yard.

"Malachi. I can't leave," she says desperately.

I swing open the door and push her in. She fights me, trying to get out of the backseat as I climb in and close the door.

"Malachi! I can't!" She shows me her arm. "This will kill me."

Base swerves out of the drive, knocking Olivia into my side and dragging a groan from me because she hit my stitches.

"We need to get you to Barry as quickly as possible," Base says when I struggle to talk or sign. "The tracker is disabled. He can cut it out."

Her lips part, and her eyes widen.

"Really?"

"Yes. Now stop distracting me so I can drive."

Breathless, we turn to stare at each other, a spark hitting her eyes as she lets out a soft cry and climbs onto my lap, grabbing my face and kissing me.

It's not gentle. It's brutal. The harsh presses of her mouth claim my lips before she desperately shoves her tongue into my mouth and devours me, a moan vibrating between our chests.

Her hand presses to where my wound is, and I wince. She pauses and looks down, then lifts her eyes to stare at me.

"Don't stop," I mouth and pull her lips back to mine.

The car swerves again, headlights shining through the back window as Tobias follows. She's swallowing each breath from me, kissing me harder as her tongue lashes against my own.

She's rocking her hips, and I'm not stopping her. I don't give a fuck that Base is here or that he's witnessing all of this. I need my girl, and I think she needs me just as much.

Her hand hits the window as Base swerves again, keeping her balance as my cock hardens beneath her.

"I need you," she breathes. "Please let me have you."

I pull my head back, shoving the fabric of her dress up to her hips and snapping the underwear clean off her body, making her whimper.

Dropping my hand between her legs, I kiss her once more as I press my thumb to her clit, sinking two fingers inside her until she rides my hand, gasping as she moves.

LEIGH RIVERS

Her hands leave my shoulders, and she rushes to get my belt undone, pulling at the buttons and freeing my hard, thick, fucking aching dick. She strokes it once, twice, three times, and my balls tingle. I don't think I'll last long. I've been deprived of her for a month—I can't even remember the last time I came without it being in her pussy or her mouth.

We don't have much time. This needs to be quick. Imagine pulling up at the safehouse with our father waiting, and I'm balls deep in my sister?

I grab one of her hips, lining my tip to her entrance, then slam her down on me. So tight and wet and fucking mine.

Unprotected. She's not on birth control anymore, but I don't care. I'll gladly watch my cum fill her and breed the shit out of her.

My cock buries in her soaking cunt over and over again.

We share sloppy yet desperate kisses while she fucks me, then she sinks her teeth into my lip and cries silently, nearly falling off my lap when Base takes a sharp right.

It hurts me, my side burning, but I don't give a fuck. I keep going, feeling the stitches pulling and tearing. Blood soaks into my shirt. I look down, touching my side, and see blood on my hand, but instead of stopping her, I grab her face and stain it red, bringing her down on my cock harder, faster, ignoring Base in front trying to get us to the destination on time.

"Tell me you love me," Olivia gasps into my mouth. "In

case we don't make it in time. I need to hear you tell me you love me."

"I love you, little sister," I reply, my words still a little unpracticed. "And I'll tell you every single fucking day after this."

I pull back, watching her ride my cock while I sign, *I love you now. I loved you yesterday. When we were kids. When we were teens. When you had me thrown in jail and when I found you again. I'll love you tomorrow. Next month. Next year. When you're mothering my child. And when we're old and gray, I'll love you even more, because I'll have had a fucking lifetime to fall more and more in love with you. Is that enough for you, Olivia? Do you need more from me?*

"You've always been enough." A tear slips down her cheek. "I want every moment with you."

"Huh?" I hear Base say, then he swears under his breath and knocks the mirror to block any reflection. "Fucking hell. Really? It's a race for life and you're deep inside your sister?"

"Yes," I breathe against her lips. "But I want to be deeper."

I snatch her lip between my teeth and groan as she sinks down to the hilt, her fingers sliding into my hair and tugging until it hurts, probably nearly as much as the opening wound on my side. Even after taking a bullet to the chest a month ago, a blade to the lung, I'm not letting any of them stop me from driving my cock up into my girl and watching her head fall back on a moan.

"Faster," I order with a forced breath against her throat.

"Fuck me faster."

Doing as she's told, Olivia grabs Base's headrest behind her and rides me with more speed, the sound of slapping skin filling my goddamn ears.

"Harder, Olivia. Drop your fucking ass down on me harder."

She lets out a harsh moan as she does just that. Her pussy tightens, and I can feel her shaking in my hold.

"Can I come in you?" I ask because I'm so close. My balls are tightening, and my spine and legs have warmth filling them. My muscles bunch, and when she fails to respond, her orgasm washes over her so hard, she freezes on top with her nails digging into my skull.

I can't hold it back either as white dots appear behind my eyes, and I push her shoulder to get as deep as possible, needing every drop of cum leaking out of me to be stuck inside her.

"Tobes. Help me," Base says into the phone pressed to his ear. "The siblings are fucking in the backseat, and I'm certain the mute just spoke."

We get there with twenty minutes to spare—no one followed us either, so Tobias pulls up just as we walk into the building. Base won't even look at me, and I feel smug that I've been able to silence the prick.

Dad grabs Olivia and pulls her in for a hug, and she cries into his chest. He looks over her head to me and mouths, "Thank you."

I lower my head with my lip flattening.

He doesn't need to thank me. I would've died to get her back here safely.

Barry has set up a table for Olivia to rest her arm on as Molly and her best friend Abigail fill the room. Dad kisses her forehead, but we all sit silent, waiting to see if Barry can do it.

Olivia holds my hand under the table, her eyes staying on me. She's terrified. If this doesn't work, then there's a chance we might lose her.

If that happens then there isn't much point in me being on this earth.

"This will hurt," Barry tells her then starts cutting into her skin.

Her eyes screw shut, and her grip on my hand tightens. Tears soak her cheeks, her teeth gritting. Then her head drops to my shoulder, and she cries and cries and fucking cries—it takes seven minutes for Barry to stop cutting into my sister's arm before drop a small metal rod on the table.

"Done."

Relief fills me as I grab Olivia's face and kiss her, not giving a fuck that everyone can see. She sobs against my lips, her hand pressing to my chest gently. "You're okay?"

My bottom lip trembles, and I swallow down the emotions as I let go of her face. *I am now.*

Tobias grabs a metal container and starts smashing it into the tracker until it's in pieces, and silence cloaks us all once more.

Because it worked.

Olivia is free, and she's holding my hand so damn tight, I don't think I'll ever let go. She covers her mouth as Abigail hugs her, shaking in each other's arms.

But then Molly launches herself at me. "I'm so glad you're okay!"

I hug her, her little head buried into me, and I look at Olivia while she cuddles our father, her friend, and then thanks everyone.

My gaze lifts to the door as Adryx walks in.

"My father is in the trunk," he says. "We'll deal with him."

"How did you get him in there?"

"A story for another time," he replies to Barry. "We need to go."

"Thank you," Olivia says to him. "I know going against your dad was hard."

He shrugs. "Not really."

Olivia puts my suit jacket on and doesn't let go of my hand as we walk out. Xander is smoking up against the car, his head down. Abigail comes out too, hugging herself, and stares at the brothers now both leaning on the car.

"All of our safe houses will be searched for my father. Olivia is no longer under any threat, and neither are any of you, but I suggest getting out of here before they catch you and assume you had a hand in my father's disappearance."

Xander lifts his head, his face filled with regret. "I'm sorry for the part I played," he says to Olivia. "Truly. I never intended for any of this to happen."

Adryx pats his little brother's chest. "Let's go."

Adryx shakes hands with Tobias and Barry. "I'll keep my word. There's one safe house that's not on any of their radars. I'll send the details to my cousin."

Base comes outside with Luciella—their hands are clasped together, her nose red from the cold weather.

"I'm taking the car." Base points to the car I just fucked my sister in. "It's faster than mine. There better not be any leftover incesty sex juice in the backseat, Kai."

Dad grimaces.

Olivia goes red.

For the first time in a while, I let out a snorted laugh and shake my head. I swear, if I ever cross paths with this guy again, I'll strangle him.

Not in a nice way.

Base salutes everyone while Luciella tells Olivia it was nice to finally meet her, then smiles at Abigail. They vanish into the car, and Tobias sighs. "I hope we don't need to meet again, Jamieson. But if we do, it better be under good circumstances."

Dad chuckles. "Take care, Tobias."

"Stop fucking your sister!" Base calls out as he slams the car door shut.

"Thank you," Olivia says to Barry, ignoring Base. "For everything."

He lowers his head and winks at Dad before he, too, climbs into the car with Tobias.

Dad and Molly go to the other car, and Olivia kisses my cheek and gets into the passenger side.

Both Reznikov brothers watch Abigail, but she walks away from them and climbs into the car too.

"Have a happy life with your girl, Malachi," Adryx says, dragging his eyes from the car back to me. "I hope we never need to meet like this again."

I nod, and he shakes my hand while his brother continues to level a deadly stare at the car.

Xander, his eye blackened by my fist, doesn't say anything as he gives me a close-lipped smile, a nod, then turns around and follows his older brother to his own car.

I get into the driver's side, my eyes closing to take a deep, well-needed breath.

"Where do we go now?" Olivia asks me.

Home, I sign.

Wherever home is for us now. It doesn't matter as long as we're together.

EPILOGUE ONE

OLIVIA

Three Years Later

"Close your eyes," Malachi tells me, and when I shake my head, he adds, "Trust me."

The tone of his voice has my eyelids closing, and the world around me goes dark. He takes my wrist, twisting it so my palm faces the ceiling.

"Don't pull away," he warns me, clearly remembering that moment in his room years ago, when he rested Spikey on my hand, and I dropped him and ran for the bed.

I gulp. "I won't."

As soon as his pet crawls onto my hand, my entire body freezes. "Malachi," I say, my voice breaking as tears instantly spring to my eyes. "Take her back. Please."

"Keep your eyes closed."

Against my entire being—which is desperate to throw her at his face and run for my life and never return to this damn house he rebuilt two years ago—I nod as a tear slides down my cheek.

He wipes it with his thumb, then I feel his breath against my mouth as his lips draw closer.

Malachi kisses me softly as his spider starts to move up from my palm to my wrist, my skin sizzling with the need to rub at it as his tongue slips between my lips and finds my own.

Mouth opening to taste him too, I kiss him back, focusing on the warmth of his tongue moving with mine, the way he sucks on my bottom lip and sinks his teeth in—it's not enough to hurt but enough to make a little whimper escape.

I try to pull my mouth away when I feel his pet nearing my shoulder, but he grabs my jaw and forces me back to his mouth at the same time he presses his hand to my chest and pushes me to lie flat on my back.

Intent on devouring me once again, he unfastens the buttons of my sleep shirt, opening it to expose my breasts. The coldness licks my skin, and my nipples harden—maybe at the feel of the frigid air, or the fact Malachi is now sliding my sleep shorts down my legs.

The absence of his mouth brings my attention back to Cordelia, my heart nearly beating out of my chest as my body seizes. She's gravitating towards my face. Every time I look, no longer able to keep my eyes closed, she's closer.

Tears sting my eyes when she passes my shoulder. "Malachi," I whisper, fear lacing my tone. "It's going to crawl to my face."

His eyes lift to see Cordelia resting near my left breast, then flicker to my horrified gaze, chest heaving erratically in terror. He doesn't take her off me, and he doesn't tell me to calm down, to stop crying, or to remain calm. No, instead, he lowers his hungry gaze between my legs, pushing his thumb against the flesh above my clit, and lets a drop of spit fall from his lips to my clit, making me tense everywhere with a moan.

My neediness and the way my core clenches have my hips rocking absently, and he rewards my bravery by parting my lips and allowing another drop of spit to land at my entrance.

Despite Malachi constantly trying to build against my fear of his pets, and this being the tenth time he's tried it this way, I can't seem to ever lose my terror of spiders. But when he's distracting me like this, I can pretend she isn't there.

"More," I moan. "Please."

Cordelia scurries back down my arm, and I try to shake her off, but Malachi glares at me, so I stay still.

Chest rising and falling in both fear and anticipation, my cheeks soaked with my tears, I rock my hips again, wanting his mouth on me regardless of my terror.

Then she moves again—she crawls off my arm, and her little legs are at my side, and when she manages to climb onto me again, I nearly die from the view of Malachi between my legs and his pet tarantula at my navel. The push and pull is there—the pull to get away from her and the push to get my husband's lips around my clit.

Technically my husband. I have a ring. I have his name, but since Dad refused to reverse either of our adoptions, we decided not to legally get married. Not that it changes anything. We still love each other dangerously.

"Such a good girl, my little sister," he says quietly then fucks his two fingers into me so hard, I gasp and nearly knock his spider off my body.

I'm shaking, I realize—I'm terrified, and my body is rattling like I'm cold, but I'm also in desperate need of more as my pussy clamps around his fingers like a strong vise.

But when he vanishes from my sight and drags his tongue against my inner thigh, not moving his digits at all, my inner walls crush his fingers more. I try to move, to rock my hips into his touch, but he bites harshly enough to stop me.

"Don't move," he says against my skin as he pushes his fingers deeper. "Or I'll put her on your face again."

He knows I love fear. My pussy just tightened around his unmoving fingers, throbbing and needy and soaked.

I'm going to die tonight. I think I might need to disobey his command and jump him, screw the repercussions of what he'll do to me for it.

I could trap his face between my legs and demand an orgasm—or wait till he's asleep and fuck him like I've tried to do on countless occasions, but he's a light sleeper and always wakes up.

He got the fun of taking from me—when is it my turn?

Then again, I like when he scares me—in fact, I love it.

It's always more intense when the fear comes from something he's doing. Whether I'm tied up in a basement, being tortured by him not fucking my pussy and only giving my ass attention, or when he chases me down and chokes me with a gas mask on, deep in the middle of a cornfield.

I try to rock into his hand once more, but I huff as he pulls his fingers out of me completely.

Looking down, I see his gaze is glued to mine as he sucks his two fingers into his mouth, tasting me like he has a million times already. His eyes close, as if he's savoring it, wrapping his tongue around each finger.

It's far too early in the morning to be doing this—I'm about to explode from the view alone.

"Why are you teasing me so much? Fuck me already."

He shakes his head and moves up my naked body, and as Cordelia moves up my ribs to my shoulder again, he's kissing the trail he's following, dragging his tongue across the underside of my breasts. The intensity of his touches have me arching my back as he takes a nipple into his mouth and sucks.

I don't know whether to moan from the intensity or scream at the feel of the spider so close to my face.

"If you don't take her off me, I'll scream."

Laughing against my skin, his gaze clashes with mine.

"You'll definitely be screaming." he says breathlessly then signs, *But not because of her.*

He palms my other breast aggressively, his spider staying in place while he squeezes and kneads and sucks and bites. Malachi's other hand slips between my legs again, and he breathes against my sensitive, pebbled nipple.

"You're terrified," he groans as he eases his fingers into me again. "But your pussy is soaked."

I whimper as he slides back down my body and drags his tongue up my inner thigh, dodging where I want him to bury his face as he ventures to the other thigh. My legs are trembling, my fingernails nearly cutting half-moons into my palms.

"Pl-Please," I cry in desperation as heat grows all over me. "I want you."

He hums and looks up at me through his dark lashes. "Am I your brother or your husband?"

"My…" I start, my voice shaking. "My husband."

I gasp as he sinks his teeth into my clit—the pain mixes with pleasure, and I think I come a little against his hand.

"Try again," he warns, breathing heavily against my pussy as he slowly starts to curl his fingers deep and thrust.

"Both," I moan, shaking as he licks, soothing the assaulted area, lapping at my clit and around it, leaving a red mark on my inner thigh before starting to tease me all over again.

Only when we're in the bedroom will we ever refer to each

other as brother and sister. It's too confusing otherwise. It's more of a dirty secret for us now. In the new town we live in, we're a couple, not the Vize siblings. No one looks at us and thinks we're weird. Molly's friends think we're married. She's adjusted to it all, and Dad also accepted us. It's like the divorce from Mom made him a better person.

Mom's gone. She's probably on husband number three now, which is sad, since her and my dad were childhood sweethearts, but I guess money and power went to her head, and she lost everything. She hasn't tried to contact me once.

Malachi's pet crawls down my ribs, grabbing my attention, and stops on top of his hand on my thigh—maybe she can smell his scent? It causes him to pause his teasing, and when his hand vanishes from my view, along with his spider, I sit up quickly. "Don't you dare put that thing there. It's basically animal abuse!"

He narrows his eyes then huffs and stands, going to Cordelia's tank—next to the other three furry spiders—and settling her inside. I sit up, naked, waiting for him to give me some attention again.

Malachi's eyes find me, and I watch as he pushes down his boxers, his thick pierced cock springing free. My mouth waters, and I want to taste the bead of precum at the tip, but I also want him to fuck me.

He's on me again in a second, the air robbed from me as he takes my throat and shoves his tongue into my mouth in a feral kiss while spreading my legs even further. Then he drags his mouth across my jaw, releasing my neck to kiss my throat and down my ribs to between my legs again.

I swear, if this asshole goes back to teasing, I'm going to—

The shrieking of my phone cuts through the room, and though I ignore it at first, whoever it is isn't taking no for an answer—a moment after it stops ringing, it starts right back up again, every time. Annoyed, I reach for it while Malachi's hands are tight on my thighs.

Then I see the name on the screen. If she's repeatedly calling, then there must be an issue.

Malachi looks like he wants to strangle me.

"Hey. Abbi. Hi."

"I'm going to kill him."

"Who—"

I'm silenced when Malachi shoves his tongue into my pussy, causing me to slam my hand over my mouth to stop my friend from hearing me moaning. He doesn't stop when I let go of my mouth and try to push his face away while Abigail yaps in my ear.

But I'm not paying attention—Malachi is full on fighting against me as I try to close my thighs, to push my palm against his forehead.

He takes my clit into his mouth and sucks while digging his long fingers into my thighs, stopping me from slamming them shut and parting me more.

He's finally giving me what I want, and I'm desperate to ride his face, to have his tongue fucking me, but words fail me when I try to tell my friend to call back. The phone slips from my ear, lying on the pillow as he parts my entrance with two fingers then pushes his middle finger inside, curling it then hammering hard enough that my body moves, the headboard slamming against the wall.

He pulls his mouth away from my clit and climbs up my body, and in one harsh thrust, he buries his cock inside me. "I'll fuck you into a coma if you don't hang up."

"Ew!" she yells loud enough for us to hear just before I snatch the phone from my pillow and hang up, tossing it aside then wrapping my arms around his neck.

He used to rarely fuck me in the missionary position before our entire lives changed. If he did, it was never romantic or slow or lovingly. He'd fuck me like he hated everything about me—he loved it when I cried, when he could taste my tears, and when I begged him to either stop or go harder.

But in the last two years, he's gone slower, taking his time with me while we had time for us. Right now, he's unmoving, throbbing within my core while he kisses me.

"We need to hurry," I mutter as my heels dig into his ass, trying to make him move. "Hurry up and fuck me like a bad little sister, Malachi."

He groans and thrusts deeper, sliding his hand from my knee to my ass, bringing me to him as each inch pushes into me.

We melt into each other's touches as he slides in and out, and I beg for more as he gives me it. He fucks me with my legs on his shoulders, on all fours, and then pushes my front down on the mattress while he fingers my ass, still burying his cock deep inside me.

When I come, he comes with me and collapses on my back. Breathless, kissing my shoulder, sweat mixing together as the temperature rises.

We don't get to have sex often, so when we do, it's always intense, and I fall asleep pretty much as soon as I finish.

"Daddy?"

At the sound of our son's voice, Malachi closes his eyes and drops his head onto my shoulder.

Isaac calls for him again, but this time his voice is shaky. He's had another nightmare. "I fucking knew we shouldn't have let Molly babysit him. She's a bad influence."

We go on dates every Thursday. Molly always babysits and Malachi, being the protective dad that he is, always blames her for his nightmares. No matter how many times he suggests someone else, he gives in when Molly calls him.

He sits up and tucks his cock into his shorts, his eyes staying on me. My husband's gaze lights up as I smile up at him. "I love that he always calls for you, but I'm starting to get a little jealous."

Rolling his eyes, he kisses my cheek and climbs off the bed, throwing his shirt on before heading to Isaac's room. I get up too, pull my sleep clothes back on, and make my way to the bedroom filled with trains and cars and boats.

Isaac is rubbing his eyes in his father's arms when I push his door open, a line of light from the hallway falling on his face.

Malachi doesn't need to say anything—not that he does much of that anyway. The odd time he'll read him a book to try to get him to sleep, and other times, we'll sing a lullaby—not the spider one—yet most of the time, being cuddled by his dad is enough to get our son to calm down.

I've been replaced as Malachi's number-one priority—I used to be his entire world, but now I'm only just a part of it, and I'm perfectly okay with that. I think he needed to feel what it was like to be loved by someone else, and Isaac loves his father unconditionally.

We're even teaching him signing. Malachi's speech has come on, but me, Isaac, Molly, and sometimes our dad are the only ones who get to hear his voice. Not because he struggles with others, but because not having a voice was his way of protecting himself, so it's saved purely for the ones who mean the most to him.

Malachi turns to face me, his hand rubbing up and down our son's back. The softness in his eyes and the gentleness of his touch speaks a thousand words for him. He's an amazing dad, and I don't think he even realizes it.

When I found out I was pregnant only a few months after the Reznikovs were dealt with, I was already far along, probably from when we were together in the car. We stood in the bathroom with ten tests, and one by one, we turned them over. He was pale, terrified, and so nervous yet went back to his therapist to ask for more help. He even asked our dad for help.

He said if he was going to become a father, the kid needed the best version of himself, and he thought no one had ever met that person. But he was wrong. No one truly has a "best" version of themselves—it's just one of life's learning curves, a feeling, an emotion, and Malachi is overflowing with them.

My bump grew, and he became obsessed with our unborn child. He made sure I was eating, drinking, resting, and even went and got a job to make sure he could lead by example.

We have more than enough money, but I knew he needed to do something. He got some training, and now he's in an animal sanctuary not far from here, much to my dad's dismay. He wanted Malachi to work with him, but since they're still building their relationship, it was best not to cross ties and create any further issues.

They're doing great, Dad and Malachi. They meet up every Tuesday and Friday at the park with Isaac, and they talk— mostly signing—and Dad will tell him about his new girlfriend and how she makes him happy. They'll push Isaac on the baby swing, and Malachi will come home and tell me that it's weird, that he's finally feeling what it's like to have a father, and how it's helping him learn how to be a father himself, despite two and a half years of being Isaac's hero.

Dad's forgiven him for what he did, and I think along the way, Malachi forgave himself too.

Mom is gone—she's not been in contact at all since Isaac was born. I thought she'd reach out when she found out she was going to be a grandma, but nothing.

I'm still not sure how I feel about that.

When Isaac was born, me and Malachi's entire existences changed. We were, are, still head over heels for each other, worshiping the ground the other walks on, and neither of us thought we could love someone else even close to the way we feel about each other.

But then this kid came along and grabbed Malachi's finger, and life has never been the same.

He's our son. But he's Malachi's best friend. His number-one reason for living.

Most nights, Malachi will sleep beside him if he wakes up, so when he lies down, and Isaac rests his head on his chest, I wait until they both fall asleep before I slip away from the door with a smile on my face.

EPILOGUE TWO
OLIVIA
Twelve Years Later

O livia's hand stays firmly in mine as we're led through the manor filled with partygoers. It's more formal than anything. A charity event where we've pledged two hundred thousand to research rare genetic diseases.

Scotland is fucking freezing. I don't know why we agreed to this. I wanted to go on vacation, but Sebastian Prince invited us here, and since I've kept in contact with Barry, the one who cut Olivia's tracker from her arm, I didn't think I could refuse to come.

She has a tiny scar, though nothing compared to my initials on her body, or the scars on my side and chest. She loves them. Kisses them whenever she can when she's traveling down to suck my dick.

"Why do you look so mad? The both of you?"

I frown deeper and look at Isaac, who looks more than pissed to be here.

His hair is styled the same as my own, much to Olivia's dismay. He also has on a fitted suit, just like me, and I hate it. I don't like wearing this shit, and my son looks like he wants to set fire to himself every time he needs to adjust his cuffs.

He's fourteen, but the terrible teens hit years ago, so we're used to his attitude and mood swings now, though I'd say we had the most placid kid out of everyone else. Isaac would rather play on his computer with his friends than go out, and even if he does, he soon calls either me or his mother to pick him up because it's too much for him.

He's like me, but at the same time he's not. The aggression that was stuck to my soul from my past trauma isn't attached to him—I had baggage on top of baggage, and it didn't help that I hated the world and myself until I met Olivia.

The kid even likes fucking spiders—could I get any luckier?

We didn't have any more children. Isaac is enough for us, and it means we can give him all our attention when it's not on each other. I don't think I could risk having a girl and her turning out like Molly with her goddamn tantrums. She's basically like a daughter anyway.

I wonder what they'd all say if they knew our mother was buried in a deep grave in the middle of nowhere?

When we get into the main party, I recognize the group in the corner.

Tobias nods to me as he leads his wife, I assume by the

wedding ring on his finger, towards Base and his friends.

There are children everywhere. I love my own, but other kids make me uneasy and, technically, I still hate them. They're loud for no reason and give me a headache.

Base has a little boy on his hip while talking to one of his friends. Kade Mitchell. I've never seen him in the flesh, but I've heard about him on the news and through constant text messages from Base.

He's the tall one with black hair. He got out of prison the same year Isaac was born, after a massive worldwide war with a corrupt cop who dragged him into the underworld. He fought his way out and got to have the girl of his dreams, and, going by the children by his side, a family.

His eyes land on me briefly as he moves to his father's partner. He kisses her cheek, and from reading his lips, I learn she's his mother.

Shit. Even Tobias got the girl, though it took him thirty years.

Her husband before him died. This entire event is for him and to fund more testing for the disease that took his life so suddenly—Ewan I think his name was.

"Abbi!" Olivia calls, and I roll my eyes at the purple-haired girl with a Reznikov brother on her arm. My wife vanishes from my side and goes to her friend, and Isaac huffs beside me.

Then his eyes land on someone by the punch bowl. "Who's that?"

I shrug.

"Can I go talk to her?"

I raise a brow at him, at the blush creeping up his face, and I gesture forward. *Good luck*, I sign, and he signs back, *I don't need luck. I'm a Vize.*

Silently laughing, I shove my hands into my pockets and watch him walk up to a girl around the same age as him. She has dark hair, and given that she looks exactly like her mother, I know who Isaac is attempting to flirt with.

A presence comes up beside me, a beer to hand.

"Keep your son away from my daughter," Kade warns.

I smirk.

Because we both know that's not going to happen.

THE END

ABOUT THE AUTHOR

Leigh Rivers is a Scottish Biomedical Scientist who has ventured into the world of writing dark, morally gray characters with rollercoaster storylines to drive her readers wild.

When she isn't reading, writing on her laptop, or gaming until ridiculous hours, she dances at the pole studio, goes to the gym, and walks her four dogs with her two sons and husband.

Find her on Instagram, Facebook and Tiktok
@authorleighrivers